BEHIND THE THRONE

LECTOR HOUSE PUBLIC DOMAIN WORKS

BEHIND THE THRONE

WILLIAM LE QUEUX

ISBN: 978-93-90314-18-8

Published: -

© 2020
LECTOR HOUSE LLP

LECTOR HOUSE LLP
E-MAIL: lectorpublishing@gmail.com

"BEHIND THE THRONE"

BY

WILLIAM LE QUEUX

CONTENTS

Chapter   *Page*

     I. The Cat's-Paw. 1

    II. Friends of her Excellency. 5

   III. In which Mary Reveals Certain Suspicions. 11

   IV. Contains a Mystery. 16

    V. Is Mainly about a Woman. 22

   VI. Discloses Certain Strange Facts. 27

  VII. An Afternoon at Thornby. 32

 VIII. The Traitor. 37

   IX. His Excellency Learns the Truth. 43

    X. "For Mary's Sake." 48

   XI. The Secret Agent. 53

  XII. Concerns some Curious Instructions. 58

 XIII. The Villa San Donato. 63

 XIV. In the Silence of Night. 68

  XV. The Peril of a Nation. 73

 XVI. Father and Daughter. 78

 XVII. The Sazarac Affair. 83

XVIII. Counting the Cost. 88

 XIX. The Sacrifice. 93

  XX. Tells the Truth. 97

XXI.	The Ear of the Minister.	102
XXII.	Concerns a Man's Duty.	107
XXIII.	The Plot.	112
XXIV.	In the Chamber of Deputies..	117
XXV.	Billy Grenfell is Philosophic..	122
XXVI.	A Millionaire's Tactics.	127
XXVII.	Vito is Inquisitive..	132
XXVIII.	"Was Sazarac your Friend?"	138
XXIX.	Around the Throne..	142
XXX.	The Path of the Tempter.	147
XXXI.	In which a Double Game is Played..	152
XXXII.	The Birth of Love..	157
XXXIII.	Mrs Fitzroy's Governess..	162
XXXIV.	In Confidence..	168
XXXV.	The Captain is Outspoken..	173
XXXVI.	In the Twilight Hour..	178
XXXVII.	At Orton Court Again.	183
XXXVIII.	"Silence for Silence!"	186
XXXIX.	Revelations.	193
XL.	The Story of Captain Solaro..	198
XLI.	A Woman's Freedom.	203

CHAPTER ONE.
THE CAT'S-PAW.

"Of course the transaction is a purely private one. There is, I suppose, no chance of the truth leaking out? If so, it might be very awkward, you know."

"None whatever. Your Excellency may rely upon me to deal with these people cautiously. Besides, they have their own reputation to consider—as well as ours."

"And how much do you say they offer?" asked His Excellency in Italian, so that the English servants, if they were listening, should not understand.

"If you accept their conditions as they stand, they pay one hundred thousand francs—four thousand pounds sterling—into your account at the Pall Mall branch of the Credit Lyonnais on Monday next," replied the other in the same language.

"And your share, my dear Angelo?"

"That is apart. I have arranged it."

"And they'll profit a million, and dress our unfortunate infantry in shoddy?"

"Possibly, but what does it really matter? A soldier's clothes are of little concern, as long as he is well armed."

"But the boots?—the contract is for boots as well."

"Your Excellency forgets that the English soldiers have more than once been sent into the field in boots made of brown paper. And they were of English make! Ours are German—and we must expect the foreigner to take advantage of us."

"Yes, but we know well the reputation of these people."

"Of course. But from the English firm we get nothing—the English are too honest;" and the thin, sallow-faced Sicilian laughed scornfully towards his superior, Signor Camillo Morini, senator of the kingdom of Italy and Minister of War.

His Excellency, a tall, well-built, well-dressed man of sixty or so, in a suit of light grey tweed, whose hair was only just turning white, whose carefully trained moustache showed but few silver threads, and whose dark, deep-set eyes were sharp and observant, stood at the window gazing thoughtfully out upon the green level English lawn where his daughter Mary and some visitors were playing tennis.

He remained silent, his back to Angelo Borselli, the man in black who had travelled from Rome to Leicestershire to urge him to accept the bribe of four thousand pounds from the German firm of army contractors. Camillo Morini was a man with a strange, adventurous history—a man who, had he not lived entirely in the political world, would have been termed a knight of industry, a self-made man who, by his own ingenious craft and cunning, had risen to become one of Italy's chief Ministers, and a senator of the kingdom. He entertained some scruples as regards honesty, both political and financial, yet General Angelo Borselli, the bureaucrat, who was Under-Secretary, for the past ten years had been busily engaged in squeezing all the profit possible out of the office he held.

Morini and Borselli had for years assisted each other, or, to be more truthful, Morini, who seemed to exercise a kind of animal magnetism over men, had used Borselli for his own ends, and the Under-Secretary had been the Minister's cat's-paw ever since the days of Victor Emmanuel when they were deputies together at Montecitorio. Upon the stormy sea of Italian politics they had sailed together, and although many times they had run before the wind towards the shoals of exposure, they had somehow always managed to escape disaster.

Borselli had, by His Excellency's clever manoeuvring, been given the rank of general although a comparatively young man, and had been appointed Under-Secretary of War, while the pair had, in secret, reaped a golden harvest, even against Morini's will. When deputy, and little better than a political adventurer, he had been compelled to make his politics pay; but as Minister, with the responsibility of office upon him, he had at first worked for the benefit of Italy. Yet, alas! so contaminating had been the corruption about him that he found it well-nigh impossible to act disinterestedly, and very soon all his highest resolves had been cast aside, and with Borselli ever scheming and ever prompting at his elbow, he was constrained, like his fellow-members of the Cabinet, to seek profit where he could.

In Italy, under the régime of the late King Humbert, Ministers soon became millionaires—in francs—and Camillo Morini was no exception.

A born leader of men, gifted with a marvellous tact, a keen, clear foresight, a wide knowledge of men, and a deep, wily cunning, he held the confidence of his sovereign, the late lamented king, and took care that nothing occurred to shake or to imperil it. He was a *poseur*, and owed his position to his ingenious methods and his plausible tongue. His highly respectable exterior was inspiring, and the veneer of elegant refinement of manner had opened to him the best social circles in Rome and Paris. He was a good linguist, and had been an advocate in Florence in the days when he made the law a stepping-stone into politics and fat emoluments.

General Angelo Borselli, the soldierly, middle-aged man of the sallow face in funereal black, always acted the part of the cringing underling, yet at heart he really hated and despised the man whom he was bound to call "His Excellency." It was, however, Borselli's active brain which evolved those neat schemes by which a portion of the public funds of poor strangled Italy went into their joint pockets, he who inspired the Press and kept at bay the horde of political opponents. It was General Borselli who made suggestions, who juggled so cleverly with figures, and who ruled the Ministry of War with a rod of iron.

The two men detested each other, yet, held together by the bond of mutual peculation, they played constantly into each other's hands, and both had become wealthy in consequence.

Noticing that the Minister remained silent, still looking forth upon the lawn,

"You are surely not becoming scrupulous! The commission is only a fair one. If those pigs of Germans want the contract they must pay for it."

Camillo Morini snapped his bony fingers, but still remained silent. At heart he longed to free himself of all this dishonesty at the expense of the comfort and safety of the army. Indeed he knew that by such transactions his country was being imperilled. Recent disasters in Abyssinia had been due directly to the defective arms and ammunition supplied to the troops. The contractors had all paid him heavy bribes, and the brave sons of Italy had gone forth armed with rubbish, and were defeated in consequence.

Yes. He longed to become honest, and yet with all his heavy expenses, his splendid palace in Rome, his magnificent old villa on the hillside outside Florence, his great tracts of wine-lands and olive-gardens in the Apennines, and that house he rented as a summer residence in England, how could he refuse these alluring presents? They were necessary for his position—for his existence. His eyes were fixed upon his daughter Mary, a neat, trim figure in a cream flannel dress; his daughter who believed so implicitly in him, and who regarded him as her ideal of probity and uprightness. He sighed.

"Perhaps you consider a hundred thousand francs not quite enough?" remarked the man behind him. "I told the agent in London yesterday, when he came to Claridge's, that I expected you would want another twenty thousand, but he said his firm could not possibly afford it. He is remaining in London until to-morrow for your decision. He intended to come down here and see you, but I forbade it."

"Quite right! Quite right! Keep all such persons as far from me as possible, Angelo," was the Minister's quick reply. "I've had more than enough of them."

The other smiled, still standing erect on the hearthrug, his back to the fireplace, his hands in his trousers pockets, smoking a cigarette.

"Of course," he said, "I tried to get all I could out of him, but a hundred thousand was his absolute limit. Indeed I wanted to make it German marks, not francs, but it was useless. I have brought with me the acceptance of the contract," he added. "The decree only requires your endorsement," and he drew from his pocket a paper which he opened and spread upon the big old-fashioned writing-table of the library.

The Minister, however, still hesitated, while his companion smiled within himself at what he regarded as a sudden and utterly unnecessary pang of conscience.

"This cheap contracting is simply sacrificing the lives of our poor men," declared Morini suddenly, turning at last from the window and facing the man who was so constantly his tempter.

"Bah! There are cheap contracts and secret commissions in all the departments—marine, public-works—even at the Ministry of Justice."

"I know, I know," groaned the Minister. "The whole system is rotten at the core. I've tried to be honest, and have failed."

"Your Excellency must admit that our department does not stand alone. It is to be regretted that our poor conscripts are half starved, and our soldiers armed with faulty ammunition, but surely we must live as well as those in the other ministries!"

"At the sacrifice of Italy?" remarked the Minister in a hard tone. "I really do not believe, Angelo, that you possess any conscience," he added bitterly.

"I possess, I think, about the same quantity as your Excellency," was the other's satirical reply, as he twisted his dark moustache. "Conscience and memory are the two most dangerous operations of the politician's intellect. Happy the man who indulges in neither."

"Then you must be very happy indeed," remarked His Excellency, with a dry laugh. "But," he added, sighing, "I suppose I must fall in with your suggestion for this, the very last time. You say that the money will be placed to my account at the Credit Lyonnais next Monday—eh?"

The Under-Secretary nodded in the affirmative, and then the Minister took up a pen and with a quick flourish scribbled his signature at the head of the document which gave slop-made uniforms and brown-paper boots to fifteen regiments of Italian infantry.

CHAPTER TWO.
FRIENDS OF HER EXCELLENCY.

Her Excellency Signora Morini was an Englishwoman, and for that reason the Minister rented Orton Court, that picturesque old Queen Anne house in Leicestershire, where, with their daughter Mary, they each year spent August and September, the two blazing months of the Italian summer.

Standing back amid wide level lawns, high box-hedges, quaint old flower-gardens, and spreading cedars, about four miles out of Rugby on the Leicester road, it dominated a wide stretch of rich, undulating pastures of bright fresh green, so pleasing to the eye after the sun-baked, thirsty land of Italy. The house, a quaint, rambling old place full of odd nooks and corners, was of time-mellowed red brick, partly ivy-covered, with a wide stone portico, spacious hall, and fine oak staircase. One wing, that which faced the tennis-lawn, was covered with roses, while around the lawn itself were iron arches over which trailing roses also grew in abundant profusion.

The Morinis kept but little company when in England. They came there for rest after the mad whirl of the Roman season, and so careful was His Excellency to keep his true position a secret, and thus avoid being compelled to make complimentary calls upon the English Ministers and officials in London, that very few persons, if indeed anyone in the neighbourhood, were really aware that the tall, courteous foreigner who came there for a few weeks each year—Mr Morini, as they called him—was actually one of the most powerful Ministers in Europe.

They were civil to their neighbours in a mild, informal way, of course. Foreigners are always regarded with suspicion in England. Madame Morini made calls which were returned, and they usually played tennis and croquet in the afternoon; for Mary, on account of her bright, cosmopolitan vivacity, was a particular favourite with everyone.

The local clergy, headed by the rural dean and his wife, were fond of drinking tea on the pretty lawn of Orton Court, and on this afternoon among the guests were several rectors and their curates, together with their women-folk. The wife of the Minister of War had been the daughter of a poor Yorkshire clergyman. She had, while acting as English governess in the family of a Roman prince, met her husband, then only a struggling advocate in the Florence courts, and, notwithstanding that she was a Protestant, they had married, and she had never for one moment repented her choice. Husband and wife, after those years of strange ups and downs, were still entirely devoted to each other; while Mary, their only child, they mutually idolised.

The scene upon that sunny lawn was picturesque and purely English.

Madame Morini, a dark-haired, well-preserved woman in pale mauve, was seated at a bamboo table in the shade serving tea and gossiping with her friends—for the game had been suspended, and cake and biscuits were being handed round by the men in flannels.

An elderly woman, wife of a retired colonel, inquired for "Mr Morini," where-upon madame answered—

"He is in the house, detained on business, I think. A gentleman has come down from London to see him." And thus was her husband's presence excused.

Ten minutes later, however, when Mary, watching her opportunity, saw her mother alone, she ran up to her, whispering in her ear—

"That man Borselli has come from Rome, mother! I saw his face at the study window. Why can't he leave father alone when we are here on holiday?"

"I suppose it is some affair of state, my dear," was her mother's calm reply. "Your father told me he was to arrive this afternoon. He is to remain the night."

"I hate the man!" declared the pretty, dark-haired girl with emphasis. "I watched him through the window just now, and saw him look so black at father behind his back. I believe they have quarrelled."

"I think not, my dear. Your father and General Borselli are very old friends, remember."

"Of course. But he's a Sicilian, and you know what you've always told me about the Livornese and the Sicilians."

"Don't be silly, Mary," exclaimed the Minister's wife, laughing. "Matters of state do not concern us women. Go and continue your game."

The girl shrugged her shoulders with the queer little foreign gesture due to her cosmopolitan upbringing, and turned away to rejoin the young man in grey flannels who stood awaiting her on the other side of the court.

She was twenty-one, with perfect, regular features, a pointed chin, dark chest-nut hair, and a pair of large, lustrous eyes in which gleamed all the fire and passion of the sunny South. Her figure, neat-waisted and well-proportioned, was always admired in the salons of Rome and Florence, and she had for the past couple of years been the reigning beauty in the official and diplomatic world of the Eternal City.

Possessed of an easy grace, a natural modesty, with a sweet, pleasant expres-sion, she had, soon after returning from school at Broadstairs, been chaperoned into Roman society by her mother, and had now, at twenty-one, become essen-tially a woman of the world, well-dressed, *chic*, and full of vivacity. A remarkable linguist—for she spoke English, Italian, French, and Spanish with equal fluency—she had quickly made her mark in that very difficult circle, Italian society, a fact which pleased her parents, and induced her father to increase her allowance until she was enabled to have her ball dresses from Paris and her tailor-made gowns from London.

affluence, saw that by dressing his daughter better than other girls he was exhibiting a prosperity that would be noticed and talked about.

As she crossed the lawn that warm August afternoon, plainly attired in her cream flannel skirt and pale blue blouse, there could be no two opinions regarding her marvellous beauty. It was of an unusual kind, a combination of the handsome classic model of the ancients with the sweet womanliness of modern life. Her carriage, too, was superb. The casual observer, watching her retreating form, would not require to look twice to recognise that she was of foreign birth; for no Englishwoman carries herself with that easy, elastic swing which is inherent in the Italian girl of the upper class. Yet, perhaps owing to her mother's English birth and teaching, she admired to the full everything that was British. She was a keen, outspoken critic of all things Italian, and was never so happy as when they were living unostentatiously in semi-privacy for those two welcome months each year in rural Leicestershire.

At heart, she hated that brilliant circle in which they were compelled to move when at home—the continual functions, the official balls, the court receptions, the gay, irresponsible world of intrigue and scandal, of dazzling uniforms and glittering decorations, in which she was so continually courted and flattered. Already she had become nauseated by its vices and its shams, and longed always for the rural peace of the country, early hours, and the ease of old frocks. Yet it was impossible, she knew. She was compelled to live in that fevered atmosphere of wealth and officialdom that revolved around the throne of His Majesty King Humbert, to receive the admiration and homage paid to her because of her striking beauty, and to act her part, as her father instructed her—a prominent part in one of the most brilliant courts of Europe.

Was it any wonder that, scarce out of her teens, she was already a *femme du monde*, with a wide knowledge of the hypocrisies of society, the tortuous ways of political intrigue, and the foetid moral atmosphere of those gilded salons and perfumed boudoirs?

"I wonder if you'll forgive me if I don't play any more, Mr Macbean?" she asked of the dark-haired young man in grey who stood, racquet in hand, awaiting her return. "I am very tired. I played in the tournament at your uncle's yesterday, you know, and we from the South are exotic plants, after all."

"Forgive you! Of course!" cried the young man gallantly. "The sun is still too warm to be comfortable. Perhaps you will show me the gardens instead?"

"Willingly," she answered. "But there's not much to see here, I fear," and they strolled together between the high box-hedges, into the well-kept flower-garden with its grey old sundial and beds edged with curbs of lichen-covered stone. Beyond lay another lawn, which rose gently until it gave entrance into a small shady wood of high old oaks and elms wherein the rooks were cawing.

The pair were comparatively strangers. A fortnight before, he had called with his uncle, the rector of Thornby, whom he was visiting, and on several occasions since they had met at tennis or at tea in the drawing-rooms of various houses in the neighbourhood.

They chatted while strolling around the great sloping lawn, and he was expressing admiration at the excellent game she had played. She inwardly reflected that he seemed a very pleasant companion—so different from those over-dressed young Roman nobles, all elegance, swagger, and pose.

To George Macbean Nature had been kind and Chance had been cruel.

He was tall, slender, and athletic, with pale, refined features and a look of thoughtful and reticent calm. People looked at him far oftener than they did at handsomer men. It was one of those faces which suggest the romance of fate, and his eyes, under their straight brows and their drooping lids, could gaze at women with an honest, open look. And yet women seldom saw him for the first time without thinking of him when he had passed from sight. He aroused at a first glance a vague speculative interest—he was a man whom women loved, and yet he was utterly unconscious of it all.

He was son of a younger son of the Macbeans of Castle Douglas; the blood of the ancient Galloway lairds ran in his veins; yet it was all that remained to him of the vanished greatness of a race that had fought so valiantly on the Border. He had, on his father's death, been compelled to come down from Cambridge only to find himself launched upon the world practically penniless, when, by good fortune, an influential friend of his father's in the City had contrived to obtain for him a situation as private secretary to Mr Morgan-Mason, a wholesale provision merchant, who, having made a fortune in business, sought to enter society by the parliamentary back door. He sat for South-West Norfolk, and was mainly distinguished in the House by his loudness of dress and his vulgar ostentation.

The post of secretary to such an impossible person was by no means a congenial occupation for a gentleman. The white-waistcoated vulgarian smiled at the poverty of the peerage, and treated his secretary as he would one of his shopmen in the Goswell Road; yet George Macbean could only "grin and bear it," for upon this aspiring merchant of cheese and bacon his very living depended. He could not afford to lose the one hundred and eighty pounds a year which the bacon merchant paid him.

It being the recess, and Mr Morgan-Mason having followed in the wake of a needy earl and his wife to Vichy, Macbean was spending a month with the Reverend Basil Sinclair, his bachelor uncle, when he had become acquainted with that bright, vivacious girl who was walking beside him.

She was speaking of Italy, and life there in winter, without, of course, mentioning the official position of her father, when he said—

"Ah! I too love Italy. I have been to Rome and Florence several times. Both cities are delightful—even to the mere visitor like myself."

"Perhaps you speak Italian?" she hazarded in that language.

"I am fairly well acquainted with it," he responded in the purest Tuscan, laughing the while. "Before I went to Cambridge I lived five years with my mother, in the mother-country, in Pisa."

"Why, you speak like a born Italian!" she laughed. "It is so difficult for us English to roll our r's—to give the exact accent, for instance, to *cane* and to *carne*. Over those two words we make ourselves ridiculous." They had entered the wood, where the damp smell of decaying leaves, so essentially English, met their nostrils, and were strolling up one of the mossy paths in the cool shadow. Yes, she was certainly lovely, he reflected. Report had not lied about her. She was more beautiful than any woman he had ever before beheld, more graceful, more cosmopolitan.

Morini? Morini? Yes, he had heard the name before. It was not at all uncommon in Tuscany. She was Anglo-Italian, and the girl born of Anglo-Italian parents is perhaps the most charming and cosmopolitan of any in Europe.

Chatting gaily, they lingered in the wood, strolled through the long range of hothouses, and then back again to the lawn, where they found the guests bidding farewell to their hostess and departing.

The Reverend Basil Sinclair was bending over Madame Morini's hand, an example which his nephew, though loth to leave the side of the girl who had so entirely charmed him, was bound to follow, and five minutes later the two men mounted into the rector's pony-cart, raised their hats, and drove away.

Later that evening, as General Borselli, ready dressed for dinner, stood, a well-set-up figure in the long, low, old-fashioned drawing-room, with its perfume of pot-pourri, awaiting the appearance of the ladies, the door suddenly opened, and there entered a dark, good-looking, brown-bearded man of about thirty, who was a guest at Orton, but having been up to London for the day, had only just returned in time to slip into his dinner-jacket.

The two men faced each other.

The new-comer, also a foreigner, started back, halting on the threshold as he recognised the sallow, sinister countenance of the other in the dim half-light. Angelo Borselli was the very last man he expected to meet beneath the Minister's roof in England, and the encounter was, to him, somewhat disconcerting.

"You!" cried the general in surprise, speaking in French. "So you actually have the audacity to pose as a friend of His Excellency, after those very plain words I spoke in the Florence Club! You accept my friend's invitation and dare pay court to mademoiselle! Is this not a dangerous game you are playing, my friend?"

"I conceive no danger in it—as far as I am concerned," replied the young Frenchman, Jules Dubard, coolly. "Besides, my private affairs are surely no concern of yours! If His Excellency does me the great honour to invite me to his English home, I shall certainly accept, even at risk of incurring your displeasure," he added, with a supercilious smile.

"You recollect what I told you?"

"Perfectly," replied the well-dressed young count, with an air of extreme politeness, as he rearranged his cravat in the mirror. "But you appear to overlook one rather important fact."

"And what is that, pray?" inquired the Sicilian, with an evil flash in his dark eyes.

"Exposure to His Excellency is synonymous with exposure of yourself in quite another quarter, my dear general," replied the guest, in a meaning tone. "You cannot afford to risk that, you know. We both of us may threaten, but it is, after all, what these English call a fool's game. Neither of us dare give each other away. So we may just as well be friends as enemies—eh?"

CHAPTER THREE.

IN WHICH MARY REVEALS CERTAIN SUSPICIONS.

Dinner, served with that same stiff stateliness that characterised everything in the Morini household, was over, and the three men had rejoined the ladies in the drawing-room.

Mary, in a pretty *décolleté* dinner-gown of pale pink chiffon, with a single tea-rose in her corsage, had, at Dubard's suggestion, gone to the piano, and in a sweet contralto had sung some of those old Florentine folk-songs, or *stornelli*, as they are called, those weirdly mediaeval songs that are still sung by the populace in the streets of Florence to-day. Then as conclusion she ran her fingers lightly over the keys and sang—

> "Fiorin Fiorello!
> Di tutti i fiorellin che fioriranno,
> Il fior del' amor mio sara il piu bello?"

"Brava! Brava!" cried the young Frenchman standing by the piano, and as she raised her eyes to his, it was patent that the pair entertained a regard for each other.

"Your songs of old Florence are so charming, so different from everything else in music, mademoiselle," he declared. "We have nothing like them in France. Our *chansons* are, after all, inharmonious rubbish. It is not surprising that you in Italy have a contempt for our literature, our music, and our drama, for it cannot compare with yours. We have had no poet like Dante, no composer like Verdi, no musician like Paganini—and," he added, dropping his voice to a low whisper as he bent quickly to her ear, "no woman so fair as Mary Morini."

She blushed, and busied herself with her music books in order to conceal her confusion. The general was chatting with her father and mother at the farther end of the long room, and therefore did not notice that swift passage of admiration on the part of Jules Dubard.

The Frenchman was a friend of the family, mainly because he had been helpful to Morini in a variety of ways, and also on account of his pleasant, easy-going manner and quiet elegance. He was from the South. The old family château—a grey, dismal place full of ghostly memories and mildewed pictures of his ancestors—stood high up in the Pyrenees above Bayonne, five miles from the Spanish frontier; yet he had always lived in Paris, and from the days when he left college on his father's death he had led the gay, irresponsible life of the modern Parisian of means, was a member of the Jockey Club, and a well-known figure at the Café Américain and at Maxim's.

As a young man about the French capital he gave frequent bachelor parties at his cosy flat in the Avenue Macmahon, and possessing a very wide circle of friends, he had been able to render the Italian Minister of War several confidential services.

Two years ago, while in Rome, he had received an invitation to dine one evening at His Excellency's splendid old palace—once the residence of a Roman prince—and from that time had been on terms of intimacy with the family and one of Mary's most ardent admirers. He spent a good deal of his time in the Eternal City, and had during the past season become a familiar figure in society.

His Excellency, quick of observation, had, however, detected Borselli's antipathy towards the young man, even though it was so cleverly concealed. And he had wondered. As fellow-guests beneath his roof they had that evening chatted and laughed together across the dinner-table, had referred to each other by their Christian names, and had fraternised as though they were the best friends in the world. Yet those words uttered by Angelo Borselli while awaiting the ladies had been full of hidden meaning.

The Morinis were in ignorance of the truth—and Mary most of all.

Dubard was not a handsome man—for it is difficult to find a man of the weak, anaemic type of modern Parisian who can be called good-looking from an English standpoint. He was thin-featured, lantern-jawed, with a pale complexion, dark eyes, and a brown moustache. He wore his hair parted in the centre, and as an *élégant* was proud of his white almost waxen hands and carefully manicured finger-nails. His dress, too, often betrayed those signs of effeminacy which in Paris just now are considered the height of good form in a man. His every movement seemed studied, yet his stiff elegance was on the most approved model of the Bois and the ballroom. He played frequently at his *cercle*, he wore the most hideous goggles and fur coat and drove his motor daily, and he indulged in *le sport* in an impossible get-up, not because he liked tramping about those horrid muddy fields, but because it was the correct thing for a gentleman to do.

But his greatest success of all had, he told himself, been the attraction of Mary Morini. All through the past winter in Rome he had danced with her, flirted with her, raised his hat to her as she had driven on the Pincio, and had joined her in her mother's box at the Constanzi. To the Quirinale he had, of course, not been bidden, but he lived in the hope of next season receiving the coveted royal command.

With Camillo Morini as his friend, everything in Italy was possible.

Yet Angelo Borselli's presence disturbed him that evening. He knew the man who had been given the post of Under-Secretary. They had met long before he had known Morini—under circumstances that in themselves formed a strange and remarkable story—a story which he feared might one day be made public.

And then?

Bah! Why anticipate such a terrible *contretemps*? he asked himself. Then he bit his under lip as he glanced at his enemy standing beneath the light of the rose-shaded lamp talking with madame, and afterwards turned again to laugh

"I lunched at the Junior United Service Club to-day with a friend of yours," he was saying; for she had risen from the piano and they had gone out upon the moon-lit verandah together, where, obtaining her permission, he lit a cigarette.

"A friend of mine?"

"Captain Houghton, the British naval attaché at Rome. He is home for a month's leave, and sent his compliments to you."

"Oh, Freddie Houghton?" she exclaimed. "He was longing to get home all the winter, but couldn't get leave. He's engaged, they say, and of course he wanted to see his enchantress. He's the best dancer in Rome."

Then suddenly lowering his voice, he asked abruptly—

"Why is Borselli here? I had no idea he was to be a guest!"

"Ah! I know you don't like the fellow," she remarked, glancing back into the room. "Neither do I. He is my father's evil genius, I believe."

"What makes you suspect that?" inquired the Frenchman, with considerable interest.

"Several circumstances," was her vague response, as she twisted her curious old snake bracelet, a genuine sixteenth-century ornament which she had bought one day in a shop on the Ponte Vecchio in Florence.

"You mistrust him—eh?"

"He poses as my father's friend, but I believe that all the time he is jealous of his position and is his bitterest enemy."

"But they are very old friends, are they not?"

"Oh yes. The general owes his present position entirely to my father; otherwise he would now be in garrison in some obscure country town."

"I only wish he were," declared Dubard fervently. "He is jealous of our friendship. Did you notice how he glared at me while you were singing?"

"And yet at table you were such good friends," she laughed.

"It is not polite to exhibit ill-feeling in a friend's house, mademoiselle," was his calm response. "Yet I admit that I entertain no greater affection for the fellow than you do."

"But why should he object to our friendship?" she exclaimed. "If he were un-married, and in love with me, it would of course be different."

"No," he said. "He hates me."

"Why?"

Jules Dubard was silent, his dark eyes were fixed away across the moon-lit lawn.

"Why?" she repeated. "Tell me!"

"Well, he has cause to hate me—that's all," and he smiled mysteriously.

"But he's a dangerous man," she declared, with quick apprehension. "You probably don't know so much of him as I do. He would betray his own father if it suited his purpose."

"I know," laughed the man drily. "I've heard sufficient stories concerning him to be quite well aware of his unscrupulous character. It is a thousand pities that he is an associate of your father's."

"Ah yes!" she sighed. "But how can it be avoided? They are in office in the same ministry, and are bound to be in constant touch with each other. The only thing I fear is that he has, by some intrigue, contrived to get my father in his power," she said confidentially.

"How? What causes you to suspect such a thing?" he inquired quickly.

"Because once or twice of late I have noticed how when he has called in Rome and in Florence my father has been disinclined to see him, and that after the fellow's departure he has seemed very thoughtful and preoccupied. More than once, too, I've heard high words between them when they've been closeted together in the study in Rome. I once heard him threaten my father," she added.

"Threaten him!" cried her companion quickly. "What did the man say? Tell me." All that the girl was telling him was confirming what, in his heart, he already suspected.

"Well," she said, in a low voice of confidence, "it was early one morning, after the last court ball, and he had driven home with us. Afterwards my father had taken him to the study, and I had said good-night, when, on going to my room half an hour later, I found my maid very unwell. Therefore I went down again, intending to get from the study the key of the medicine cupboard, when I heard voices within, and naturally stopped to listen. I heard my father say distinctly, 'I won't. I'll never be a party to such a piece of audacious robbery—why, it's treason—treason, do you hear? No, Angelo, not even you can induce me to betray my country!' Then in reply I heard the general say, 'Very well. I have told you the course I intend to adopt. Your refusal places me in a critical situation, and I shall therefore save myself.' 'At my expense?' asked my father in a low, hoarse voice. 'Yes,' the man replied. 'I shall certainly not fall without an effort to retain my place, my liberty, depend upon it. And when the truth is out regarding the Sazarac affair, this high moral standard that you are now adopting will avail you but little.' Then there was a silence. At last my father asked in a tone of reproach, 'You actually intend to betray me, Angelo?—you, who owe your rank, your position, everything to me! Tell me, you are surely joking?' 'No,' replied the fellow, 'I am in earnest. You must act as I have suggested, or take the consequences'?"

"You are certain—quite certain—that Borselli mentioned the Sazarac affair?" asked the Frenchman, in deep earnestness and surprise. "I mean that you distinctly heard the name of Sazarac mentioned?"

"Distinctly. Why?"

But the Frenchman made no reply. How could he tell her? What she had related revealed to him a strange and startling truth—a truth which held him amazed,

CHAPTER FOUR.

CONTAINS A MYSTERY.

In the rector's cosy little study at Thornby, George Macbean sat that same evening smoking his pipe, perplexed and puzzled.

In the zone of light shed by the green-shaded reading-lamp the rector, a stout, good-humoured, round-faced man of forty, sat writing a letter, while his nephew, lounging back in the old leather arm-chair before the fireplace, drew heavy whiffs at his pipe, with his eyes fixed straight upon the well-filled bookcase before him.

That day he had become a changed man.

From the first moment he had bowed to Mary Morini, when his uncle had introduced him at Orton, he had been struck by her marvellous grace and beauty, and this admiration had daily increased until now he was compelled to acknowledge within himself that he was deeply in love with her.

He smiled bitterly as the truth made itself manifest. He had been over head and ears in love with half a dozen women in his time, but he had always in a few weeks discovered their defects, their ambitions, and their lack of womanliness, without which a woman is no woman. He supposed it would be the same again, for he was not a man who wore his heart upon his sleeve.

And yet he had discovered that a mystery surrounded her—a mystery that attracted him.

The dead quiet of the night was unbroken save for the scratching of the rector's pen, for the village of Thornby, like all agricultural villages, goes to bed early and rises with the dawn. The solemn bell in the old church-tower struck ten as Mr Sinclair scribbled the superscription, blotted it, and rose from the table to fill his own pipe.

"Why, George, my boy, you're glum to-night. What's the matter?"

"I really didn't know I was," laughed his nephew. "I was only thinking. And I didn't want to disturb you."

"Nothing disturbs me—except babies in church," declared the big fellow, laughing deeply. He was a good type of the easy-going bachelor parson in the enjoyment of a comfortable living and popularity in local society. He was fond of golf and cricket, was a good judge of a horse, a good shot, and frequently rode to hounds.

He filled his well-coloured briar carefully, lit it, and then casting himself into the chair opposite his nephew, said with a laugh—

"I noticed you were very chummy with Mary Morini. Well, what do you think

"Very charming," responded the young man, rather annoyed at his uncle's chaff.

"All the men about here rave over her beauty—and they have cause to, no doubt. She's a very entertaining companion and possesses a keen sense of humour—one of those girls who attract a man without being aware of it. That's the chief essential in a woman's grace."

"But who are these Morinis?" inquired Macbean, removing his pipe from his mouth. "Nobody seems to know exactly who or what they are."

"You're quite right," responded his uncle, in a rather changed tone. "Quite between ourselves, I've heard that question asked a good many times. Morini himself seems a bit of a recluse, for he seldom goes anywhere. Indeed, I haven't spoken to him more than half a dozen times in my life. But Madame Morini and her daughter are taken up by the local people because of their apparent affluence and because they rent Orton from Lady Straker."

"What kind of man is this Morini?" asked Macbean, in an idle tone.

"Oh, rather gentlemanly, with a lot of elegant pose. Speaks English very well for a foreigner, and smokes a very excellent brand of cigar. But, if the truth were told, he's looked upon here with a good deal of suspicion. Ill-natured people say that he's a foreign adventurer who comes here in hiding from the police," he added, laughing.

The young man blew a long cloud of smoke from his lips, and remained silent. He was trying to recall a face he had seen—the face of a man, evidently a foreigner, who had passed them in a dogcart as they were on the road home from Orton. The man's features had puzzled him ever since. They were familiar, yet he could not recollect in what circumstances they had met before.

In his position as secretary to the Member for South-West Norfolk he met many men, yet somehow he held a distinct idea that in the misty past this man had created upon him some impression of evil.

"You recollect," he exclaimed at last, "that just before we came to the crossroads to Calthorpe we passed a dogcart coming out from Rugby, with a groom in dark green livery."

"Yes. It was Morini's cart. The man in it is a guest at Orton," was the rector's reply. "More than that," he added, "he's said to be engaged—or about to be engaged—to the girl you admire so much."

"Oh, that's interesting!" remarked Macbean. "Do you know the man's name?"

"He's a young French count named Dubard. I've met him here several times; he seems quite a decent fellow for a Frenchman."

"Dubard? Dubard?" repeated the young man aloud, starting forward as though a sudden revelation had flashed upon him. "Surely he can't be Jules Dubard, the—"

"The what?" asked the rector quickly.

His nephew hesitated, recognising how he had narrowly betrayed the secret of that recognition. Then he added quite coolly—

"The Frenchman."

Basil Sinclair, disappointed at this clever evasion, looked his nephew straight in the face, and from the pallor of his cheeks saw that whatever recollections had been conjured up by mention of that name they were evidently the reverse of pleasing.

"His name is certainly Jules, and he is a Frenchman," he said gravely. "But you know something about him. I see it in your face."

The young man smiled, and lolling back again in the big easy-chair, answered with admirable coolness, considering the bewildering truth that had at that moment flashed upon him—

"I am only surprised that Miss Morini should become engaged to a Frenchman. She told me to-day that her greatest regret is that they cannot live in England always."

"Ah, my boy, she's a thorough-going cosmopolitan," replied the rector, his pipe still between his teeth. "Such women always marry foreigners. I daresay her father would object if she wanted to marry an Englishman. He's a man who evidently means his daughter to marry a title."

"In Italy it is rather a claim to distinction not to possess a title," laughed his nephew, recollecting how many penniless counts and marquises he had come across during those happy years when he lived with his Uncle Pietro in the white, half-deserted old city of Pisa.

"Morini is Italian to the backbone, with all the Italian's admiration for England and yet with all the Italian's prejudices. You'll say so when you know him."

"But this count?" exclaimed Macbean. "Tell me what you know about him."

"You know more than I do, my dear George," declared Sinclair, with a sly smile, "only you don't choose to tell me. You hold an opinion that he is not a fit and proper person to become the husband of Morini's daughter. Admit it."

"I don't yet know who Morini really is," responded his nephew, with a clever diplomacy. "You have not yet told me the general impression in the neighbourhood regarding the family."

"As I have already said, they're looked upon with distinct suspicion."

"Because they are foreigners—eh?"

"Possibly. We are very insular here in Leicestershire, notwithstanding the increasing foreign element in the hunting-field."

George slowly knocked the ashes from his pipe, saying—

"We English hold the foreigner in too great contempt. We are apt to forget that there are other Powers constantly conspiring to undermine our strength and to [illegible] security that is really childish in its simplicity, and if we have not a wise king, a strong Cabinet, and shrewd men in our diplomatic service, the mine must explode some day, depend upon it."

"Ah," laughed the rector, "I suppose it's your parliamentary associations that make you talk like that. You told me you sometimes prepare speeches for Morgan-Mason to deliver to his constituents. Is that one of his texts?"

"No, not exactly," replied the other, with a good-humoured smile. "I only speak what I think. The ignorance of the public regarding foreigners is simply appalling. They are in utter ignorance of the state of advancement of certain foreign nations as compared with our own. We are always slow and conservative, while they are quick to adopt new inventions, new ideas, and new schemes of progress."

"Mostly gingerbread," remarked the rector.

"Argument upon that point is unnecessary," said Macbean, growing serious. "I only emphasise the fact that a foreign family in England is at a far greater disadvantage than an English family on the Continent. The former is held in suspicion or shunned, while the latter is fêted and welcomed. Ah, my dear uncle, society, with all its sins and vices, is full of amazing prejudices."

"But of course there is another side to the question of the Morinis," his uncle said. "It got abroad last year that Morini held some very high position in Rome. Young Barton, the schoolmaster at Kilworth, went with one of Lunn's tours to Italy, and when he came back he told an extraordinary story of how the party were being shown the outside of one of the public offices when a gentleman descended from a carriage which drove into the courtyard, and as he entered the sentries saluted. To his surprise he recognised him as Mr Morini, and on inquiry understood from one of the doorkeepers that he was His Excellency the Minister of War. Of course nobody believed him. But I've looked in 'Whitaker,' and, strangely enough, it gives Signor Camillo Morini as Minister of War!"

"Ah, my dear uncle," laughed Macbean, "of course regard it as entirely confidential, but what Barton discovered is the truth. Signor Morini is a member of the Italian Cabinet, and one of the most prominent personages in Italy—and they actually believe him *here* to be an adventurer!" he laughed. "But," he added, "you haven't told me about Dubard."

"I know practically nothing, except that he stayed at Orton for a month last summer, and was very attentive to Mary. And as he's here again this season, the gossips say they are engaged. He is a rich man, I hear, with estates in the Pyrenees."

George Macbean's lip curled slightly, and he gave vent to a distinct sniff of dissatisfaction. He had recognised him as they had passed on the highroad, and yet, until his uncle had mentioned the name of Dubard, he had been puzzled as to the man's actual identity.

To him, the fact that the Frenchman was guest at Orton, and engaged to the Minister's daughter, was utterly staggering. Yet rumour did not say there was really an engagement—or at least it had not been formally announced.

The young man relit his pipe and smoked on in silence, his brows knit, his mind full of a certain scene of the past—a scene conjured up in his memory by sight of that pale, narrow face with the brown moustache—a scene that caused his hands to clench themselves and his teeth to close together firmly.

"Do tell me what you know about the Frenchman," urged the rector.

"No, thank you, my dear uncle," responded the other. "I know too well these gossiping villages, and I hold the law of slander in too great a dread. The count is all right," he laughed. "A very nice fellow, you said."

His uncle saw that he had no intention of saying a word against the visitor at Orton, and yet at the same time it was apparent that he held him in distinct mistrust. Yet, after all, reflected the rector, it was curious that George had not recognised him at once.

Macbean sat back watching the smoke curl slowly up, plunged in deep reflection. That man of all others was to marry Mary Morini! What a cruel vagary of Fate! Did she really love the fellow? he wondered. Had his elegant airs and graces, his stiff poses, and French effeminacy really attracted her? To him it seemed impossible. She was too sweet and womanly, too modest and full of the higher ideals of life, to allow that veneer of polish to deceive her. It might be, of course, that the marriage was to be one of convenience—that the Minister wished his daughter to become a French countess with an ancient title like that of Dubard—yet he could not conceive that she would of her own free will marry such a man.

Evidently His Excellency Camillo Morini was in blind ignorance of the character of his guest, or he would never for a moment entertain him in the bosom of his family.

If they were really engaged, then her future was at stake. He alone knew the truth—that ghastly, amazing truth—and it was therefore his bounden duty to go to her and frankly tell her all that he knew—or better, to seek an interview with the Minister and place the facts before him.

When he had bidden his uncle good-night and mounted to the small old-fashioned bedroom, he blew out the candle and sat at the open window gazing out upon the wide stretch of pasture land white in the moonbeams, reviewing the whole situation and endeavouring to decide upon the best course of action.

Mary Morini had charmed him with her sweet face and piquante cosmopolitan manner, yet at that same moment he had made a discovery that held him dumb in amazement. He recognised that she was in deadly peril—how deadly she little dreamed, and that to save her—to save the honour of her family—he must tell the truth.

He saw before him the tragedy of silence, and yet, alas! his lips were sealed.

To utter one single word of what he knew would be to bring upon himself opprobrium, disgrace, ruin!

CHAPTER FIVE.

IS MAINLY ABOUT A WOMAN.

George Macbean had, after a long, sleepless night, made up his mind.

When he descended to breakfast next morning he announced to his uncle his intention of cycling into Rugby, well knowing that the rector had to give a lesson in religious instruction in the village school, and would therefore not be able to accompany him.

So, in determination to meet the Frenchman face to face, to expose him and thus save Mary, even at risk of his own disgrace, he mounted and rode away down the white, dusty highroad.

Instead of going into Rugby, however, he turned off at Lilbourne, and rode over the road along which they had driven the previous evening, to Orton.

Eleven o'clock was certainly a rather unconventional hour for calling, but as he dismounted at the gates and walked his machine up the long, well-kept drive he had already invented an excuse. As he passed the study window he saw within a tall, elderly, grave-faced man in a suit of light grey tweed, and at once recognised that it was His Excellency himself.

In answer to his ring at the door, a young English footman appeared, whereupon he asked—

"Is Count Dubard at home?"

"The count left this morning by the nine o'clock train."

"Left!" echoed Macbean. "And is he not returning?"

"I think not, sir. He took his luggage. But I will inquire if you'll step in a moment."

The man had conducted him across the wide old-fashioned stone hall into a pleasant morning-room which looked out upon the flower-garden and was flooded with sunshine, and after the lapse of a few moments the door reopened and there entered Mary herself, a charming figure in a fresh white blouse and linen skirt.

"Why, Mr Macbean!" she cried, extending her hand gaily. "You are quite an unexpected visitor! Davis says you want to see Count Dubard. He left for Paris this morning."

"And is he not coming back?"

"No, I believe not," was her answer. "He received a letter this morning calling him to Paris at once, and dashed off to try and catch the eleven o'clock service from Charing Cross. He just looked tired, and said He was anxious to see you, I think."

"Anxious to see me—why?" asked Macbean quickly.

"Last night he told me that he recognised you as you were driving home with Mr Sinclair, and asked if I knew you. I, of course, told him that you had been playing tennis here. He seemed very eager to see you, and made quite a lot of inquiries about you."

Her companion was silent. The recognition had been mutual, then, and the story of the urgent letter was only an excuse of the Frenchman's to escape from a very ugly and compromising position! His flight showed Macbean that the fellow was in fear of him, and yet he had fortunately avoided a scene between them, and a result which, in all probability, might have caused his own ruin.

He looked at the bright, sweet-faced woman before him, and wondered—wondered how she could allow her affection to be attracted towards such a fellow. And yet what an admirable actor the man was! She was, alas! in ignorance of it all.

How could he tell her? To explain, would only be to condemn himself. No. He resolved that for the present he must conceal his secret—for his own sake. Nevertheless how strange it was, he thought, that he should thus suddenly be drawn so closely towards her. Yesterday she was a mere acquaintance of the tea-table and the tennis-lawn, like dozens of other girls he knew, while to-day he was there as her friend and protector, the man who intended to save her and her family from the ingenious trap that he now saw was already prepared.

"I'm sorry he's gone," he remarked in a tone of regret, adding, "I knew him long ago, and only after we had passed, my uncle told me that he was a guest here."

"He too said he wanted very much to see you," she remarked brightly. "But you'll meet again very soon, no doubt. I shall tell him of your inquiries when I write, for he spoke of you in the warmest terms. I did not know your address in London, so I gave him Mr Sinclair's. I'm so sorry he's gone," she added. "We were to have all gone for a picnic to-day over to Kenilworth."

"And instead of that the central attraction has disappeared," he hazarded, with a smile.

"What do you mean by 'central attraction'?" she asked, flushing slightly.

"My friend Dubard, of course. I suppose what everyone says is correct, Miss Morini, and therefore I may be permitted to congratulate you upon your engagement to my friend?"

"Oh, there is no engagement, I assure you," was her reply, as she looked at him with open frankness, her cheeks betraying a slightly heightened colour. "I know there's quite a lot of gossip about it, but the rumours are entirely without foundation," she laughed; and as she sat there in the deep old window-seat, he recognised that, notwithstanding the refined and dignified beauty of a woman who was brilliant in a brilliant court, she still retained a soft simplicity and a virgin innocence; she was a woman whose first tears would spring from compassion, "suffering with those that she saw suffer." She had no acquired scruples of honour, no coy concealments, no assumed dignity standing in its own defence. Her bashfulness as they spoke together was less a quality than an instinct; like the self-folding flower, spontaneous and unconscious. Cosmopolitan life in that glare and glitter of aristocratic Rome—that circle where, from the innate distrust women have of each other, the dread of the betrayed confidence and jealous rivalry, they made no friends, and were indeed ignorant of the true meaning of friendship, where flattery and hypocrisy were the very air and atmosphere and mistrust lay in every hand-clasp and lurked in every glance—had already opened Mary Morini's eyes to the hollow shams, the manifold hypocrisies, and the lamentable insincerity of social intimacies, and she had recoiled from it with disgust.

She had retained her woman's heart, for that was unalterable and inalienable as a part of her being; but her looks, her language, her thoughts, assumed to George Macbean, as he stood there beneath the spell of her beauty, the cast of the pure ideal.

And yet she loved Jules Dubard!

He bit his lip and gazed out of the old diamond panes upon the tangle of red and white roses around the lawn.

Ah! how he longed to speak to her in confidence—to reveal to her the secret that now oppressed his heart until he seemed stifled by its ghastliness.

But it was utterly impossible, he told himself. Now that Dubard had fled, he must find other and secret means by which to acquaint her with the truth, and at the same time shield himself from the Frenchman's crushing revenge.

He contrived to conceal the storm of emotion that tore his heart, and laughed with her about the unfounded rumours that had got abroad concerning her engagement, saying—

"Of course in a rural neighbourhood like this the villagers invent all kinds of reports based upon their own surmises."

"Yes," she declared. "They really know more about our business than we do ourselves. Only fancy! That I am engaged to marry Count Dubard—ridiculous!"

"Why ridiculous?" he asked, standing before her.

"Well—because it is!" she laughed, her fine eyes meeting his quite frankly. "I'm not engaged, Mr Macbean. So if you hear such a report again you can just flatly deny it."

"I shall certainly do so," he declared, "and I shall reserve my congratulations for a future occasion."

She then turned the conversation to tennis, evidently being averse to the further discussion of the man who had courted and flattered her so assiduously—the man who was her father's friend—and presently she took Macbean out across the lawn to introduce him to her father, who had seated himself in a long cane chair beneath the great cedar, and was reading his Italian paper.

His Excellency looked up as they approached, whereupon Mary exclaimed—

This is Mr Macbean, father. He wishes to salute you. He was here yesterday playing tennis, but you were not visible."

"Very glad to meet you, sir," exclaimed Camillo Morini, rising, grasping the young man's hand, and raising his grey felt hat. "You know," he explained, as he reseated himself, "I am a busy man, and so I have but little opportunity of meeting my wife's English friends. But," he added, in very good English, after a slight pause, as he readjusted his gold-rimmed glasses and looked harder at the young man, "if I am not mistaken, we have met before, have we not? I seem to recognise your face."

"Yes, your Excellency," laughed Macbean, whereupon both Mary and her father started in surprise, for it was apparent that their visitor was aware of Morini's true position. "I had the honour of having an audience of your Excellency in Rome. I am secretary to Mr Morgan-Mason, and accompanied him to Rome on the deputation which waited upon you regarding the concession of supplying army stores in Abyssinia."

"Of course, of course!" exclaimed the Minister, suddenly interested. "I recollect quite well. You introduced the deputation, and I remember remarking how well you spoke Italian for an Englishman. Ah yes. I could not give the concession, as it had already been given to a German firm," he added, omitting, however, the real reason, namely, because the English company had offered no secret commission. "And you are secretary to Morgan-Mason? He is a deputy, I believe."

Macbean explained that his employer sat for South-West Norfolk, and in response to other inquiries gave certain information concerning his politics and his social influence, facts of which the clever Minister made a note; for an idea had occurred to him that the monied provision-dealer whose pompousness had struck him as he had sat in his private cabinet at the Ministry of War might be one day of service to him.

All through his career it had been part of Camillo Morini's creed to note persons who might be of assistance to him, and to afterwards use their influence, or their weaknesses, to his advantage. A keen judge of character, he read men's minds as he would an open book. He had recognised the weakness of that white-waistcoated Englishman who was struggling into society, and he resolved that one day both the Member of Parliament and his secretary should be put to their proper uses.

"Mr Macbean called to see Count Dubard, who is a friend of his," his daughter explained.

"Oh, you are acquainted! How curious!" exclaimed His Excellency. "Dubard unfortunately left this morning—because he received a letter which recalled him at once to Paris. But as my valet tells me that no letters arrived for the count this morning, I can only surmise that he was tired of us here, and found country life in England too dull," he laughed knowingly. "I've received the same fictitious letter myself before now, when I've been tired of a host and hostess."

And they all three laughed in chorus. His Excellency was of course unaware of the real reason of Jules Dubard's flight, and the young Englishman smiled within himself as he reflected upon the staggering surprise it would cause that calm, astute man who was such a power in the south of Europe if he knew the actual truth.

"Of course," added Signor Morini, turning to the young man, "you will do me one kind favour? You will not mention to anyone here my true position. I come to England each year for rest and quiet, and if I am unknown no political significance can be attached to my summer visits—you understand?"

"Certainly, your Excellency, I shall respect your wishes," was Macbean's reply, and a few minutes later he took leave of the great statesman and his daughter, and, full of strange conflicting reflections, rode out upon the broad highway back to Thornby.

CHAPTER SIX.
DISCLOSES CERTAIN STRANGE FACTS.

As Big Ben boomed forth twelve o'clock over London that same night the supper-room at the Savoy was filled to overflowing with a boisterous, well-dressed crowd of after-theatre revellers. The scene was brighter and gayer perhaps than any other scene at that hour in all the giant city. The "smart set," that slangy, vulgar result of society's degeneration, was as largely represented as usual; the women were fair, the jewels sparkled, the dresses were rich, and in the atmosphere was that restlessness, that perpetual craze for excitement which proves so attractive to habitués of the place.

Every table in the great room was engaged, and the company was essentially *le monde ou l'on s'amuse.* But you probably have sat there amid the hurrying of the waiters, the hum of voices, the loud laughter of "smart women," the clinking of champagne-glasses, that babel of noise drowned by the waltzes played by the Hungarian band. The air was heavy with the combined odour of a hundred perfumes, the fresh flowers drooped upon the tables, and the merry company crowded into that last half-hour all the merriment they could before the lights were lowered.

At such places one sees exhibited in public the full, true, and sole omnipotence of money—how it wins the impoverished great ones to be guests of its possessor, how it purchases the smiles of the haughtiest, the favours of the most exclusive.

Lazily watching that animated scene, the two men who had been guests at Orton, Dubard and Borselli, were sitting apart at a small table near the window. A bottle of Krug stood between them, and as they leaned their elbows on the table they criticised their fellow-guests, speaking in Italian, so that their remarks should not be understood by their neighbours.

The band had just concluded Desgranges' "Jalouse," that air so reminiscent of the terrace of the Café de Paris at Monte Carlo, the leader had bowed to the company, and the waiters were busy collecting the banknotes with which the bills were in most cases paid, when the Italian drained his glass, saying—

"Let us go! I've had enough of this! Come on to Claridge's with me for a final cigar."

"A moment?" exclaimed Dubard, his eyes fixed across the room. "Do you see over there, just behind the column, two ladies with a stout man with grey side-whiskers? One of the ladies is in blue. What a terrible vulgarian the fellow is! I've been watching him."

The general glanced in the direction indicated and replied—

"Oh yes, I noticed him as we came in. You're right, my dear Jules, that fellow is a vulgarian. I met him once in Rome. His name is Morgan-Mason, a deputy and very wealthy."

"Morgan-Mason!" echoed the Frenchman, looking hard at him. "Ah!" he added, "I've heard of him, of course. Yes. Let us go," and they both rose, descended by the lift, and drove in a hansom to Claridge's.

In the Under-Secretary's elegant little sitting-room—the room wherein that afternoon he had accepted the German contractor's bribe on Morini's behalf—he drew forth a box of choice cigars, and they both commenced to smoke.

A brief and rather painful silence fell between them. Both men had that evening exhibited towards each other a strained politeness, each knowing that the other hated him. Dubard's defiance on the previous night had upset all the calculations of that past-master of intrigue, Angelo Borselli, whose dark eyes now darted a swift glance at his companion lolling back in the big arm-chair apparently perfectly at his ease.

To Borselli's surprise, and believing that his departure had been due to his threat on the previous night, Dubard had left Rugby for London an hour before he had, but at four o'clock that afternoon he had sent an invitation to the Carlton, suggesting that they should spend the evening together at a theatre, which they had done.

There was a mystery in the Frenchman's sudden departure from Orton, and in it Borselli suspected an ingenious move. Throughout the whole day he had reasoned within himself, finally coming to the conclusion that it was better to be friendly with such a man as Jules Dubard than to be his enemy.

Dubard had seen during the evening that his companion wished to speak with him but was hesitating. At last, however, after they had smoked in silence for some minutes, the crafty Sicilian stroked his moustache and exclaimed—

"I fear, my dear Jules, that I was rather hasty, perhaps rude, last night. Yet, after all, I am very glad that you took my hint and left Orton."

The Frenchman opened his eyes widely at the man's calm audacity.

"I did not take your hint in the least, I assure you," he exclaimed, with quick indignation. "I left Orton for quite another reason."

The sallow-faced man smiled, as though quite unconscious of his companion's anger.

"Yes," he said. "I know. You cannot deceive me."

"You know?" cried the Frenchman, starting to his feet. "What do you know? Have you invited me up here to threaten me again?"

"I merely say that I know the reason why you received the letter calling you to Paris this morning," replied the Under-Secretary in a cold, calm voice. "It was because you met and were recognised by a certain Englishman named Macbean, the secretary of that vulgar fellow we saw eating his supper half an hour ago."

Dubard's jaw fell. He saw that by some utterly unaccountable means his ene-

Was it possible that he could know the whole truth? No; it was impossible. Macbean dare not speak. Of that he felt quite assured.

"Ah?" continued the general, a grim smile crossing his thin, hard features as he narrowly watched his companion. "You see I am not quite as ignorant of the past as you believe, my dear Jules."

"Nor am I!" cried the Frenchman, turning upon him savagely. "Last night you threatened me, remember!"

"And to-night I have invited you here, my dear friend, to arrive at some amicable agreement that will be to our mutual advantage," answered the clever Under-Secretary, with a suavity of manner which showed him to be a born diplomat.

"Yes, I know," answered the other in a dry, hard voice. "This is not the first time you and I have discussed matters, General Borselli. I know that if it suited you you'd betray your own mother. You have no conscience, no code of honour?"

"My code of honour is exactly the same as yours, *caro mio*," replied the Italian, laughing. "I try to turn all I can into profit for myself, just as you are trying to do. My maxim is 'self first.'"

"And for that reason you are plotting the downfall of Morini and the whole Ministry!"

"A work in which you are actively assisting," added the Under-Secretary.

"I did not come here to be insulted," Dubard protested.

"Neither did I invite you here to pose as a censor of political morality," responded his shrewd companion, looking straight and determinedly into his pale face. "But why should we quarrel, when it is to our mutual interests to remain friendly?"

"I have not quarrelled. Last night you objected to me visiting the Morinis."

"Because I am well aware of your object."

"I admit that I intend to marry Mary," and he removed his cigar from his mouth and examined it.

"And you have also a further object in view, my dear count—one that is even more interesting," declared Borselli, "a plan that I can very easily frustrate."

"Well, you told me that last night," he said. "And I, on my part, frankly declare that I do not in the least fear any revelations you can make."

"Not of the affair of General Sazarac?" whispered the cunning Italian, his dark eyes fixed upon the younger man as he bent towards him. "Have you so completely forgotten certain events which, if recalled, would mean—well, they would mean that you would neither marry Morini's daughter nor be successful in the next very ingenious trick by which you intend to make a grand *coup* at the expense of my country."

At the mention of the name of General Sazarac the other's face blanched, and holding his breath he stood glaring at the man who with raised eyebrows smiled so calmly at him. He saw that this political adventurer was aware of a certain deep, terrible secret of the past which he believed was buried for ever. His enemy's attitude of cool confidence was sufficient to bring him at once to a sense of his insecurity.

"Well?" he managed to gasp. "And what is your proposal?"

"Ah, my dear friend, I am glad you are ready to listen to reason," responded the Sicilian. "We must both face the future unshrinkingly, you know. You have your own schemes; I have mine. By acting in accord we shall succeed, but if we are enemies then we shall commit the very foolish and unpardonable error of exposing each other. I know quite well that there are certain rather unfortunate incidents regarding my own career, those disagreeable little matters of which you have knowledge, and by which you could retaliate. You see, I do not for a single moment intend to deny them. On the contrary, I frankly suggest that by an agreement of silence we can be helpful in each other's interests. We both desire advancement, and can gain it through the medium of Morini. Are you not agreed?"

Dubard, slowly convinced that without the general's aid he must be powerless and in peril, nodded in the affirmative. He did not discern the wily man's ulterior motive, or the secret reason of the proposed compact.

"Your primary object, my dear Jules, is of course money," the general went on. "Now, by a simple written declaration I shall absolve you from all connection with the Sazarac affair, while you, on your part, will deny my connection with that ugly little matter in Rome two years ago. Both of us will then emerge again honest and upright—models of virtue. Bygones will be bygones. I shall go my way, you will go yours; I to assist you, and you to help me—a perfectly reciprocal arrangement. I shall become Minister, while you—well, you will by a single *coup* become a rich man, and at the same time gain a very charming wife."

"And Morini?"

The Under-Secretary elevated his shoulders and exhibited his palms.

"And the Englishman Macbean?"

"He is a mere fly in amber," declared the Sicilian, with a sinister smile. "Fortune lies before us in Italy, my dear Jules—for you wealth and a wife; for me, office and distinction. By acting in accord we have nothing whatever to fear. Morini dare not disobey us, and Macbean, being a poor man, will easily fall into our power. Leave him entirely to me. I have a scheme by which he will shortly discover that his whole future depends upon his silence, and that a single indiscreet word will mean his ruin."

"And if that fails?"

"Then there is still that effective method which was adopted towards Sazarac—you understand?"

The Frenchman nodded, darting a swift glance at the thin-featured man before him.

CHAPTER SEVEN.
AN AFTERNOON AT THORNBY.

The Thornby Flower-Show was held a week later in the rectory grounds, the work of arrangement chiefly devolving upon the bluff, good-natured rector and his nephew George.

The little rural fête, encouraged by the richer residents, was, like other village flower-shows, the annual occasion for the cottagers to exhibit their "twelve best varieties of vegetables," their "six best pot-plants," the ferns from their windows, and such-like horticultural possessions. Though quite a small show, it was typically English, well managed, and therefore always attended by people from the big houses in the neighbourhood, whose gardeners themselves competed in the open classes.

The judges—three gardeners from a distance—had inspected the exhibits in the marquee, and having made their awards, had, together with the committee, consisting of the local butcher and baker and two or three cottagers, all in their Sunday clothes and wearing blue rosettes, been entertained to luncheon by Mr Sinclair, when just before two o'clock the village band in uniform filed in at the garden-gate and put up their music-stands on the lawn. Then, as the church clock struck two, the villagers were admitted, each exhibitor making a rush for the tent, anxious to ascertain whether his exhibit bore the coloured card indicative of a prize.

At half-past two several smart carriages had driven up, and at last came the Morini landau, containing Mr Morini and his wife and daughter Mary. Basil Sinclair and George having welcomed them at the gate, Mr Morini was conducted to a small platform on the lawn, where, after a few words of introduction from the rector, he made a short speech in fairly good English, declaring the flower-show open.

Afterwards the party were conducted round the show by Sinclair, while George, of course, walked with Mary, who looked cool and sweet in a simple gown of pale grey voile, with a large grey hat to match.

As they walked around the tent, close beneath the noonday sun and heavy with the odour of vegetables and perfume of flowers, she congratulated him upon the success of the show.

Thornby always looked forward to the flower-show, for it was a gala day for the village; its four shops were closed, across the road at the top of the hill the committee stretched a string of gay bunting, and when dusk came the rectory garden was illuminated and there was dancing on the lawn. Thornby made every occasion an excuse for a dance, and the annual dress ball on the rectory lawn was the chief event of the year.

It was His Excellency's first visit to the rectory, therefore Mr Sinclair showed him the old-fashioned house, the grounds, the quaint old fifteenth-century church with its curious sculptured tombs, old carved oak and monumental brasses, while Mrs Morini, meeting several ladies of her acquaintance on the lawn, left Mary free to walk and talk with George Macbean.

For a whole long week of never-ending days he had been eagerly anticipating that meeting. Never for one moment had he ceased to think of her. The sweet, fair-faced girl was in peril, he knew, and if it were possible he intended to save her. But how? Ah! that was the question.

Although so deeply in love with her, he was judicious enough to save appearances, knowing well that the eyes of the whole countryside were upon him. The rustic is ever on the alert to discover defects in his master, and gossip in a village generally errs on the side of ill-nature. Therefore he was careful to appear gallant, and yet not too pressing in his attentions—a somewhat difficult feat with the strong ardour of love burning within him.

They were strolling together through the quaint old flower-garden sloping gently away towards the placid river, where they found themselves alone, when Mary, turning her beautiful face to him, suddenly said—

"I had no idea, Mr Macbean, that you had met my father in Rome. He was very much interested the other day, and after you had gone made quite a lot of inquiries about you."

"It was very kind of him," was the young man's laughing reply. "I merely went as interpreter to Mr Morgan-Mason, who had business at your Ministry of War."

Then, as they halted beneath the trees at the water's edge, where there was a cool, refreshing breeze, she exclaimed suddenly, with a slight sigh, "Ah, how I wish we always lived in dear old England! I always look back upon my schooldays by the sea as the happiest in all my life; but now,"—and she drew a long breath again. "It is so different in Italy."

Yes. She was sad, he recognised—very sad. But why? Her young heart seemed oppressed by some hidden grief. He saw it in her fine dark eyes at the moments when she was serious. Time after time, as he spoke to her and she answered, he recognised that upon her mind rested some heavy burden which oppressed and crushed her. Her resolute yet gentle spirit, her simple, serious, domestic turn of mind distinguished her from all the other women of his acquaintance. Her reveries, her simplicity, her melancholy, her sensibility, her fortitude, her perfectly feminine bearing, even though that of a cosmopolitan, were the characteristics of a womanly woman—a woman who would struggle unsubdued against the strangest vicissitudes of fortune, meeting with unshaken constancy reverses and disasters such as would break the most masculine spirit.

George Macbean recognised all this, and more. He saw that she was at heart a thoroughly English girl, fond of tennis, hockey, and a country life, who had been transplanted into an artificial world of glare and glitter, of empty etiquette and false friendships, and yet who, at the same time, seemed to be held transfixed by some secret upon her conscience.

What was it? he wondered. Was he, after all, mistaken?

The longer he remained in her company, the more mystified did he become. He knew too well the character of Jules Dubard; he knew that she was marked down a victim, and he intended to stand as her friend—her champion if need be—even at peril to himself.

As she leaned over the old wooden rail at the river brink, gazing across the calm, unruffled waters, she chatted with gay vivacity about their mutual friends in the neighbourhood, and related her failure at a tennis tournament held on the previous day by a colonel's wife on the other side of Rugby.

"I suppose you often see Count Dubard in Rome," he said at last, with some attempt at indifference. "He is in Italy a great deal nowadays, I have heard."

"He was in Rome this winter," she answered. "He often came to my mother's receptions."

"He has a very wide circle of acquaintances, has he not?"

"Yes, mostly military men. He seems to know half of the officers in Rome. I thought I knew a good many, for crowds come to us every Thursday, but he knows far more."

"And of course your father sends him cards for the official receptions at the Ministry of War?"

"Certainly—why?" she asked, glancing quickly at her companion with some surprise.

"Oh, nothing," he laughed uneasily. "I was only reflecting that he must have a very pleasant time in Italy, that's all."

"I believe he enjoys himself," she said. "But every foreigner who has money and is recognised by his Embassy can have a pleasant time in Rome if he likes."

"But not every foreigner enjoys the friendship of the Minister of War," he remarked—"nor of his daughter," he added, with a smile.

Her cheeks flushed slightly.

"Ah!" she protested, with one of those quaint little foreign gestures. "There you are again, Mr Macbean! Teasing me because these ignorant people here say that I'm engaged to the count. It is really too bad of you! Did I not assure you the other day that it is quite untrue?"

"Forgive me!" he exclaimed, raising his panama hat, bowing as though she were an entire stranger, and yet laughing the while. "I had no intention of giving offence. Envy is permitted, however—is it not?"

"Oh, it hasn't given me offence at all?" she laughed frankly. "You see, there's

Her words struck him as very strange. They seemed to convey that if the engagement were really a fact it would cause her regret and annoyance.

"I wanted to meet Dubard so much," he remarked in a tone of regret. "I suppose there is no chance he will return to Orton?"

"Not this summer, I think. He left us to go direct to Paris, and then I believe he goes to his estate in the Pyrenees."

"But he came here intending to spend a week or so at Orton, did he not?"

"Yes; but he received a letter recalling him to France," she said. "Father says he didn't receive any letter. If he really didn't, he surely could have left without telling us a lie."

Macbean smiled. How little she knew of the real character of Jules Dubard, the plausible *élégant* who was such a prominent character at the Jockey Club and in the Bois.

"Very soon," she added, in a tone of regret, "we shall have to return. My father is due back at the Ministry on the fourth of next month, and while he is there we shall go up to San Donato, our villa above Florence, and stay for the vintage, which, to me, is the best time in Italy in all the year."

"Ah yes," he sighed. "I have always heard so. Myself I love Italy—I only wish I could escape from this country with its long dismal winters and live in sunshine always."

"You would very soon tire of it," she assured him, looking him straight in the face with her fine eyes. "Even our bright sun gives one fever, and our blue sky becomes so monotonous that one longs for the calm of a grey English day."

"I would like to try it for a year or two," he declared wistfully.

"Then why don't you?"

He was silent, and their eyes met again.

"Because I am not my own master, Miss Morini," was his low response. "My living, such as it is, lies here in England. I am the factotum of a man who has elevated money to be his god, and I am compelled to serve him in silence and without complaint because it happens to be my lot in life."

"A rather unhappy and uncomfortable one, I should imagine," she remarked, suddenly growing grave.

"At times, yes," was his brief reply. He did not wish to burden her with his own disappointments and misfortunes. She knew what was his position, a mere secretary, and that was sufficient. What hope could he ever have of daring to aspire to her hand? He might stand as her friend, but become her lover, never!

And when, a week later, he called at Orton to wish her farewell, as his vacation was at an end and he was compelled to return to his chambers in the Temple, and to that room in Mr Morgan-Mason's flat in Queen Anne's Mansions, he looked in vain in her eyes for some sign of genuine regret. There was none. No, she too had realised that on account of his position love was forbidden him.

"We shall meet here again, I hope, Mr Macbean—next summer," she exclaimed, laughing airily, as she gave him her small white hand.

"I hope so," was his fervent reply in a low, meaning voice, as their hands clasped.

And then, with sinking heart and full of grave apprehensions regarding her future, he bowed and left her, left her, alas! to Jules Dubard—Jules Dubard of all men!

CHAPTER EIGHT.

THE TRAITOR.

Camillo Morini stood at the big window of his private cabinet in the Ministry of War at Rome, gazing down upon the silent courtyard, white in the glaring heat of afternoon.

He was dressed in a cool suit of clean white linen, as is the summer mode in the South, and as he stood gazing out at the sentry standing in his box motionless as a statue, he calmly smoked his after-luncheon cigar—a good Havanna he had brought from England. The man who was so constantly juggling with a nation's future pressed his lips together, and afterwards heaved a big sigh—a sigh that echoed through the big, lofty room.

The Minister's cabinet, like all the rooms in the new War Office, was big and bare, with a marble floor for summer, and a high stove of white terra-cotta with broad brass bands for winter. Upon the ceiling were fine modern frescoes; the walls, however, unlike those of the other rooms, which were mostly colour-washed, were papered dark red, and the heavy furniture was covered with thick red plush; while in one corner was a handsome marble bust of Victor Emmanuel upon a pedestal, and above hung a large framed portrait of King Umberto, the reigning sovereign, and a huge shield bearing the arms of Italy. In the centre stood a huge writing-table of carved walnut, with a great high-backed chair, the seat of the man who ruled the army of Italy.

The doors were double, with a wide space between, so that the messenger in uniform who lounged outside should overhear nothing, while so hemmed in by secretaries was the Minister that he was as difficult of approach as the very sovereign himself.

That huge square block of new stuccoed buildings, with long corridors, enormous clerks' room, and big courtyard, the echoes of which were awakened day and night by the regular tramp of the sentries and the clank of arms, was at that moment a veritable hive of industry—for of all the government departments in Rome, the War Office, with its tremendous responsibilities, is the best conducted.

His Excellency was reflecting upon something that Angelo Borselli, the Under-Secretary, had told him while they had been lunching together at the club. He recognised the seriousness of it all, and he sighed in consequence.

Presently, while his eyes were still fixed upon that sentry erect and motionless in his box, upon which the sun beat down so fiercely, there was a rap at the door, and there entered the uniformed messenger who had been on guard outside, who saluted, saying—

"General Arturo Valentini of the 6th Alpine Regiment, together with a captain of the same regiment, crave an audience with your Excellency."

"What is the captain's name?" grunted the Minister of War.

The messenger looked at the card that had been given him, and replied—

"Captain Felice Solaro, your Excellency."

"Ah! Solaro! Solaro!" exclaimed Morini, tossing away his cigar. "Show them in."

And as he passed before the tiny mirror he glanced at himself to adjust his cravat and see that not a single hair was awry—a habit of his before giving audience.

A few moments later two men in uniform were ushered in. The general, short of stature, white-haired, with firm military step, a red face, and white moustache, saluted and stood at attention as he entered the Minister's presence; while the captain, a smart-looking, dark-haired man of forty, followed his superior's example, yet as Morini darted a quick glance at him, he visibly trembled at it. The captain's face was white as death, and as he stood for a moment in the awkward silence that followed, his gloved fingers chafed his sword hilt nervously.

"Well, general?" inquired the Minister, who had never before met that distinguished officer, but whom he, of course, knew well by repute. Valentini had been Inspector-General of Genio fifteen years ago, and had served Italy well in those fierce campaigns of the early sixties, as his row of medals and decorations showed. "Why do you wish for audience?" he asked sharply.

"Your Excellency, I am here to crave for a more merciful sentence upon this man," the kindly old officer answered, turning to the captain, who stood with head bowed at his side. "I am his commanding officer, and in justice I wish to intercede for him."

The Minister raised his eyes in surprise, and asked—

"And what is this man's name, pray?"

"I am Felice Solaro, your Excellency," faltered the captain, as though fearing to pronounce his own name. "My general has travelled with me from Piedmont to obtain audience and to implore your mercy."

"Solaro!" echoed the Minister, looking straight at him. "Ah yes, I remember!" Then turning to the general, Morini added in a hard, impatient tone—

"I cannot see why you should have troubled yourself to come to Rome on such an errand—and without leave too! I thought this man was under arrest? Is this the way you execute military justice in the north?"

"I took it upon myself to bring the captain here," was the fine old officer's answer.

"And he wears his sword, I see!" remarked the Minister, with a sneer. "I suppose you have taken it upon yourself to give it back to him—eh?"

"I returned him his sword temporarily, your Excellency, in order that during

and further, in order that he should stand before you in the full possession of his rights as an officer, and ask your leave to explain."

"I have no time to hear any explanations from men who have been condemned by court-martial, General Valentini. It is your duty to hear his excuses—not mine. The whole matter is quite clear. I have had the papers before me, and have gone through them carefully. They were sent to me in England. And if you ask me my private opinion, general, I think that dismissal from the army and fifteen years' imprisonment is a very light sentence upon a traitor. Had I been on the court-martial I should have given a life sentence."

"But, your Excellency!" gasped the unhappy captain, his face blanched, his hands trembling, "I am innocent. I am the victim of some clever conspiracy, by which the real culprit has shielded himself. I had no chance of defending myself at the court-martial, for—"

"Silence!" cried the Minister. "You have been tried and found guilty of treason against your king and country. The evidence is as plain as the light of day, and yet you deny your guilt?"

"I do deny it," declared the unhappy captain. "They refused to hear my explanation."

"That is true, your Excellency," interposed the general. "The court sat for four days in Turin with closed doors, and as three of the officers composing it were due to go on their annual leave, the sitting on the fourth day was terminated hurriedly, sentence was given, and sent to you for confirmation. Your Excellency has confirmed it, therefore Captain Solaro has no appeal except to yourself."

"You, as his commanding officer, were not a member of the court?"

"No, your Excellency."

"Then why should you interest yourself in a matter which does not concern you, pray?" inquired Morini impatiently.

"Because this unfortunate affair reflects upon the honour of my command."

"Oh, of course. It is all very well to speak heroically after the event!" exclaimed the Minister of War, with a hard, dry laugh. "The mischief has been done, and one of your officers has been found guilty of treason—of selling a military secret to a foreign power."

"Found guilty, yes," exclaimed the unfortunate captain. "But innocent, nevertheless!"

Morini shrugged his shoulders, and seating himself in his writing-chair took some official memoranda from a drawer in the table. Then, having glanced quickly at it, he said—

"The facts are quite plain. This man, Felice Solaro, of the 6th Alpine Regiment, is in garrison on Mont Gran Paradiso in the Alps, where on the other side of the mountain, at Tresenta, we have recently constructed a new fortress, for the protection of the frontier at that point. This fortress, which is sunk out of sight, has taken four and a half years to construct, and was only completed and garrisoned six months ago. It commands the Oreo valley, which, in the event of hostilities with France, would be one of the most vulnerable points on the frontier. French agents have, time after time, endeavoured to learn something of our works up there; but so well has the spot been guarded that only two agents have succeeded in obtaining sight of it, and both were arrested and are now in prison as spies. And yet, in spite of all this, there was found in Solaro's quarters by an orderly fragments of a curious letter in French addressed to 'Mon cher Felice,' acknowledging receipt of the plans, thanking him, and enclosing the sum agreed upon in Italian banknotes."

"The letter was never addressed to me," the captain cried. "I know nothing of it. The whole thing was a conspiracy to ruin and disgrace me!"

"But there are other facts supplied by the secret service," went on the Minister in a dry, hard tone, turning to the accused man. "You spent your last leave in Paris; you were seen by one of our agents in the company of a man well-known to be a French spy. You went to various places of amusement with him, drank with him at the Hôtel Chatham, at the Grand Café, and other places, and," added Morini, looking him straight in the face, "and what is more, he lent you money. Do you deny that?"

The captain stood glaring at his accuser, utterly dumbfounded. This latter truth had not been given in evidence against him. The Minister therefore held certain secret information of which he was in entire ignorance. He had been watched in Paris! He held his breath, and was silent. Even the general looked at him in surprise and suspicion.

"No," he answered hoarsely at last, "I do not deny it. The man did lend me money."

"For what purpose—eh? In order to obtain from you in secret the plans of the Tresenta fortress," declared His Excellency. "French agents do not lend money to Italian officers without some *quid pro quo*."

"I did not know that the fellow was a spy until afterwards."

"Until it was too late, I suppose. You were entrapped, so you were compelled to give the plans to France. Now admit it."

"I assert that I am entirely innocent," he declared. "It is true that I spent my leave in Paris, where I met a man who called himself Georges Latrobe, an engineer from Bordeaux, who spoke Italian I ran short of cash, and he lent me five hundred francs, which I repaid to him ten days after my return to barracks. It was only on the last day when I was with him that my suspicions were aroused regarding his real character. We were sitting together in the Café Terminus, when he turned the conversation to our defences on the Alpine frontier, expressing a desire to visit me at Gran Paradiso. I at once told him that the admission of strangers within the military zone was prohibited. But he pressed me, and even went so far as to offer me a receipt for the money he had lent me, together with a like sum if I could gain him admission, in order, so he said, to see the latest feat of Italian engineering. But [illegible] and from that day I have not seen him."

"But you furnished him with plans and details of the fortifications?" snapped the Minister of War.

"I did not," denied the captain stoutly. "I admit that I very narrowly escaped falling into a clever trap, but fortunately saved myself. If the plans have actually been furnished, then they have been given by someone else, not by me; and that letter was placed in my quarters in order to divert suspicion from the guilty person."

"Ah, a very ingenious story!" the Minister laughed incredulously. "You admit being friendly with the spy?"

"I admit all that is the truth, your Excellency, but I flatly deny that I am a traitor to my king," was the accused man's quick, response.

"But you see you were watched while on leave," the Minister went on, referring to his report. "On your return from Paris you travelled by way of Milan to Bologna, where you visited a certain Signora Nodari and her daughter."

"The latter was my betrothed," the unhappy man explained.

"Exactly. Then how do you account for the agent Latrobe calling upon her a month later and obtaining from her a packet which she had received by post from the garrison of Gran Paradiso? It was only afterwards that this fact was known, otherwise the spy would not have escaped from Italy."

Captain Solaro stood rigid.

"Have you really proof of this, your Excellency?" he demanded in a low, hoarse voice. "I—I cannot think that she would betray me."

"Ah! Never trust a woman," observed the Minister, with a grim smile. "She has made a statement—a statement which proves everything."

"Which proves?" he cried wildly. "Which proves I am innocent."

"No," declared Morini calmly. "Which proves that you are guilty."

"Ah, but let me tell you how—"

"No more!" cried Morini, rising with quick anger from his chair and snapping his fingers in impatience. "You have been found guilty and sentenced, and I think that even your general, after your own admissions, is now convinced of his injudicious and ridiculous attempt to shield a traitor."

"Ah!" cried the unfortunate man, hot tears springing to his eyes, "I see now how I have been betrayed—and I know by whom!"

"I have no further time to waste upon hearing any counter-charges," abruptly answered the Minister. "From to-day you are dismissed the army in disgrace. My decree will appear in to-night's *Gazette*, and, General Valentini," he added meaningly, turning to the stern old officer who had writhed beneath the civilian's rebuke, "convey your prisoner back to Turin, and do not again become the gaoler of a traitor."

"You absolutely refuse to hear me further, then!" cried the captain in wild desperation, dismayed to find that all attempt to clear his character had failed.

"I do."

The accused man with set teeth drew his sword, and with one quick wrench across his knee broke the gleaming blade and cast it ringing upon the marble floor.

"Take my sword!" he cried, drawing himself up to the salute. "Take my honour—take my life! But you—even you, Camillo Morini—cannot condemn me with justice! One day you shall know that I am innocent—you hear!—innocent!"

And with firm tread he strode out of the Minister's private room, followed by his general, who merely saluted in stiff silence, his scabbard trailing upon the marble.

CHAPTER NINE.

HIS EXCELLENCY LEARNS THE TRUTH.

The Minister of War was seated busily writing beneath the green-shaded reading-lamp in the big library of the great old Antinori Palace, his handsome residence in Rome.

Five years ago he had bought that enormous old place in the Via Nazionale—a place full of historic interest—together with its old furniture, its gallery of cinquecento paintings, and its corridor filled with armour. It was a high, square, ponderous place of princely dimensions, with a great central courtyard where an old fountain plashed on in the silence as it had done for three centuries or more, while around the arched cloisters were the carved arms of the various families through whose hands the place had passed in generations bygone.

The library was a high room on the first floor, with long cases filled with parchment-covered books, many of them illuminated codices and rare editions, a fine frescoed ceiling, and a great open hearth over which was an ornamentation of carved marble of the Renaissance with a grinning mascherino. The floor was of marble, except that the littered writing-table was set upon an oasis of thick Turkey carpet, giving to the room an austere character of comfortless grandeur, like everything else in that huge old palace of the days when every house of the Roman nobility was a fortress.

An Italian Minister's life is not by any means an easy one, as Camillo Morini had long ago discovered. He was often in his private cabinet at the Ministry of War at nine o'clock in the morning, and frequently sent home by his private secretary urgent papers which he could examine and initial after dinner, as he had done that day. His wife and daughter were up at the villa near Florence for the vintage, and he was alone and undisturbed. He had not even troubled to change for dinner, but was still in the linen suit he had worn during the day, and had merely exchanged his white coat for an easy black alpaca one.

As Minister of War, his salary was one thousand pounds sterling per annum, an amount quite inadequate for his needs. True, he travelled free in his private saloon on the railway, but yet he had a most uncomfortable time of it owing to the fact that he was expected by his friends to repay them for services rendered with the gift of offices, favours, introductions, and recommendations. Wherever he went he was besieged by a host of people who wanted favours, exemptions of their sons from military service, increased stipend, or the redressing of some act of official injustice or petty tyranny.

His wife, too, was pestered with "recommendations" to him; for without recommendations nothing could be obtained. If he went to inspect the garrison of a provincial town, the prefect, the mayor, the head of the *carabinieri*, and the most prominent citizens called on him every day; while when in the country the wheezy village band played operatic airs outside his window every evening, alternated with a chorus of children from the elementary schools.

His sovereign, King Humbert, although good-natured and brave, was too easy-going and lacking in moral stamina to make a really strong monarch, hence the whole Cabinet, from the Prime Minister downwards, were guilty of grave irregularities, if not of actual corruption. The fault, however, lay with the system, rather than with the men. How could a Cabinet Minister entertain lavishly and keep up appearances upon a mere thousand pounds a year, when he had no private means?

Happily, the present hard-working, cultivated king, Victor Emmanuel the Third, has mastered all the details of state business, and has swept his Cabinet clean of those men who abused their position under his lamented father, until the whole face of Italian politics has entirely changed since the days when Camillo Morini held office as head of the army.

Under the late King Humbert, Ministers were often chosen, not because they were capable statesmen, but simply because it was necessary that a particular region should be represented in the Cabinet, so as not to arouse local jealousies. In any case, their tenure of office was too precarious and too short to enable them to do much good work, and whatever the Minister managed to do would probably be undone by his successor.

Morini would have gone out of office half a dozen times had he not succeeded, by judicious bribery, in obtaining protection from his enemies. Indeed, he only retained office by dint of his own ingenuity and clever diplomacy towards those who were ever trying to hound him down. Not only did he bear the great responsibility of the army, but, in common with other members of the Cabinet, the greater part of his activity was absorbed in the manipulation of party groups in the Chamber and in studying parliamentary exigencies. He had to judiciously subsidise certain newspapers in view of a general election, make use of the secret service fund in certain quarters, and be careful not to shower too many favours on one province; for if he offended any particular town, the local deputy, hitherto a staunch ministerialist, would turn and rend him.

Truly his position, head of an army costing sixteen millions annually, and with a multitude of people bent on getting something out of him, was the reverse of comfortable. He would have resigned long ago had he dared, but resignation or dismissal from office would, he knew only too well, spell ruin to him. So he was held there in an office of bribery and dishonesty, which he had grown to regard with bitter hatred. He had served through three administrations, it was true, and was a trusted servant of his king, yet the daily worry of it all, the ever-present fear of exposure and of downfall, held him in constant apprehension of a future ruin and obscurity.

The dead silence of the night was unbroken save by the scratching of his quill as he scribbled his signature upon one after another of the pile of various papers

He wrote mechanically, for he was reflecting upon that scene in his cabinet when the captain of Cacciatori Alpini had broken his sword across his knee.

"A clever fellow!" he murmured. "He thought to bluff me, but he did not know how closely I had had him watched. If I did not know all that I do, I really believe I should have thought him innocent. A good actor. I will send his broken sword as a present to that doddering old fool, his general—as a souvenir of his visit to Rome without leave!" he laughed to himself, still continuing to sign the commissions and decrees.

Of a sudden there was a rap at the big white doors at the end of the dimly lit room, and a gorgeously dressed man-servant in stockings and gold-laced coat advanced to the table, saying—

"The Onorevole Ricci desires to see your Excellency."

"Pig's head! Didn't I give orders that I was not at home?" he cried, turning furiously upon the man.

"But your Excellency is always at home to the Signor Deputato?" the servant reminded him, surprised at the sudden outburst of anger.

"Ah!" growled his master. "Yes, you are right, Antonio! I forgot that I told you I was always at home to him. I must see him, I suppose," he sighed, and when the man had gone his brow contracted, his teeth clenched; yet almost before he could recover his self-possession the long white doors reopened, and his visitor—a short, dark-bearded, middle-aged man in evening dress—was ushered in.

"Ah, my dear Camillo!" he cried enthusiastically, advancing towards the Minister, who rose and took his hand. "I only arrived in Rome this afternoon, and heard you had returned from England. Well, and how are you after your holiday? I suppose I may take a cigar?" he asked, crossing to the cigar-box, opening it, and selecting one.

"The rest was welcome," answered the other calmly, stretching his arms above his head and glancing furtively at the new-comer as though he held him in some suspicion. He was a pleasant-looking man, a trifle stout, with a round, sun-bronzed face, as though fond of good living, while his perfectly fitting dress-suit was cut in a style which showed it to be the garment of a London tailor. He possessed the careless, easy manner of the gentleman, striking a match and lighting his cigar with a familiarity which showed that he was no stranger to the Minister's roof.

"I too have been in the country for quite a long while," he said—"at Asti. I have to visit the electors now and then just to make them promises and put them in a good-humour."

"Or they would hound you out, Vito—eh?—just as the Socialists would throw me out if they could," laughed His Excellency drily, walking to the cigar-box, selecting one, and lighting it.

"And Her Excellency and the signorina?" inquired the deputy.

"They are up at the villa. They always go there for the vintage."

"Of course, Rome in September is only fit for us politicians and the English tourists. I wonder you are back so early."

"Duty, my dear Vito," replied the other. "One day, when you are Minister, you will find that you had much more leisure as advocate in Turin and deputy for Asti."

"I suppose so," he laughed. Then he added, "I met Angelo in the club an hour ago. He has also been in England, it seems. I think I shall go to England next summer—if you invite me."

"Which is not likely."

"Why?"

"Because when I am in England I like to be away from all my official duties," frankly answered Morini. "They don't even know who or what I am—and I delight in keeping them in ignorance."

"Then why did you invite Angelo? I am jealous, you see."

"Because I wished to consult him upon a confidential matter."

"Regarding an army contract tendered you by a German firm," replied the other, carelessly blowing a cloud of smoke from his lips as he stood with his back to the huge open grate. "You may as well tell the truth, my dear friend."

The Minister, starting, looked at him sharply, and asked—

"How did you know?"

"Never mind how I know, Camillo. It is, as you see, useless for you to try and deceive me. You have given the contract to those Germans—for a consideration. But don't think that I blame you. Why, I should do the very same thing myself. I get a little in my own small way out of certain people in Asti, but not enough. That's why I am compelled, so much against my will, to come to you."

"Ah!" groaned the Minister, facing him quickly and determinedly. "The same old story—eh? Money."

"Like air, it is a necessity of life," he replied, smiling. "I have been in want of it for a month past, but preferred to wait rather than to trouble you while you were on holiday."

"But you surely get enough now!" protested His Excellency. "I've obtained a dozen different favours for you; I've given you appointments; I've allowed you to make recommendations for military decorations in Piedmont; I've allowed you to handle the secret service funds; and I've done all I could so as to place you in a position to receive secret commission. But of course, if you fail to make use of your opportunities, it is not my fault."

"Never fear. I do not stir a finger without some consideration," he laughed. "You surely know me too well after all these years. No; I find that it is not sufficient. Money I want, and money I must have. Recollect what services I have rendered to you in the Camera, my dear Camillo," he went on. "You surely do not

the various groups and inducing them to pass a vote of confidence! You never were nearer downfall than you were that afternoon—except, perhaps, to-night. You have enemies, my dear friend—enemies in the Socialist groups, who declare that you have held office too long," he added.

"I know," exclaimed the other hoarsely. "I know that," and he tossed his cigar away with a quick, impatient gesture.

"While you've been abroad I have been active in secretly ascertaining the real state of political opinion in the north, and much as I regret to tell you, it is distinctly antagonistic. Now that Milan is such a strong Socialist centre the other large towns are following, and an agitation is spreading against you. They want a fresh man in office as Minister of War—the man who is so cleverly scheming to replace you."

"To replace me!" exclaimed Morini. "And who is this man, pray?"

The words which Vito Ricci had spoken sank like iron into his soul. He knew, alas! how very precarious was his office.

"The man is our friend Angelo," slowly replied the crafty deputy. "Already in the north he is looked upon as your successor. If the groups in the Camera fall asunder, then your dismissal is imminent. I know this is a very unwelcome piece of news, my dear Camillo, but it is a hard fact which I have come here to-night to reveal to you."

CHAPTER TEN.
"FOR MARY'S SAKE."

His Excellency's face fell. He was silent for several moments.

The easy-going, well-dressed political adventurer before him was, he knew, in the secrets of the strong party who were his opponents and who were ever plotting his downfall. He had, since his return to Rome, heard rumours through certain quarters in which secret service money was spent that an agitation had been set afoot by his antagonists, but he had never dreamed that the prime mover of it all was the very man in whom he had so implicitly trusted, one of the men who owed everything to him—Angelo Borselli! The revelation staggered him. He really could not believe it to be actually true.

"And so he intends to become Minister—eh?" remarked Morini bitterly, when he at last found tongue.

"He is working for that end," replied Ricci. "I was in Milan and Parma a week ago, and on every hand I saw how cleverly he was stirring up ill-feeling against you. He is secretly allied to the Socialists—of that I am certain."

"Because he sees that through them he can obtain office," replied His Excellency, his pale face now very serious. "You have done well to tell me this, *caro mio*," he added. "I shall know now how to deal with the man who learns my secrets and then seeks to betray me."

"But your position is daily becoming one of graver peril," exclaimed the wily advocate, placing his hand confidentially upon the Minister's arm. "The agitation is widespread. The Socialists intend that the Government shall fall."

"But you will help me, Vito, as before?" Morini urged quickly. "Those shrieking Socialist maniacs shall not gain the ascendency?" he declared, clenching his hands and pacing the room quickly.

Vito Ricci, deputy for the town of Asti, shrugged his shoulders, but did not reply. In the Italian Camera every politician of any prominence had a small body of adherents, and political ability consisted in so manipulating a number of these bodies as to form a majority; therefore for this purpose each Minister secretly bribed one or more of the most unscrupulous deputies to juggle with the party. A group might to-day be on the side of the Government, and to-morrow with the Opposition. There were no real political principles at stake in the policy of these groups, and the only important question was that of party management and judicious bribery.

Vito Ricci was a professional politician, with whom politics was a regular trade. The Government granted him a free railway pass—as it did all the other [illegible] enabled him to obtain many favours for himself and his friends. The system of recommendations and parliamentary influence was one of the worst features of Italian political life, for it was generally regarded as one of the deputy's chief duties that, for a consideration, he should help his friends and constituents to procure favours, promotions, decorations, and concessions of contracts which would not be otherwise obtainable. Political jobbery was regarded as inevitable.

Indeed, Vito Ricci lived upon the bribes he received—and lived well.

"You are silent," remarked His Excellency, looking him straight in his face. "Why?"

"Because I have nothing to say."

"You don't promise to assist me!" he exclaimed. "You don't declare your readiness to unite the groups again in our favour!"

"Because I fear it would be a useless task," responded the other in a calm, mechanical voice.

"A useless task!" gasped the elder man, whose face was blanched. "What do you mean?"

"I mean that matters have assumed an ugly appearance," replied the deputy. "Even the journals who have received so much money from you are silent when they ought to be loudest in your eulogy. They are evidently awaiting the advent of their new masters."

"Then you actually anticipate a catastrophe?" exclaimed Morini hoarsely, halting before the man who had rendered him so many valuable services—the clever, unscrupulous adventurer who had several times turned the parliamentary tide in his favour.

Vito nodded slowly, his bearded face grave and hard set.

"If what you say is really true regarding Angelo, then I am fully aware of the great peril in which I stand," the Minister exclaimed at last, his voice faltering in his agitation. "Borselli will hesitate at nothing in order to gain power."

"Ah, I told you so a year ago, my dear Camillo," was the deputy's reply. "But you would not listen. He was your friend, you said—as though there was such a thing as friendship in any of the ministries."

"I have been deceived," admitted the other in a low voice.

A silence fell between the pair, until the deputy suddenly said hesitatingly—

"I suppose Angelo could make some rather awkward revelations—eh?"

The Minister slowly nodded.

"H'm. I thought as much from what I gathered in Milan. He would denounce you, and by reason of his big Socialist following he would come out with clean hands. He has laid his plans well, without a doubt. Sirena, the Socialist deputy for Pesaro, told me, in confidence, all that is intended."

"They mean to strike a blow at me?"

"Yes, by criticising the army, and by bringing forward some curious story about the plans of the fortress of Tresenta in the Alps being sold to France. Do you know anything about it?"

"Yes. The plans have unfortunately been given to France by a captain named Solaro, who has been dismissed the army and sent to prison. So they intend to make political capital out of that, do they?"

"It seems so," was the other's answer.

Morini slowly repaced the room, his chin upon his breast, deep in thought, the dead silence being broken only by his footsteps upon the marble floor.

"Borselli has formed a plot against me—a deep, dastardly plot!" he exclaimed in a desperate tone, halting again suddenly, a determined look upon his grey features. "He intends that I shall fall. But you, Vito, can save me, if you will—you know you can. With a little of this," and he rubbed his thumb and forefinger together, "you can unite the groups as you did before, and show the country that the Minister of War still possesses the confidence of the kingdom."

"I doubt it," answered Ricci dubiously.

"But you will not desert me now?" implored His Excellency, laying his hand firmly upon the deputy's shoulder. "Recollect the past, Vito. Remember the day when you, a lieutenant, prevented my horse throwing me at the manoeuvres in the Chianti. That was long ago, but both of us have had cause to congratulate ourselves upon that meeting."

Ricci nodded. He recollected well how the Minister, then only a few months in office, had allowed him to resign from the army and complete his studies as an advocate, and how, by a clever stroke of political jobbery, he had been elected deputy for Asti, in order that he should serve the Minister as his secret agent in the Camera. He had become rich in a few years, owing to the various grants and concessions His Excellency had made to him, yet somehow his personal extravagance kept him always poor, always in want of money. He feared to calculate how much of the secret service funds had already found its way into his pocket, and yet with wily ingenuity he was there again for a grant, not from the secret service fund—for he knew well that the sum voted for the present year was already exhausted—but from Camillo Morini's own private purse.

Vito Ricci, with all the outward appearance of a gentleman, was utterly unscrupulous. He worked in the Camera for the master who paid him best—a fact which Morini knew too well. If the Socialists were prepared to pay his price, then the man whom he had trained so cleverly and promoted to place and power would calmly throw him over, and hound him down with just as great an enthusiasm as he now supported him.

"I suppose," he went on at last, "it is, as usual, a matter of price with you—eh,

Vito?"

"Well, I must live, just as you must," responded the other with a faint smile as given him. "I have no private income, and therefore must make money somehow."

"You have made plenty of it," the other remarked. "Only three months ago you had fifty thousand lire out of the secret service fund."

"And I am now badly in want of an exactly similar amount," the deputy declared.

"Ah! so that is the price—eh? Fifty thousand?"

"Yes. But of course I cannot guarantee success for that sum. It may cost more. I have to bribe the leaders of each of the groups in the Chamber, and I flatter myself that I am the only man who can work them in favour of the Ministry."

"I admit that, my dear Vito. You are a marvel of tact and cunning. What a pity you did not enter the Diplomatic service! But the price. It is too high. I can't really afford to pay so much. Ah! if you knew how heavy my personal expenses are, and how—"

"Of course," the other cried, interrupting. "You made the same excuse last time, but you paid these screaming hounds all the same. It is surely useless to waste breath upon argument. The facts are quite plain, as I've already told you. If you pay for triumph you will probably receive it; if you don't, you must fall, and Angelo Borselli will be given your portfolio. Pardon me for saying it, Camillo, but of late you have lived with your eyes shut. I have watched, and I have observed certain things. Recently you have held me aloof from you, just at a moment when I could be of greatest service. This, I confess, has hurt me. I believed you reposed confidence in me, but it seems that you mistrust me."

"I mistrust all blackmailers," was the Minister's quick reply, his dark eyes flashing at the speaker.

"Because you are one yourself," the other retorted quickly, with a grin. "You yourself taught me the gentle art of blackmailing. But no! do not let us revile each other. Rather let us face the critical situation. I tell you that you are blind—otherwise you would realise how cleverly and with what devilish ingenuity your power is being undermined. You must bribe the groups—you must pay the sum I ask. It is your duty, not only for your own sake, but for that of your family—the signora and the Signorina Mary."

The Minister of War stood undecided. Mention of his family brought home to him the terrible responsibility upon him. Ruin, exposure, condemnation, disgrace, all stared him in the face. Yet by paying what his creature demanded he could once again steer clear of the shoals of the stormy parliamentary waters, and the country would have renewed confidence in Camillo Morini.

He knew that he was—as indeed he had been for years—entirely at the mercy of this man whom he had trained as his secret agent both in the Camera and out of it.

"Well," he answered at last in a deep, hoarse, broken voice, "and suppose I pay? What then?"

"Then I shall do my best," was Vito's response. "I can't, of course, be certain that I shall succeed, but as the groups require my influence in another quarter, they will probably render me assistance in this."

Morini was pacing the room again. His appearance was that of a man filled with apprehension. He saw that the situation was most critical, and recognised that ruin was before him. He glanced across at his writing-table, when his lips compressed and a strange, half-triumphant smile overspread his grey countenance.

"Very well," he exclaimed, and his sigh ran through the great old chamber. "I suppose you must have the money to throw to those howling dogs. Call at the Ministry to-morrow and you shall have a draft."

"For sixty thousand," said the deputy quickly. "Better be on the safe side. I shall have to distribute money freely this time, you know."

But the Minister refused, knowing that the extra ten thousand lire would go into Vito's pocket. Then they argued, long and hotly, Ricci, the accomplished blackmailer, refusing openly to lend his influence for any less sum, until at length the man who was so completely in his power was reluctantly compelled to yield — for the sake of his wife and Mary, he said in sheer desperation.

"And now that you are again reposing confidence in me, my dear friend," said the deputy, "let me give you a word of warning."

"Speak. I am all attention."

"Last season there was here in Rome a man named Dubard. You introduced us one night when I dined here. I have since heard that he is aspiring to your daughter's hand."

"Well?"

"Watch him, and you will discover something that will surprise you. I shall say no more. The future is in your own hands."

CHAPTER ELEVEN.
THE SECRET AGENT.

A fat waiter conducted a well-dressed, lady-like girl up the great marble staircase of the Hôtel Brun, in Bologna, rapped lightly at the door of a private sitting-room, and ushered her in.

Angelo Borselli, who rose to meet her, bowed politely, with a smile on his sallow face, and welcomed his visitor.

She was about twenty-three, with very dark hair, fine big eyes, and a well-formed figure, rather stout, as are most of the Bolognese.

"I had given you up, signorina," he said. "I have waited for you over an hour."

"I could not get away before," she replied somewhat timidly. "At home they seemed suspicious, and I had the greatest difficulty in coming here." And she smiled, a faint flush suffusing her sunburnt cheeks.

"You came in a closed cab?"

"No, I went to the station and drove here in the hotel omnibus, as though I had arrived by train. I thought it would excite less suspicion."

"Excellent!" laughed the Under-Secretary, glancing to see that the door was closed. "You are clever—always clever, Filoména. You will make a first-class agent of the Ministry some day," he added approvingly.

She laughed as she seated herself in the chair he politely offered, and laid the little fan she carried upon the table, replying—

"I always do my best. But my mother watches so closely that I have to be most cautious."

"You have done exceedingly well," declared the schemer. "In this last affair you have rendered me the greatest assistance. Without you we should have failed. But I have invited you here to learn all the details. I was in Paris at the time, and all I have gathered is from the official reports of the court-martial. They did not call you up to Turin, I hope?"

"No. They took my evidence in secret at the barracks here."

"And what did you tell them?"

"I described exactly what had happened. How the captain had a year ago declared his love for me, and how he came to Bologna from Paris."

"And what else?"

"I described how I had received in confidence the mysterious packet from him, with instructions to hand it to a friend of his, a Frenchman, who would make an appointment to meet me. What I told the three officers who took down my statement seemed to create a great impression upon them."

"Of course it would, because it is your statement that has condemned Solaro."

"Condemned!" she gasped in blank surprise. "What, has he already been tried?"

"Yes, and dismissed the army."

"But he is—"

"There are no buts, signorina," he quickly interrupted in a hard voice. "If you render secret service to the Ministry you must never reason as to the why or the wherefore. Always rest assured that we are acting solely for the benefit and safety of Italy."

She thought deeply for a moment.

"When I met the Frenchman by appointment at a seat in the Montagnola garden, and gave him the packet, he broke it open, and I saw that some tracings were inside."

"And what did the Frenchman say?" inquired Borselli. "Oh, he was very polite," she laughed, blushing slightly. "We walked about the garden for nearly half an hour; for he was a pleasant man, who spoke Italian exceedingly well—evidently an officer."

"Most of the men in the French secret service are recruited from the army or the detective police," he remarked. "But I intend that Italy, like Russia, shall in future rely upon the shrewdness of clever women like yourself. This Frenchman said nothing regarding Solaro?"

"He merely remarked that he supposed the captain trusted me implicitly, and I, of course, replied in the affirmative. He wrote to me from the Hôtel National in Lucerne, making the appointment in the Montagnola, indicating a certain seat, which showed that he was well acquainted with Bologna."

"Did he mention me?"

"No. He urged me, however, to deny all knowledge of the mysterious packet if taxed with receiving it. From that I concluded that he was in ignorance of how the whole affair had been arranged."

"Of course," he answered, with a laugh. "It would never do for France to learn our motives. We allow them to have the secrets of Tresenta because we have other ends in view. What they are you will know later."

"And in the meantime Felice Solaro is dismissed the army in disgrace?"

The sallow-faced man nodded. He did not tell her that he had been sentenced to fifteen years' imprisonment, for he knew how soft-hearted women are towards the innocent.

"Do you know," she said presently, "I have a suspicion which I think I ought to tell you. It is that the address upon the envelope which contained the packet of papers was not in Captain Solaro's own handwriting."

He looked quickly into her face, frowning slightly and saying—

"Suspicions do not concern you, signorina. When I give you orders, it is for you first to execute them as secretly and expeditiously as possible, and secondly to have a care that your association with me is never discovered. You understand? I am merely Filipo Florena, shipping agent, of Genoa, and you write to me always to my office in the Via Balbi. Should you ever be in real peril, you have that code address by which a telegram will find me, either at home or abroad."

She saw that her remark caused him annoyance, therefore she began to apologise and declare her readiness to serve the War Department of her country in every way possible.

"As I have already said," he remarked in a quiet voice, obtaining her permission to smoke, "you have shown yourself in every way adapted to the responsible office I intend that you shall hold. You come of good family, although at present in straitened circumstances; you possess good looks, and you are a perfect model of all the virtues. Your mother, the widow of my old friend, Colonel Nodari, would, of course, object to the capacity in which you have once or twice served Italy. Yet it is for the honour and safety of your country, recollect. You are an agent of the Ministry of War, and being in its employ should act obediently, without expressing any surprise at the information you are asked to obtain, or attempting to deduct any logical conclusion."

She sat silent, listening to the advice the schemer gave her. Her late father, a colonel of cavalry, had been the Under-Secretary's friend, and the latter had been a frequent guest at their house. Indeed, she had known General Borselli ever since she had been a child, and of late, by clever ruses, this man had contrived to use her quick woman's intelligence for his own ends. In recognition of her services, he had sent her small sums of money, which she found very useful for her dress bills, and on one or two occasions had sent her little trinkets, which she had locked up carefully from her mother's prying eyes.

The Under-Secretary for War, far-seeing and deeply scheming always, recognised in her a very valuable assistant. She was known to the officers of a dozen garrisons, for she had been reared in the military atmosphere, therefore she was enabled to discover for him facts about persons that it would otherwise have been impossible for the Ministry to obtain.

A dozen times had she been successful in elucidating various sources of discontent, and gaining other information of greatest value to the War Office in Rome, information which Borselli used for his own ends and with the purpose of undermining the power of the Minister Camillo Morini. As the dead colonel's daughter, and very popular on account of her bright disposition and good looks, she was the last person suspected of collecting that information which so mysteriously found its way to headquarters. And yet, under Borselli's secret tuition, she had become as clever and ingenious an agent as any the Government employed.

Truth to tell, however, the part she had played in the Solaro affair, now that she realised how the unfortunate captain had been entrapped, caused her a deep pang of conscience. Several months before, in that very room, she had met the Under-Secretary by appointment, and he had, after some preliminaries, remarked upon her acquaintance with Captain Solaro, whereupon she blushingly explained that they had known each other for some years, ever since her father was in garrison on the frontier at Ventimiglia. He put some direct questions to her, and discovered that, although they corresponded frequently, she was in no way in love with him. Then he gave her instructions how to act, declaring that the captain was strongly suspected of secret dealing with a French agent, and that if she received a sealed packet by post from the Alpine garrison she was to hold it, and deal with it exactly in the manner which the captain ordered, but in the meantime she was also to communicate with the supposed shipping agent in the Via Balbi in Genoa—himself. In brief, she was to appear very friendly with the captain, inspire him with every confidence, and yet betray him into the hands of the authorities. To her, the suggestion was a very unwelcome one, but Borselli urged her to carry out the delicate negotiation from patriotic motives—as daughter of a brave soldier who had served Italy so faithfully and well in the struggles of the sixties. It was this claptrap appeal to her loyalty that had caused her to become a secret agent of the Under-Secretary, which had now resulted, she knew, in the disgrace of an innocent man.

Why had the trap been baited so cunningly? she wondered within herself. There was some hidden motive in the expulsion of Solaro from the army; what could it be? Surely that packet she had given the polite Frenchman had not really contained plans, for it was not likely that the War Office would actually connive at its own betrayal to France?

"I know that this recent little affair in the north has puzzled you, signorina," the general remarked slowly, his eyes fixed upon her. "But you will see that we have right on our side one day. Act with care, exercise a wise discretion always, and you will not only be able to assist us, but you will, in future, receive a secret payment from the Ministry of seven thousand lire per annum, together with a fair allowance for expenses. The first payment has already been made to you in recognition of your tact towards Solaro," he added, and taking from his wallet a slip of paper, he handed it to her, adding, "This is a draft on the Bank of Italy for the amount. Leave it in the bank if you wish—you will probably find it useful one day. You see it is upon the private account of Filipo Florena."

She, wondering, held the draft between her fingers. It was the first she had ever seen, and she told him so.

"Put it away in your writing-desk or your jewel-case. And when you want it you can cash it on sight at any branch of the Bank of Italy—or, indeed, at any moneychanger's."

She folded it carefully, and slowly placed it in her purse, while he, glancing at her furtively and seeing that possession of such a sum had given her confidence, suddenly exclaimed—

[illegible]

CHAPTER TWELVE.
CONCERNS SOME CURIOUS INSTRUCTIONS.

"Well?" she asked, as he paused and looked at her. "Why are you in Bologna?"

"I am here," he answered, "for the purpose of sending you to England."

"To England!" she echoed, half rising from her chair.

"Yes. You speak English quite well, therefore I have obtained for you a situation as governess in a highly respectable and wealthy family," he said. "You remember you asked me a year ago to arrange that you might leave home and become your own mistress, for you told me you were tired of living on your mother's narrow means."

"But I—"

"As I have already said, signorina," he interrupted, "there are no buts where the safety of Italy is concerned. You are wanted to go to England for two reasons: the change will be beneficial to you, and you will render a service to the Ministry."

"Then I am to accept the post with an ulterior object in view?" she remarked quickly.

"Of course," he replied, with a smile. "There are certain matters of which we desire information, and it lies with you to supply it. You are well educated, a good linguist, and just the stamp of young lady who goes as governess in a wealthy family. Therefore, the post being vacant, I at once secured it for you by giving you a very strong recommendation."

"I would rather remain in Italy," the girl implored, recognising almost for the first time how entirely she was in that man's hands.

"No," he declared. "They expect you in England next week. The young lady, your pupil, is to begin her studies at once—while you will commence to study other matters on our behalf," he added, his dark face relaxing into a meaning grin.

She was silent, twisting her handkerchief nervously in her gloved hand. She realised that so cleverly during the past three years had this man weaved a net about her she was now bound to obey him. But she had never dreamed that the services she rendered to the Ministry of War were to take her abroad—to England.

There, in Bologna, her status as the daughter of a colonel who had served with distinction and had died a commendatore gave her the *entrée* into what was a select circle of society for a provincial town, but strange perhaps to English ideas—a society composed mostly of needy counts and seedy countesses, marquises who lived in bare, half-furnished palaces upon the remnant of what past generations

with the officers of the garrison. It was a degrading thing that she should go out as a governess, yet if it were really necessary, she must, she knew, bow to the inevitable.

At first she resisted his request, urging that it was impossible. She had only made the suggestion as a joke; she was ready to serve the Ministry of War at home in her own small way, but to go abroad, to become a secret agent of Italy in England, was quite another matter.

He smoked on in silence, standing at the window and pretending to be interested in the people passing in the street below.

"My dear signorina," he exclaimed at last, turning his thin, unprepossessing face to her, and looking straight at her with his dark, crafty eyes, "I quite admit that to leave your home and friends is not a pleasant outlook. But you see it is imperative—absolutely imperative. You can render us most valuable assistance. Indeed, we are relying entirely upon you."

"My mother will never consent to it," she assured him.

"Leave the signora to me," he laughed drily. "She will believe that you have become companion to an English lady. I will arrange it all. You know what entire confidence the signora has in me!"

Filoména smiled. This man, who held such a high office in the Ministry, had always been a friend of her family. Indeed, the colonel's widow was greatly indebted to him, for, through him, the War Office now paid her a small sum annually in recognition of her late husband's services to the kingdom, a payment which was not legal, but which had been ordered by Borselli and made law by decree of the Minister Morini himself.

"You will have a very pleasant time of it in England, I assure you," he went on. "As governess you will, of course, be treated as an underling, but remain patient, watchful, and attentive always to your instructions. Remember that upon you depends much, that you may render greater service to Italy than even her ambassadors. Knowledge is power, is an old and trite saying—and knowledge is in no place more powerful than the Ministry of War."

He treated her with a certain fatherly solicitude and confidence which impressed her. Four years ago, when she left the convent school at Ravenna and resumed the acquaintance formed in her childhood, he had gradually taken her into his confidence. He required certain information regarding certain officers in the Bologna garrison which with her woman's subtle way of learning secrets she could obtain, while on his part he was ready to further her interests, to obtain that very necessary income for her mother—to act, in fact, as her friend, and to place her, in secret, under the protection of the Ministry of War. But secrecy was to be observed—secrecy in everything. To him alone was she to report, by letter or verbally. She was to act the spy on his behalf with cunning, care, and caution.

In the various tasks he had set her she had acquitted herself well, more especially in the mysterious affair of Captain Solaro, the man who, to his cost, had fallen in love with her. At heart she hated herself for the despicable part she had been compelled to play, yet she had become Borselli's spy in order that she and her mother should receive that small but very necessary pension from the War Department.

In character she was one of those silent, watchful women whom nothing escapes, and who note every look and every gesture—one of the few women, indeed, who can keep a secret. Borselli, the man who used the Minister Morini as his cat's-paw, and was as cunning an adventurer as there was in all the length of Italy, had recognised these qualities as those of a secret agent of the most successful type, and therefore had resolved to turn to account his ascendency over her.

She had taken up her little fan and was fanning herself with quick nervousness. The evening was a stifling one in September, for in that month Bologna, with its long streets of stucco porticos, is a veritable oven.

"The address of your new mistress is here," remarked the Under-Secretary, producing a card from his pocket-book, whereon was written in pencil in an English hand: "Mrs Charles Fitzroy, 186, Brook Street, Grosvenor Square, W."

"It is in the best and most fashionable part of London," he added. "And they have a fine place out in the country. The child whom you are to teach is aged eight—a little friend of mine. So you see I have arranged it all for you. You have only to go there and commence your duties."

She shrugged her shoulders. The idea of taking a situation as governess did not appeal to her. She would, indeed, have refused point-blank if she dared, only refusal might mean the cessation of her mother's slender income.

She knew Angelo Borselli's wife and son, and had visited them in Rome. The Signora Borselli was a stout woman of rather coarse type, proud of her position, fond of crude colours and a dazzling show. Her carriage in Rome was painted a bright grass green, and the livery of her servants was a blue-grey with yellow cockades. She dressed expensively, but without taste, as might be expected of one who was daughter of a straw hat manufacturer at Sancasciano. The son was aged eighteen, a superb young cub, who was now at the University of Ferrara studying law. Filoména Nodari was of gentle birth, and therefore despised the woman who had treated her so patronisingly. She looked upon Angelo Borselli as her dead father's most devoted friend and her mother's benefactor, but the wife of the Under-Secretary she held in disdain as an uncouth countrywoman aspiring to a great position—as indeed she really was.

"England is a long way off, signore," she remarked in a blank voice, after a long pause, the silence being unbroken save for the strains of the military band playing outside in the piazzi, as it does every evening in summer. "Cannot you send someone else?" she begged.

"There is no one so well adapted as yourself," he declared. "You know English and French, and could act the part of governess to perfection. I admit that to accept a menial office is not really pleasant, yet you must recollect that as a servant of the Ministry you are acting your part for the benefit of Italy—just as your poor father

She sighed, and lapsed again into thought. Like a thousand other girls living at home upon slender means, she had often longed for a change of life and for sight of those foreign places about which she had read so much—and most of all of London. And here, he pointed out, was an opportunity of serving Italy abroad.

She believed all that he told her—how the information she furnished was necessary for the successful conduct of the Ministry in order to thwart the machinations of Italy's enemies. She had no idea that her actions and inquiries, directed by him, were always with one end in view—to oust from office the Minister himself.

On the one hand, Filoména Nodari was extremely clever and far-seeing, a veritable genius in the discovery of secrets, while on the other she was as wax in the hands of this man whom for so many years she had regarded as her friend.

"Am I to write to this person, my employer?" she asked with a slight sigh, still holding the card in her hand.

"Only to announce the day and hour of your arrival in London—at the station of Charing Cross, remember. I told Mrs Fitzroy who and what you are—that you are tired of sleepy Bologna, that you were an officer's daughter, and all the rest of it. Your wages are seven hundred francs a year, or twenty-four pounds in English money, with your railway fare paid to London, and your return fare if you don't suit. But," he added, with a meaning laugh, "you will suit, signorina—you must suit, recollect?"

She shrugged her shoulders dubiously, saying—

"Of course, if it is really necessary, I will go. But I fear I may fail."

"Not if you are determined to succeed," he assured her. "You have good looks, and they go such a very long way. That is why a pretty woman is so successful as a secret agent."

She flushed slightly at his flattery.

"Well, and what am I to do? What information do you require?" she asked, speaking almost mechanically and gazing fixedly across the room.

"The facts, simply told, are these," he said, tossing his cigarette into the ashtray and halting before her. "This Mrs Fitzroy is the wife of a Mr Charles Fitzroy, a London fur merchant, and Alderman of the City, and sister to a man named Morgan-Mason, a member of the English House of Commons. This man you must watch. Recollect his name. Although he is a bachelor and lives in an apartment in Westminster, he spends much of his time at his sister's house; hence you will have an opportunity of forming his acquaintance and keeping observation upon his movements. He is clever, crafty, and quite unscrupulous, therefore be cautious in all your movements. You must try and seize an opportunity to get a glimpse through his private papers if possible, and see if there are any documents in Italian of an unusual character."

"Then you suspect him to be an enemy of Italy?" she remarked seriously.

"We suspect that this blatant, pompous orator, who is now gathering such a following in the House of Commons, is forming certain plans to undermine our strength, to turn English opinion against an Italian alliance. Therefore it is necessary that we should be in possession of all the details, and you alone can obtain knowledge of the truth. He does not know Italian, a fact which gives you distinct advantage. Watch him very carefully, and report each week to Genoa; while, on my part, if I have any important instructions to send, I shall address the letter to the Poste Restante at Charing Cross—which is opposite the railway station. Your aim must be to find out all you can; to discover with whom this man is in association in Italy, remembering that whatever secret information, or more especially any documentary evidence you can secure, will be of the utmost service to us. Go, my dear signorina," he added, placing his hand upon her shoulder, "go to London, and carry with you my very best wishes for success."

The woman sat silent, thinking over his instructions, while through the open window on the evening air came the strains of military music.

And as he watched her his thin, sallow face slowly relaxed into a sinister smile, when he reflected within himself the real reason why he was sending the pretty spy to England.

CHAPTER THIRTEEN.
THE VILLA SAN DONATO.

The sky was aflame in all the crimson glory of the Tuscan sunset.

The Angelus of a sudden clashed forth from the high castellated tower of the village church away over the Arno, winding deep in its beautiful fertile valley, that veritable paradise of green vale and purple mountain, and was echoed by a dozen other bells clanging discordantly from the hillsides, while from afar came up the deep-toned note of the big bell in the campanile of brown old Florence.

It was the hour of the *venti-tre*, and those patient toilers, the *contadini*, in the vineyards, who had been busy since dawn plucking the rich red grapes that hung everywhere in such luscious profusion, crossed themselves with a murmured prayer to the Madonna, and prodded their ox-teams homeward with the last load for the presses. All day long "babbo," with his wife and children of all ages, had worked on beneath that fiery sun, singing as they laboured; for the grape harvest was a rich one, the wine would be abundant, and they, sharing half the profits with the padrone in lieu of payment, would receive a good round sum.

Like most of the great estates in Tuscany, that of San Donato, the property of His Excellency Camillo Morini, was held by the peasantry on what is known as the *messeria* system, by which the whole of the land was divided into a number of fields, or *poderi*, half the produce of which was retained by the *mezzadro*, or peasant who cultivated the soil, and the other half went to the landlord as rent. The *poderi* varied in size, but were usually about thirty acres in extent, each with its *contadino's* house colour-washed in pale pink, and upon the wall, painted in distemper, a heraldic shield bearing the bull's head erased argent, the arms of the proprietor.

The estate of San Donato, with its huge old fourteenth-century villa—a great castellated place with high, square towers, that would in England be called a castle, on the crest of a hill—and its *fattoria*, or residence of the bailiff, another great rambling place with its oil mills and wine-presses, in the valley below, was one of the largest in Tuscany.

The villa, with its long façade of many windows, its flanking towers, its enormous salons of the cinquecento, its splendid frescoes, its antique marbles, its grey old terraces and broken statuary, was indeed in a delightful situation. Perched on the summit of a lofty and broken eminence, it looked down upon the vale of the Arno and commanded Florence with all its domes, towers, and palaces, the villas that encircle it and the roads that lead to it. The recesses, swells, and breaks of the hill on which it stood were covered with groves of pines, ilex, and cypress. Behind, deep below, lay quiet old Pistoja in the distance, and still farther off swelled the giant Apennines.

From the villa ran a broad open road, straight to the ancient gate of the little walled village of San Donato itself—a remote, ancient place, almost the same to-day as when in the days of Dante it guarded the valley against the incursions of the Pisans. From its high brown walls, now crumbling to decay, the view was, like that from the villa of its lord, without rival in all Italy. Its tiny piazza was grass-grown, and outside the walls, in a shady cypress grove, stood a ruined calvary with some of Gerino's wonderful frescoes.

San Donato, though only seven miles from Florence as the crow flies, was an un-get-at-able place, inaccessible to the crowd of inquisitive English, and therefore unchanged and its people unspoilt. Indeed, in winter a week often went by without communication with the world below; for the post did not reach there, and the little place was self-supporting. The people, descendants of the men who had shot their arrows from those narrow slits in the walls, were proud that they had the great Minister of War for their lord, and that the estate was not like that adjoining, going to decay through the neglect and gambling propensities of its owner, who had not visited it for twenty years! On the contrary, San Donato, still almost feudal, was prosperous under a generous padrone, and the few weeks each year which the Minister and his family spent there was always a time of rejoicing with the whole countryside. Then the *contadini* made excuse for many festas, and there was much dancing, playing of mandolines, and chanting of *siomelli*. The padrone delighted to see his people happy, and the signorina was always so good to the poor and the afflicted.

Out upon the great wide stone terrace that ran the whole length of the villa, where spread such a wonderful panorama of river and mountain, Mary was standing beneath an arbour of trailing vines; for even though the *venti-tre* was ringing, the sun's rays were still too strong to stand in them bareheaded. She presented a slim, neat figure, delightfully cool in her plain white washing gown with a bow of pale blue tulle at the throat, yet, as her face was turned towards the far-distant heights of Vallombrosa, there was in her handsome countenance a look of deep anxiety.

Jules Dubard, leaning against the grey old wall at her side, noticed it and wondered. He too was dressed all in white, in a suit of linen so necessary in the blazing Tuscan summer, and as he folded his arms he smiled within himself at the effect of his words upon her.

"But you don't really anticipate that my father's enemies are plotting his downfall?" she asked seriously turning her great dark eyes upon him.

"Unfortunately, I fear they are," was his reply. "What I heard in Paris is sufficient to show that here, in Italy, you are on the eve of some grave political crisis."

"For what reason?" she inquired earnestly. "Tell me all you know, for your information may be of the greatest use to my father. I will write to him to-night," she added, in a voice full of apprehension.

"No. Do not write," he urged. "You will see him in a week or ten days, and then you can tell him the rumours I have heard. It seems," he went on, "that there [illegible] formed a most ingenious conspiracy to secure its downfall. Other men, rivals of the present Ministry, are eager for office and for the pecuniary advantages to be thereby obtained."

"What is the character of the conspiracy?" she inquired seriously. "Perhaps my father can thwart it."

"It is to be hoped that he can, but I confess I doubt it very much," was his slow answer. "Downfall seems imminent. Indeed, a friend of mine, whom I met the other day in Biffi's café, in Milan, was discussing it openly. It seems that our French secret service has been at work on your Alpine frontier, and that the plans of the new fortress at Tresenta have been sold by one of the officers of the garrison. Out of this the Opposition intend to make capital, by charging your father with neglect, even connivance at the traitorous dealings with France, and thereby hounding him from office."

"But it is unjust!" cried the girl wildly. "It is disgraceful! If the spies of France have been successful, it is surely not my father's fault, but the fault of the officer who prepared and sold them. What is his name?"

"I hear it is Solaro."

"Solaro!" she gasped hoarsely. "Not Captain Felice Solaro, of the Alpine Regiment?"

"Yes, signorina, that was the name."

She stood staring at him, utterly amazed and mystified. Felice Solaro! — a traitor!

"But it is impossible!" she declared quickly. "There must surely be some mistake!"

"I heard it on the very best authority," was the young Frenchman's calm answer. "A court-martial has, it seems, been held with closed doors, and as a result the man Solaro has been dismissed and sentenced to imprisonment for a term of fifteen years."

"Dismissed the army!" she exclaimed blankly. "Then the court-martial found him guilty?"

"Certainly. But did you know the man?"

She hesitated a moment, then faltered —

"Yes, I knew him once. But what you tell me seems utterly impossible. He was the very last man to betray Italy."

"They say that a woman induced him to prepare the plans," remarked the Frenchman. "But how far that is true I have no idea."

Mary's face was paler than before. Her brows were contracted, and in her dark, luminous eyes was a look of quick determination.

"Is my father aware of all this?" she demanded.

"Undoubtedly. He, of course, must have signed the decree dismissing Solaro from the army. I believe the matter is being kept as quiet as possible, but unfortunately the Socialists have somehow obtained knowledge of the true facts, and will go to the country with the cry that Italy, under the present Cabinet, is in danger." Then, after a slight pause, he went on, "I look upon your father as my friend, you know, signorina, therefore I think he ought to know the plot being formed against him. They intend to make certain distinct charges against him, of bribery, of receiving money from contractors who have supplied inferior goods, and of being directly responsible for the recent reverses in Abyssinia. If they do—" Pausing, he elevated his shoulders without concluding the sentence.

"But it is impossible, Count Dubard, that the man you name could have sold our military secrets?"

"You know him sufficiently well, then, to be aware of his loyalty?" sniffed her companion suspiciously.

"I know that he would never be guilty of an act of treason," she answered quickly. "Therefore if he really has been convicted of such an offence, he must be the victim himself of some conspiracy."

The count regarded her heated declaration as the involuntary demonstration of a bond of friendship, and looked into her eyes in undisguised wonder. She stood facing him, her white hand upon the broken marble of an ancient vase, yellow and worn smooth by time.

"You appear to repose the utmost confidence in him," he remarked, surprised. "Why?"

"Because I am certain that he has fallen the victim of a plot," she declared, her face hard set and desperate. "If those enemies of my father's are endeavouring so cleverly to oust him from office, is it not quite feasible that they have laid the blame purposely upon Captain Solaro?"

"Why purposely?"

She paused, and again his eyes met hers.

"Because they knew that if Captain Solaro were accused," she said slowly, "my father, as Minister, would show him no clemency."

"Why?"

"There is a reason," she responded hoarsely, adding, "I know that he is innocent—he *must* be innocent."

"But he has been tried by a competent court-martial, and found guilty," remarked her companion.

"With closed doors?"

"And is not that the usual procedure in cases of grave offence? It would never do for the public to learn that the loyalty of Italy's officers had been found wanting. That would shake the confidence of the country."

"And yet my father's enemies are preparing to strike a crushing blow at him by making capital out of it?" she exclaimed. "Ah yes. I see—I see it all!" she cried.

man—a second case of Dreyfus!"

The Frenchman shrugged his shoulders but made no reply.

"You said that a woman's name had been mentioned in connection with the affair," she went on. "Was her name Nodari—Filoména Nodari—and does she not live in Bologna?"

Her companion's lips pressed themselves together, but so slightly that she did not notice the almost imperceptible expression of annoyance upon his face.

"I do not know," he declared. "I merely heard that there was a woman in the case, and that she had given certain evidence before the military court that left no doubt of the guilt of the accused. But," he added, half apologetically, "I had no idea, signorina, that Solaro was a friend of yours."

"Oh, he is not a friend, only an acquaintance," she protested.

"Then why are you so intensely interested in his welfare?" he inquired.

"Because I have certain reasons. An injustice has been done, and I shall at once ask my father to have the most searching inquiry made. He will do so, if it is my wish," she added confidently.

"Then you intend to champion the cause of the man who is accused of being a traitor to Italy?" remarked the wily Parisian, regarding her furtively as he spoke. "I fear, signorina, if you adopt any such course you will only place in the hands of your father's enemies a further weapon against him. No; if you desire to assist His Excellency at this very critical moment, you must refrain from taking any action which they could construe into your own desire, or your father's intention, to liberate the man who is convicted of having sold his country to its enemy."

"But it is unjust! He is innocent."

"Be that how it may, your duty surely is to help your father, not to act in a manner which would convince the public that he had connived at the sale of the military secrets of Tresenta."

Her dark eyes fixed themselves upon the distant towers and cupolas of Florence, down where the grey mists were now rising. They were filled with tears, and her chest beneath her laces heaved slowly and then fell again.

And the man lounging at her side with studied grace laughed within himself, triumphant at his own clever diplomacy.

CHAPTER FOURTEEN.

IN THE SILENCE OF NIGHT.

Dinner at the Villa San Donato was always a stately meal, served in that huge, lofty *sala di pranzo*, or dining-room, with its marble floor, its high prison-like windows closely barred with iron, its antique frescoed walls, and old low settees covered with dark green damask running right round the apartment.

In that enormous echoing room nothing had been touched for two hundred years. The old oak furniture had been well-preserved, the great high-backed chairs, covered with leather and studded with big brass nails, the fine carved buffet, and the graven shield over the door bearing the arms of the princely house that had once owned the place, all spoke of a brilliant magnificence of days bygone when those huge halls had echoed to the tread of armed men, and the lord of San Donato entertained his retainers and bravoes with princely generosity. The villa was so huge that the guest easily lost himself in its ramifications, its long corridors and huge salons each leading from one to the other. Like all the fortified villas of the cinquecento, every window on the ground floor was closely barred, and this, combined with the bareness of the rooms, gave to them an aspect of austerity. Over the whole place was a comfortless air, like that of most Italian houses, save in Madame Morini's rose boudoir, and the little sitting-room which Mary had arranged in English style, and called her own.

In the great dining-room there was sitting accommodation for two hundred, and yet on that evening the party only numbered six: Her Excellency, Mary, Jules Dubard, an English schoolfellow of Mary's named Violet Walters, the fair-haired daughter of an eminent KC, and two sisters, named Anna and Eva Fry, daughters of an English merchant at Genoa whom Her Excellency had invited up for the vintage.

The voices of the little party echoed strangely in that enormous old apartment, and from time to time a peal of laughter came back from the corners of the place with weird and startling repetition. The party had that day made an excursion over to another estate which the Minister possessed above the Arno, at Empoli, where the vintage was in full swing. The trip had been delightful, and the peasantry had received them with that deep homage and generous hospitality which the Tuscan *contadini* extend to their lord.

All were in good spirits except Mary, who, in a gown of pale carnation pink, sat conversing mechanically in English with her friend Violet, a pretty girl, about a year her senior, but within herself reflecting deeply upon what the man sitting opposite her had told her when out upon the terrace an hour before.

Her father was in peril; it was her duty to warn him. Felice Solaro had fallen a victim of some dastardly plot, [illegible]

She longed to explain to her father all that the count had told her, but in reply to a question, her mother had said that she did not expect him to leave Rome for at least a fortnight. Therefore she remained thoughtful, apprehensive, and undecided how to act. At first she had contemplated explaining everything to her mother, but on reflection she saw that there were certain reasons why her anxiety should not be aroused. Her Excellency was in very delicate health, and while in London had consulted a physician, who had told her that she must have as little mental worry as possible. For that reason Mary resolved to hide the serious truth from her.

Dubard, with his studied elegance of manner, was entertaining the ladies with droll stories, for he was something of a humourist, and essentially a ladies' man. Once or twice as Mary's eyes met his he saw in them an expression of deep anxiety, and of course knew well the reason.

The Fry girls were particularly interested in the young Frenchman, of whom they had heard as a new star in the social firmament in Rome during the previous season, but, being provincials, they had not met him. Both were dark and fairly good-looking; Eva aged about twenty-one, and Anna two years her senior. Their father, Henry Fry, was an exporter of marble and of olive oil, who, like his father before him, carried on business in Genoa, and had amassed a considerable fortune; but Mrs Fry's death three years previously had left the girls to shift for themselves in the social world, and their mother having long been an intimate friend of Her Excellency, the latter each year invited the girls up to San Donato as company for Mary.

Dinner ended at last, and the little party passed through the three great salons lit by the thousand wax candles in their antique sconces, into the minor drawing-room beyond, which was always used of an evening because it was cosier and small enough to be carpeted.

The Fry girls were clever mandolinists, and taking up their instruments at Madame Morini's invitation, played and sang that sweet old Tuscan serenade—

> "Io ti amerò finchè le Rondinelle
> Avranno fatto il nido dell' amore;
> Io ti amero fin che nel Cielo stelle
> Vi saran sempre a illuminarmi il cora.
> Io ti amerò,
> Io ti amerò,
> Fin che avrò vita
> Mio bel tesor!"

As they sang, Dubard stood beside Mary and looked into her dark eyes for some responding glance.

But there was none. She was not thinking of him, but of that unfortunate man convicted of treason, disgraced and languishing in gaol—and of Filoména Nodari, the woman who had foully betrayed him.

"You are sad to-night," he managed to whisper to her as they turned together from the singers.

She nodded, but no response escaped her lips.

Her feelings towards Jules Dubard were mixed ones. She found him a very pleasant and entertaining companion, always courteous, elegant of manner, and excessively polite—the kind of man who at once attracted a woman. And yet somehow, when she came to calmly analyse her regard for him, she found it to be based merely upon his attractive personality; or, in other words, it was little more than a mere flirtation, which may be forgiven of every woman who is courted and flattered as she was.

True, he had, in a kind of joking manner, more than once declared his love for her. But she had always affected to treat his words as empty and meaningless, and to assume that they were good friends and nothing more. At heart, however, she knew that both her parents would be pleased to see her marry this man; for not only would she be the wife of a wealthy landowner, but would also obtain the ancient and honoured title of Comtesse Dubard.

Sometimes, in the secrecy of her room, she sat and reflected upon the whole situation, but on each occasion she arrived at the same distinct and unalterable conclusion. She admired Jules; she was fond of his society, and he was, even though his Gallic elegance of manner was a trifle forced, nevertheless a perfect gentleman. But surely there was a great breach between admiration and actual affection.

What he had told her out on the terrace in the sundown, however, showed plainly that he was really her father's friend. And yet, strangely enough, he did not wish her to alarm her father unduly. Why? she wondered. If that grave peril actually existed he should surely be forewarned!

"What I told you this evening has, I fear, upset you, signorina," Dubard said in a low, sympathetic voice. "But do not be disquieted. I will assist your father in thwarting this conspiracy against him. Do not tell Her Excellency a word. It would be harmful for her, you know."

"I shall say nothing," was her reply. "But," she added, "I cannot help feeling anxious, especially as you suggest that I shall not write to my father and warn him."

"Oh, write if you wish," he exclaimed quickly. "Only recollect all that I have told you is only hearsay. Therefore, I think it unwise to arouse your father's apprehensions if the rumour of the conspiracy is baseless. No?" he went on. "Remain patient, and leave everything to me."

She sighed, without replying; then, in order to reassure her, he whispered, at the same time looking into her eyes intensely—

"You know, Mary, that I will do my very best—for your sake. You know me sufficiently well for that."

He would have continued his protestations of affection had not the singers at that moment ceased, and they were both compelled to rejoin the little group, much to Mary's relief, for at that moment she had another, which could of the time.

She did not exactly mistrust the count, yet some strange intuition told her that his solicitude for her father's safety was feigned. What made her think so she knew not, but she experienced that evening a strange, unaccountable presage of evil.

He asked her to sing, and then, being pressed by the others, she responded, chanting one of those old *stornelli* of the countryfolk which she was so fond of collecting and writing in a book, the weird love-chants that have been handed down from the Middle Ages. It was one she had taken down from the lips of a *contadino* at Castellina a few days previously—

> "Giovanottino dal cappel di paglia,
> Non ti voglio amar più, non n'ho più voglia...
> Voglio piuttosto vincer la battaglia!"

And while she sang, Violet Walters, standing with Dubard, looked at him with an expression which told him that he had created a favourable impression upon her. Thus the evening passed quietly, until the bell over the private chapel of the castle tolled eleven, and the guests rose and parted to their rooms, being conducted through the long ghostly corridors by the domestics with candles.

Mary allowed her Italian maid Teresa to brush her long brown tresses before the mirror, as was her habit, but the faithful servant remarked in surprise upon the signorina's preoccupied look.

"I'm very tired, that's all," Mary replied, and as quickly as possible dismissed the girl and locked her door.

Her room she had furnished in English style with furniture she had chosen in London. It was a delightful little place, bright with clean chintzes and a carpet of pastel blue. Upon the toilet-table was a handsome set of silver-mounted bottles and brushes, a birthday gift from her devoted father, and around the bed, suspended like a canopy from the ceiling, were the long white mosquito curtains.

For a long time she sat before the glass in her pale blue dressing-gown, her pointed chin sunk upon her breast in thought. Ruin was before her father—and if so, it meant ruin for them all!

Should she disregard the count's suggestion and write to him, urging him to come from Rome and see her; or if not, to allow her to travel alone to Rome? Should she write in secret?

How long she remained pondering, she had no idea. Twice the clock struck solemnly over the deep dark valley that spread beneath her window, until presently, with her mind made up, she rose and crossed to her little writing-table on the opposite side of the apartment, but was dismayed to find the stationery rack empty of notepaper.

If she wrote, it was necessary to do so at once in order to give the letter to Teresa when she came with the coffee in the morning, for the young peasant who took the postbag each day left at eight in the morning, so as to catch the midday mail from Pistoja. There was paper in the library at the farther end of the mansion, therefore she resolved to go and obtain some.

Wrapping a white shawl about her shoulders, she took her candle, and opening her door noiselessly, crept down the long marble corridor past her mother's door, and then, turning at right angles, proceeded to the door at the end which gave entrance to the splendid book-lined room full of priceless editions.

As she crept along in her little felt-soled slippers she suddenly halted, fancying that she heard an unusual noise. The peasantry entertained an absurd belief that at night supernatural noises were heard in the place, but of course she did not believe in them. In fact, she believed that the story had been invented by the agent, and circulated among the superstitious folk in order to give the house better protection against thieves.

She listened intently, her ears strained to catch every sound.

Yes, someone was moving in the library!

Her first thought was of burglars, but holding her breath and determined to first make certain before raising the alarm, she advanced cautiously to the door, placed her candle upon the floor, and peered through the keyhole.

She was not mistaken.

A light shone within. The great green door of her father's safe stood open before her, revealing the nest of iron drawers within, while someone was moving at the writing-table a little distance away, beyond her range of vision.

Her heart beat quickly as her eye was glued to the keyhole.

The thieves, whoever they were, had opened the safe with a key and were calmly rifling it!

She heard a noise as of crisp papers being turned over slowly, and then a few seconds later a dark figure crossed to the safe and took a further packet from one of the drawers.

As the man turned towards her his face became revealed in the dim light. Sight of it staggered her.

The man who had opened the safe, and who was methodically examining her father's confidential papers in secret, was none other than Jules Dubard!

CHAPTER FIFTEEN.
THE PERIL OF A NATION.

The revelation of the truth that Jules Dubard was making a methodical examination of her father's private papers held Mary spellbound.

From where she bent her eye at the big old-fashioned keyhole, she saw that the ponderous steel door had been opened by a key, for it was still in the shining lock. Within that safe her father kept a number of important state papers relating to the army, and quantities of correspondence had, from time to time, been brought up from Rome by official secretaries and he had placed them there for safety.

Once, while she had been helping him to arrange a quantity of technical documents and tie them in bundles with pink tape, he had remarked—

"These are safer here than in Rome, my dear. There are thousands who long to get sight of them, but they would never think of looking here."

But there had been a still further curious incident, one which she recalled vividly at that moment as she watched the man intently examining the documents by the light of his candle. It had happened back in April, when some matters connected with the estate called His Excellency from Rome, and he had brought Mary with him up to San Donato, where they had remained only two days. The country was delightful in the bright springtime, and Mary had desired to remain longer, but it was impossible, for her father's official duties took him back to the Eternal City—and besides, to live in the country in spring is not considered fashionable.

On the second night, while they were at the villa, he being alone, she sat with him in the library after dinner watching him rearrange a series of papers in the safe. It was eleven o'clock when he concluded and locked the great green door, then, carrying the key in his hand, he crossed to where she sat, and said in a calm, earnest voice—

"Mary, I know that you will keep a secret if I reveal one to you, won't you?"

"Most certainly, father," was her answer, not without some surprise.

"Then put on your cloak and a shawl around your head, my dear. I want to take you out."

Her curiosity was increased, for although it was moonlight it was late to walk in the country. Nevertheless she obeyed, and together they passed down the steep, narrow bypath through the dark pine woods, deeper and deeper, until before them in the silence the Arno spread shimmering in the moonbeams.

At the river's edge His Excellency suddenly halted, saying—

"Mary, I wish you to bear witness to my action, so that if you are ever questioned you may be able to tell the truth. Recollect that to-night is the ninth of April—is it not?"

"Yes; why?" she inquired, more puzzled than ever.

"Because I have decided that that safe in the library shall never again be reopened while I live. See! Here is the key!" and he gave it into her hand, urging her to examine it, which she did under the bright moonbeams.

Then he took it from her hand, and with a sudden movement tossed it as far as he could towards the centre of the deep stream, where it fell with a splash.

He sighed, as though a great weight had been lifted from his mind, and as they turned to re-ascend the hill he said with a grim laugh—

"If anyone wishes to open it now, he'll have a good deal of difficulty, I think."

That was all. She had never questioned him further. She had been witness of the wilful concealment of the key, but the reason she knew not. There were state secrets, she supposed, and she always regarded them as mysterious and inexplicable.

Yet the safe had been reopened—if not by the actual key flung into the river, then by a copy.

But what motive had Dubard in coming there on a visit during the Minister's absence, and making careful examination of the documents which had been so zealously hidden?

Out on the terrace that evening Dubard had, by giving her that warning, shown himself to be her father's friend. Yet surely this secret prying was no act of friendship?

And this was the man who had courted and flattered her—the man whom more than once she had believed that she could love!

Her heart beat quickly, for she scarce dared to breathe, lest she should betray her presence. The silence was unbroken save that within the room was the rustle of papers as the man carefully glanced over folio after folio.

The writing-table stood a little to the left, beyond the range of her sight, therefore he was for a long time invisible to her. Yet in the dead silence she could distinctly hear the scratching of a pen, as though he were making some extracts or memoranda. He had evidently lit the lamp upon the table, for his candle still stood on the floor before the open safe.

As she listened she heard him laugh lightly to himself, a harsh, low, mocking laugh, which echoed through the big old room, and then he rose and carried back the bundle of documents carefully retied, and placed them in their drawer, afterwards taking out another, and looking at the docket upon it.

From the latter he saw it was of no interest to him, therefore he tossed it back, as he did a second and a third. He seemed to be searching for something he could not find, and his failure caused him considerable chagrin.

His actions held her utterly dumbfounded. Although she had been attracted women possess, regarded him with some vague distrust. What she now discovered made it plain that she had not been mistaken. Her father had welcomed him to his house, had entertained him, and had regarded him as a man of sterling worth, notwithstanding his Parisian elegance of manner and foppishness of attire.

In their family circle her father had, indeed, more than once expressed admiration of the count's high qualities, which showed how completely the man had insinuated himself into the Minister's confidence. But the truth was now revealed, and he was unmasked.

Her natural indignation that he, a comparative stranger, should seek to inquire into her father's most carefully guarded private affairs, prompted her to burst in upon him and demand the reason of his duplicity; but as she watched, she recognised that the most judicious course would be to remain silent, and to describe to her father all that she had witnessed.

Therefore she remained motionless with strained eyes, set teeth, and quickly beating heart, gazing upon the man who had accepted her mother's hospitality only to make an examination of her father's secrets.

An hour passed. The deep-toned clock struck the hour of four, followed by the far-distant bell of Florence. She was cramped, chilled, and in darkness, for she had extinguished her light in order that he should not be attracted by it shining beneath the door.

Presently, however, she saw from his dark, heavy countenance, lit by the uncertain light of the candle, that he was deeply disappointed. He had searched, but had evidently failed to find what he expected. Therefore he commenced busily to rearrange the packets in the steel drawers, just as he had found them, preparatory to relocking the safe and retiring to his room.

She recognised that he had concluded his search—for that night, at any rate—for there still remained four or five drawers full of papers unexamined. Servants rise early in Italy, and he feared, perhaps, that he might be discovered. The remaining papers he reserved for the following night.

She watched him close the safe door and place the key in his pocket, then she rose, caught up her candle, and sped along the corridors back to her own room.

She relit her candle, and as she did so caught the reflection of her own face in the long mirror, and was startled to see how ghastly pale it was.

The discovery amazed her. She realised that the man who courted her so assiduously and who flattered her so constantly was in search of something which he believed to be in her father's possession. How he had recovered that key which had been thrown deep into the Arno at that lonely reach of the river beneath the tall cypresses, was an utter mystery.

Should she go to her mother and tell her of all she had seen? Her first impulse was to reveal everything, and seek her mother's counsel; yet on reflection she deemed it wiser to tell her father all she knew. The natural impulse of a daughter was, of course, to take her mother into her confidence, but one fact alone prevented this—only a few days previously her mother had been so loud in praise of the count, in order, it seemed, to recommend him to her daughter. Madame Morini was, with her husband, equally eager to see a formal engagement between the pair, and was surprised and disappointed to notice the cold, imperturbable manner in which Mary always treated him. Mary had realised this long ago, and for that reason now hesitated to tell her mother the truth.

Next morning, while she was puzzling over what excuse she could make to go to Rome, her mother came to her with an open letter in her hand, saying that her father had been called to Naples to be present at an official reception of King Humbert by that city, and would not return to the Ministry for three days. This news caused Mary's heart to sink within her, for she saw the uselessness of going to Rome until he returned.

That day she avoided Dubard, making an excuse that she had a headache, and spending most of the time alone in her little boudoir. The Frenchman took the other girls for an excursion through the woods, and during his absence she entered the great old library and carefully examined the lock of the safe.

It showed no sign of having been tampered with, having evidently been opened with its proper key—or an exact copy of it. The waste-paper basket was empty, the maid having taken it away that morning; but the blotting-pad caught her eye, and she held it before the long old empire mirror and tried to read the impressions of the words he had copied. But in vain. One or two disjointed words in French she made out, but they told her absolutely nothing. He had evidently made memoranda of the documents in French, or else the documents themselves had been written in French.

She knew, by his actions on the previous night, that he intended to return and conclude his investigations, and a sudden idea occurred to her to thwart his plans. The real object of his search he had apparently not discovered, therefore it was her duty to prevent him from obtaining it, and yet at the same time remain secret and appear to possess no knowledge of his attempt. She reflected for some time how best to accomplish this, when at last a mode essentially feminine suggested itself—one which she hoped would be effective.

Again she crossed to that huge green-painted safe let into the wall, which contained her father's secrets—and many of the military secrets of the kingdom of Italy—and taking a hairpin from her tightly bound tresses—always the most handy feminine object—she broke off a piece of the wire about an inch long, which she carefully inserted in the keyhole, poking it well in by means of the other portion of the pin until she heard it fall with a click into the delicate mechanism of the lock.

Then, smiling to herself, she withdrew, knowing that whatever attempt Dubard now made to reopen that door would be without avail. There was nothing to show that anyone had interfered with the mechanism, therefore he would be entirely unsuspecting, and would attribute the non-working to some defect in the lock itself, or in the key.

That night she sat next him at dinner, bearing herself as bravely bright and

he, on his part, thought her more charming than ever.

The evening passed as usual in the small drawing-room with music and gossip, and later, after all had retired and one o'clock had struck, Mary crept out in the darkness to the library, where, sure enough, she saw, on peering through the keyhole, the man who was so cleverly courting her actively trying to open the safe door.

The key would only half turn, and in French he muttered some low words of chagrin and despair. He tried and tried, and tried again, but all to no purpose. He withdrew the key, blew into the barrel, examined it in the light, and then tried once more.

But the lock had become jammed, and neither by force nor by light manoeuvring could he turn the key sufficiently to shoot back the huge shining bolts that held the door on every side.

Mary's effort had been successful. By that tiny piece of wire her father's secrets were held in safety.

CHAPTER SIXTEEN.

FATHER AND DAUGHTER.

"My dear child, you really must have been dreaming, walking in your sleep!" declared Camillo Morini, looking at his daughter and laughing forcedly.

"I was not, father!" she declared very seriously. "I saw the man take out those bundles of papers I helped you to tie up."

"But the key! There was only one made, and you know where it is. You saw me do away with it."

"He has a duplicate."

The Minister of War shook his head dubiously. What his daughter had told him about Jules Dubard was utterly inconceivable. He could not believe her. Truth to tell, he half believed that she had invented the story as an excuse against her engagement to him. Though so clever and far-seeing as a politician he was often unsuspicious of his enemies. Good-nature was his fault. He believed ill of nobody, and more especially of a man like Dubard, who had already shown himself a friend in several ways, and had rendered him a number of important services.

"And you say that you put a piece of your hairpin in the lock, and that prevented him reopening it on the second night?"

"Yes. Had it not been for that he would have made a complete examination of everything," she said. "If he had done so, would he have discovered much of importance?"

His Excellency hesitated, and his grey brows contracted.

"Yes, Mary," he answered, after a brief pause. "He would. There are secrets there—secrets which if revealed might imperil the safety of Italy."

"And they are in your keeping?"

"They are in my keeping as Minister of War."

"And some of them affect you—personally? Tell me the truth," she urged, her gloved hand laid upon the edge of the table.

"They affect me both as Minister and as a loyal subject of His Majesty," was His Excellency's response, his face growing a trifle paler.

If the truths contained within that safe really leaked out, the result, he knew, would be irretrievable ruin. Even the contemplation of such a catastrophe caused him to hold his breath.

"Then I assure you, father, that nearly half the documents within have been carefully and methodically examined by this man who poses as your friend."

And to tell you the truth, dear, I cannot believe that no one would open the door, unless he recovered it from the Arno—which is not likely. They never dredge that part, for it is too deep. Besides, that portion of the river is my own property, and before it could be dredged they would have to give me notice."

"But a duplicate—could he not possess one?"

"Impossible. That safe was specially manufactured in London for me, and is one of the strongest ever constructed. I had it made specially of treble strength which will resist any drill or wedge—even dynamite would only break the lock and leave the bolts shot. The only manner it could be forced without the key would be to place it in a furnace or apply electrical heat, which would cause the steel to give. The makers specially designed it so that no second key could ever be fitted."

"Then you disbelieve me?" she said, looking into her father's face.

"No, I don't actually disbelieve you, my dear," he responded, placing his hand tenderly upon hers; "only the whole affair seems so absolutely incredible."

"Everything is credible in the present situation," she said, and then went on to relate what Dubard had told her regarding the conspiracy of the Socialists, who intended to hound the Ministry from office.

She was seated in her father's private cabinet at the Ministry of War, in the large leather-covered chair opposite his big littered table, the chair in which sat so many high officials day after day discussing the military matters of the Italian nation. The double doors were closed, as they always were, against eavesdroppers.

She had, at her own request, managed to have a telegram sent her by him, and with Teresa had arrived in Rome only an hour ago. She had driven straight to the Ministry, and on her arrival Morini had quickly dismissed the general commanding in Sicily, to whom at that moment he was giving audience.

The story his daughter had related seemed utterly incredible. He knew from Ricci of the deep plot against him, but that the safe should really have been opened, and by Dubard of all men, staggered belief. That was why, in his astonishment, he declared that she must have been dreaming.

But in a few moments he became convinced, by her manner, that it was no dream, but an actual fact. Dubard, who had shown himself a friend, had actually pried into what was hidden from all. Why?

What had he discovered? That was the question.

Mary told him of the memoranda, and of the impressions upon the blotting-pad, whereupon he exclaimed quickly—

"I'll send someone up to San Donato to-night to bring the blotting-pad here. Granati, the handwriting expert, shall examine it." Then after a brief pause, he bent towards her, saying, "You do not believe that he really discovered what he was in search of?"

"No; he seemed disappointed."

His Excellency heaved a sigh of relief. If Jules Dubard really had opened the safe, then he feared too well the reason—the motive of the search was plain enough to him.

His teeth set themselves hard, his face blanched at thought of it; and he brushed the scanty grey hair from his forehead with his hand.

And yet it seemed impossible—utterly impossible—that the safe could really have been opened and its contents examined.

"I can't understand Count Dubard's reason for accepting our hospitality and then acting as a thief during your absence, father," the girl remarked, looking him full in the face. "I've told mother nothing, as I preferred to come straight to you. That is why I asked you to call me here by telegraph."

"Quite right, my dear; quite right," he said. "It would upset your mother unnecessarily."

"But there is another matter about which I want to talk," she said, after some hesitation; "something that the count has told me in confidence."

"Oh! What's that?" he asked quickly.

"It concerns yourself, father. He says that there is a deep political plot against you—to secure the downfall of the Cabinet and to bring certain unfounded charges against you personally."

Her father smiled quite calmly.

"That news, my dear, is scarcely fresh," he replied. "For twenty-five years my political enemies have been seeking to oust me from every office I've ever held. Therefore that they should be doing so now is only natural."

"I know! I know!" she said, with earnest apprehension. "But he says that the plot is so formed that its result will reflect upon you personally," and then she went on to describe exactly what Dubard had told her.

His Excellency, nervously toying with the quill, listened, and as he did so reflected upon what Ricci had already told him.

How was it, he wondered, that the Frenchman, who was outside the inner ring of Italian politics, knew all this? He must have some secret source of knowledge. That was plain.

Morini looked into his daughter's great brown eyes, and read the deep anxiety there. Within his own heart he was full of apprehension for the future lest the Socialists might defeat the Government; yet, with the tact of the old political hand, he betrayed no concern before her. What she told him, however, revealed certain things that he had not hitherto suspected, and rendered the outlook far blacker than he had before regarded it.

"The count has also told me that there is a charge of treason against Captain

Solaro."

Instantly her father's face changed.

"Well?" he snapped.

"The captain is innocent," she declared. "He must be. He would never betray the military secrets of his country."

"That is a matter which does not concern you, Mary," he exclaimed quickly. "He has been tried by court-martial and been dismissed the army."

"But you surely will not allow an innocent man to suffer, father!" she urged in a voice of quick reproach.

"It is not a matter that concerns either of us, my dear," he answered in a hard tone. "He has been found guilty—that is sufficient."

She was silent, for suddenly she recollected what the count had said, namely, that any effort on her part to prove poor Solaro's innocence must reflect upon her father, whose enemies would use the fact to prove that Italy had been betrayed with the connivance of the Minister of War.

She sighed. She had suspicions—grave ones; but she knew that at least Felice Solaro had been made the scapegoat of some cunning plot, and that his sentence was unjust. Yet what could she do in such circumstances? She was powerless. She could only remain patient and wait—wait, perhaps, for the final blow to fall upon her father and her house! A silence fell, broken only by the low ticking of the marble clock and the measured tramp of the sentry down in the sun-baked courtyard.

Her father sighed, rose from his chair, and with his hands behind his back paced anxiously up and down the room.

"Mary!" he exclaimed suddenly, in a changed voice, hoarsely in earnest, "if the secrets hidden in that safe have actually fallen into the hands of my enemies, then I must resign from office?" His face was now blanched to the lips, for all his self-possession seemed to have deserted him in an instant as the ghastly truth became revealed. "I know—I know too well—how cleverly the conspiracy has been formed, but I never dreamed that that safe could be opened, and the truth known. No," he said in a low voice of despair, his chin sunk upon his breast; "it would be better to resign, and fly from Italy."

His daughter looked at him in silence and surprise. She had never seen him plunged in such despair. A bond of sympathy had always existed between father and daughter ever since her infancy.

"Then you dare not face your enemies if they are actually in possession of what is contained in the safe?" she said slowly, rising and placing her hand tenderly upon her father's shoulder. She realised for the first time that her father, the man whom she had trusted so implicitly since her childhood, held some guilty secret.

"No, my dear, I dare not," was his reply, placing his trembling hand upon her arm.

"But you are unaware of how much knowledge Count Dubard has obtained," she pointed out.

"Sufficient in any case to cause my ruin," replied the grey-haired Minister of War. "That is, of course, if he is not after all my friend."

"But he is your friend, father," she was compelled to exclaim, in order to give him courage, for she had never in her life seen him so overcome.

"Those midnight investigations are, as you have said, a curious way of demonstrating friendship," he remarked blankly. "No," he added in a dry, hard tone. "To-day is the beginning of the end. These are my last days of office, Mary. The vote may be taken in the Chamber any day, and then—" and his eyes wandered involuntarily to that drawer in his writing-table wherein reposed his revolver, which, alas! more than once of late he had handled so fondly.

"And after that—what?" his daughter asked anxiously.

But only a deep sigh ran through the lofty room, and then she realised that her father's kindly eyes were filled with tears.

CHAPTER SEVENTEEN.
THE SAZARAC AFFAIR.

The great gilded ballroom of the French Embassy in Rome was thronged by a brilliant crowd, even though it was out of the season and the majority of the official and diplomatic world were still absent from the Eternal City, in the mountains or at the baths.

The bright uniforms, the glittering stars and coloured ribbons worn by the men, and the magnificent toilettes of the women, combined to form a perfect phantasmagoria of colour beneath the huge crystal electroliers.

The orchestra was playing a waltz, and many of the guests were dancing; for the floor at the Farnese Palace was the best in Rome. Camillo Morini, though in no mood for gaiety and obliged to attend, was wandering aimlessly through the rooms, exchanging salutes with the men he knew and now and then bowing low over a woman's hand. In his brilliant uniform as Minister of War, with the cerise and white ribbon of the Order of the Crown of Italy and a number of minor decorations, he presented a strikingly handsome figure, tall, erect, and distinguished-looking, as he strode through the huge painted salons dazzling with their heavy gilt mirrors and giant palms, a man of power in that complex nation, modern Italy.

After Mary had sought him and revealed the amazing fact of Dubard's secret investigations, she had gone on home to the palace with her maid Teresa, where he had joined her about six o'clock.

Father and daughter had dined alone in the long, high, old frescoed room. Few words they exchanged, for both felt that a crisis was imminent, and that if the blow fell the catastrophe must be overwhelming and complete. A true bond of deepest sympathy had always existed between them, for, as an only child, he had lavished upon her all his affection, while she, in turn, regarded him with a strong affection unusual in these decadent days. More than once since she had returned from the Broadstairs school she had been his assistant and adviser in the hours when she had found him alone and agitated as he so often was. More than once, indeed, he had confided in her, telling her of affairs which he withheld even from his wife for fear of unduly disturbing her in her delicate state of health. Often he had, of his own accord, sought his daughter's counsel. Hence she was in possession of many confidential facts concerning persons and politics in Rome, and with her woman's keen perception had already in consequence become a trained diplomat.

In the long and painful silence during dinner he urged her to accompany him to the French Ambassador's reception, adding with a sigh, "I would rather remain at home with you, my dear; but I must go. It will not do for me to betray any sign of fear."

"Go, certainly. It is your duty, father. But I am really too tired after my journey."

And so she excused herself from accompanying him, and went off early to her room.

His Excellency had been chatting with the Prince Demidoff, the Russian Ambassador, and was passing into the great ballroom, where the gaiety was then at its height, when he came face to face with Angelo Borselli, gorgeous in his brilliant general's uniform.

"Ah, my dear Camillo!" exclaimed the latter. "I only returned from Paris to-day, and called upon you on my way here. I must see you at once—privately."

The Minister, who had not met the Under-Secretary since the adventurer Ricci had revealed to him the truth regarding the Socialist conspiracy, controlled his feelings with marvellous calmness, and greeted his friend effusively.

"Why?" asked His Excellency under his breath. "Has anything happened?"

"A good deal. But here the very walls have ears," was the answer. "I have come in search of you."

"Well?" asked the Minister of War in abrupt surprise, recollecting the warning Ricci had already given him.

"Come with me. I know my way about this place," Borselli said. "There is an anteroom at the end of the south corridor where we can talk without risk of eavesdroppers."

Their host, Baron Riboulet, the French Ambassador, a tall, handsome, brown-bearded man, stopped and greeted the pair at that moment, while several other personages well-known in Roman society came up to pay their respects to His Excellency the Minister. Then at last the Under-Secretary managed to whisper—

"Let's get away. I must see you without further delay. Come."

And together they strolled through the magnificent salons with their brilliant crowds and presently entered a small, barely furnished room in a distant part of the historic old palace which is now the residence of the representative of the French Republic. As soon as they were within Borselli switched on the electric light, closed the door and locked it.

When he turned to the Minister the latter saw that his countenance had changed. He was pale and anxious, as though he had information of the highest importance to impart.

"Well?" asked Morini, wondering why he had brought him there so mysteriously.

"I have been in London again," the other exclaimed. "The truth of the Sazarac affair is known!"

Camillo Morini held his breath, his brows knit themselves, and his teeth were set hard. If this were a fact, then Borselli himself must have revealed the truth, for he alone knew it. What Ricci had told him had opened his eyes to this fellow's secret intentions. This was, no doubt, part of the vile, despicable conspiracy to secure the downfall of the Ministry. He knew that Angelo Borselli, the ambitious schemer with the rank of general, who owed everything to him, was his bitterest opponent, and he now saw an opportunity of fathoming the ingenious ramifications of the plot that was to effect his ruin. He was, however, too well versed in statesmanship to betray in his face the inner workings of his mind, and Borselli, notwithstanding that consummate craft which was his most prominent characteristic, had no suspicion that his chief was aware of the conspiracy.

"If the truth regarding General Sazarac is out, my dear Angelo," he said quite calmly, "then you must forgive me for suspecting that the catastrophe is due to your own indiscretion."

"Ah, my dear friend, there you are entirely wrong!" the other declared in a low, intense voice. "A man whom you know in England is well aware of the whole of the facts."

"And who is he, pray?" inquired the Minister, still preserving an outward calm that was perfect.

"The young Englishman George Macbean—the man who was staying with Sinclair of Thornby."

"Macbean?" slowly repeated His Excellency, gradually recalling to his memory the young Englishman whom Mary had introduced to him upon his own lawn. "Ah, of course! I recollect. He is Sinclair's nephew, and secretary to that fellow Morgan-Mason who came to Rome to see us about provisioning."

"The same. He knows everything."

The Minister was silent. His brows were knit. He recollected Macbean quite well, and wondered whether what Borselli was telling him were the actual truth. Since Vito Ricci had revealed the amazing cunning with which the Under-Secretary was working, he naturally mistrusted him.

"Well, and what does it matter?" asked Morini, still quite cool.

"Matter?" gasped the other. "Matter? Why, if he reveals what he knows it will mean ruin for us both—ruin?"

"You have expressed fear several times, my dear Angelo," laughed the Minister, leaning easily with his back to the table. "For myself, I entertain no fear. How did you discover that he held this knowledge?"

"I had my suspicions, and I therefore returned to England and found him in London. I did not approach him myself, of course, but from information I gathered I know that he must be aware of the whole truth. That being so, we must not risk any revelations."

"But even if he really does know, what motive could he ever have in bringing any distinct charge?" queried Morini, facing the man who, he knew, intended to himself occupy the post of Minister of War.

"You forget that he is secretary to that overbearing parvenu Morgan-Mason, and that the latter was Sazarac's most intimate friend."

Camillo Morini bit his lip. He had never thought of that. The affair of General Sazarac was to the public a mystery—one which the English Member of Parliament had actively endeavoured to solve. The young Englishman Macbean, if he really knew the truth, might be induced by his employer to speak! In an instant he recognised a further peril in a quarter hitherto entirely unexpected.

"You are quite certain he knows?"

"Absolutely."

"By what means did he learn the truth?"

"Ah, that is not clear!" responded the thin-faced man. "He knows; but how, is more than we can tell. The merchant of provisions, his employer, was the general's friend. Therefore the general probably knew the secretary, and may have taken him into his confidence! Cannot you therefore see that the fellow must be given an appointment in our Ministry? We cannot afford to allow him to remain the secretary of this parvenu, treated worse than a dog, ill-paid and sneered at on account of his superior birth and education. We must run no risk."

"Then the English Member of Parliament is not a very good employer—eh?"

"The reverse; a very bad one. He is a man who rose from being an assistant in a grocer's shop in a London suburb to be what he is, the greatest dealer in provisions in all the world—a man who is worshipped in London society because of his millions, and upon whose smile even an English duchess will hang. Ah, my dear Camillo! You, although you have a house in England, do not know those English. They are a people of millions; and in society they count their virtues by the millions they possess. I know a man who was a waiter in an hotel in South Africa a few years ago who now has the proud English nobility—their milords and their miladies—around his table. They eat his dinners, they shoot his birds, they use his yacht, they beg of him for loans—and yet they jeer and laugh at him behind his back. It is so with this member of the English Parliament to whom our young friend now acts as secretary."

"I cannot see your point," said the Minister of War, his uniform-hat tucked beneath his arm.

"Cannot you see that if this Englishman really knows the story of Sazarac it is to our mutual interests that he should not speak of it? It might mean ruin for us," Borselli pointed out in a low, earnest voice. "Cannot you see that, being in the employ of that pompous hog-merchant Morgan-Mason, and badly paid for his services he is longing for a higher and more lucrative position? Is it not but natural? He knows Italy, and would be only too eager to accept an appointment in the Ministry—where we really want a good English secretary. Such a man would be of the utmost value to both of us."

"Then you suggest that we should offer him an appointment?"

"Exactly," was Borselli's reply. "If you agree to give the fellow a secretaryship, leave the rest to me. He will be only too eager to accept an appointment under the Government, and once in Rome and in our employ, he will never dare to open his mouth regarding the ugly affair."

CHAPTER EIGHTEEN.
COUNTING THE COST.

Next day at noon Mary, who was out driving in the smart English victoria, called at the Ministry and again sat alone with her father trying to persuade him to order an inquiry into the case of the unfortunate Felice Solaro.

"It is useless, my dear," was his impatient answer. "He has already been here himself, but the case is proved up to the very hilt. I therefore cannot interfere."

"Proved by that woman Nodari?" she cried, with fierce indignation. Then, after a pause, she leaned towards him and said in a low, earnest voice, "You will not allow an inquiry because you fear its result, father?"

"Hush! Who told you that?" he gasped, staring at her.

"No one. It is only a logical conclusion. The captain is the victim of a wicked conspiracy, and he is suffering in silence because he knows the utter futility of appeal."

"He has already appealed to me."

"And you have refused him justice!" was his daughter's quick reproachful declaration. "You are surely not unjust, father? You cannot be."

The tall, distinguished-looking man was silent, and rising, walked up the long strip of carpet placed upon the marble floor. Then slowly he returned to her, and looking straight into her face, said—

"My hands are tied, my girl. I am powerless, I confess to you."

"But in your heart you believe that he is innocent? Tell me the truth."

"Yes," he whispered in a broken voice. "I do—I do."

She made no response. His admission was full of a poignant meaning. She saw that he was somehow fettered, held in some mysterious bondage of which she was in ignorance.

Again she spoke of the examination of the safe by Dubard, but this matter he seemed disinclined to discuss, and pleading other affairs, he urged her to return home and await him at luncheon.

At three o'clock, after eating his midday meal with her, he went forth again to make a round of official calls, when, a quarter of an hour later, the Italian footman threw open the long white doors of the small salon where Mary was sitting writing letters, and announced—

"Comte Dubard!"

She started quickly, held her breath, and rose to greet her visitor, who, foppishly dressed in a pale grey flannel suit, came forward smiling, and, drawing his heels together, bowed low over her white hand. The man's calm impertinence and cool unscrupulousness held her speechless.

"I thought you were still at San Donato," she stammered, when at last she found tongue. "I had no idea you were here, in Rome."

"I have followed you," he declared, smiling. "You left the villa unknown to me, and therefore I have come to you."

"For what reason?" she inquired, her brows slightly elevated.

"Because—well, because I fear that the reason of your sudden journey is to reveal to your father those things which I told you in confidence the other day. Remember the future rests entirely in your own hands. He must know nothing—at least at present."

"And is that the only reason you are here, count?" she asked meaningly, standing before him with her hands behind her back, her splendid dark eyes fixed upon him.

"I come here as your friend to warn you that silence is best at this moment. A word to your father will precipitate the crisis. I know," he went on, "that you are convinced that an injustice has been done in the case of poor Solaro. Your attitude the other evening showed me that. But I beg of you to make no effort to clear his character, because, in the first place, any such attempt must of necessity fail; and secondly, your father's enemies would at once shriek of the insecurity of the French frontier. No," he argued, speaking in a low tone in French, "you must keep your own counsel, mademoiselle. If this catastrophe is to be averted, if the Cabinet is to be saved, then it must be by some ingenious means that are not apparent to your father's enemies."

She stood listening to this declaration of friendship by the man who had pried into her father's secrets. It was on the tip of her tongue to openly charge him with ulterior motives, nevertheless her better judgment prevailed. She recognised, as her father had pointed out, that no good end could be served by showing her hand at that juncture, therefore she allowed him to argue without raising her voice in protest. He had followed her from Tuscany because he was apprehensive lest she should tell her father the truth. Why? He was in fear of something; of what, she could not tell.

A great conspiracy, ingenious and widespread, was afoot to encompass her father's ruin, therefore she resolved to remain at his side and at any cost face the perils of exposure. The few hours she had spent in her father's society had shown that, so full was he of his responsible official duties and affairs concerning the army of Italy, he had, in a few weeks, become an entirely changed man. His face was now pale and drawn, and when he sat alone with her there rested upon his countenance a haunted look—the look of a man who was face to face with ruin. Loving her father, she had been quick to recognise the truth. At first it had staggered her, but her surprise and horror had given place to a deep filial sympathy, and while determined to hide her secret from her mother, she had become at the same time her father's confidante and friend.

"I am quite well aware of the intentions of the Opposition," she answered coldly, after a painful pause. "But I am not in the least apprehensive. My father has for so many years been a faithful servant of his sovereign that the Italian people still have confidence in him. Neither the country nor the Camera can fail to recognise the many reforms he has introduced into the army, or how he has alleviated the lot of the common conscript."

"Ah!" he exclaimed, with a deep sigh. "I am glad that you recognise your father's strong position—the strongest of any man in the Italian Government. Nevertheless," he added, "those shrieking firebrands can, if they so desire, set Italy aflame. We have that truth to face, and we must face it."

Her lips were pressed together, for she saw how cleverly he was changing his tactics towards her. She also recognised how, by appearing to have confidence in the future, she could place him off his guard. Her father's honour was, she felt, in her hands, and the magnitude of the issue aroused within her all her woman's innate tact and courage.

"I came to Rome because my father telegraphed to me," she said quite simply. "He wanted to take me with him to Palermo to visit my aunt, but the king's programme is changed, so we are not going after all. I intend to return to San Donato the day after to-morrow. It is still too hot in Rome."

"Ah! then I own myself quite mistaken," he laughed. "I have been unduly anxious, for I attributed your sudden departure to your natural desire to tell His Excellency all that I had explained in confidence. We men, you know, are in the habit of saying that women cannot keep secrets."

"I can keep one," she declared.

"Yes," he answered. "I know you can. Upon your secrecy in this affair the very fate of the Ministry depends, believe me. You know that I am your father's true friend—as well as yours."

She held her breath, and her eyes met his.

"You have told me that several times before," she remarked in a quiet, mechanical voice and with an assumed air of unconcern.

"And I mean it," he said earnestly. "Only you had better not tell your father that I am here. It is, perhaps, unwise to let him know that I have followed you from San Donato—he may suspect."

"Suspect what?"

"Well, suspect the reason of my visit to you to-day," he said, surprised at her quick question. "You see I have come here because—well, to tell you the truth," he faltered, "I am here to tell you something which I wanted to say at San Donato— yet I dared not."

"What—is it bad news?" she asked, looking at him with some apprehension.

A long silence fell between them. He was watching her, hesitating whether he should speak. At length, however, he suddenly took her hand and said

"As I have told you, I am your father's friend. You may doubt me; probably you do. But one day I shall prove to you that I am acting solely from motives of friendship—that I am endeavouring to shield your father from the impending blow."

"If you are, why do you not go to my father and tell him everything?" she asked, inwardly filled with doubt and mistrust.

"Because, as I have told you, it is impolitic to do so at this moment. We must wait."

"And while we wait his enemies may take advantage."

"No, not yet. Their plans are not yet complete," he answered. "I was at the Camera last evening, and discovered the exact situation. If we are patient and watchful we may yet turn the weapon of our enemies against themselves."

He saw that she was grave and thoughtful, that his advice caused her to reflect; while she, on her part, did not divulge what she had already told His Excellency.

They stood together at the window, where the long green sun-shutters were closed to keep out the blazing heat of afternoon, and as he looked upon her handsome profile in that dim half-light he saw that her face and figure in her cool white dress was the most perfect that he had ever gazed upon even in the *haut monde* of Paris. In the air was the stifling oppression of the storm-cloud: "You are sad," he said presently in a calm, low voice as he leaned against the broad marble sill of the window, where a welcome breath of air reached them from the silent sun-baked street below.

Her dark eyes were fixed upon the opposite wall, and her hands were clasped in pensive attitude; for his manner had mystified her, knowing all that he had done in the silence of the night at San Donato.

"I fear the future," she declared frankly, starting at his words and turning her gaze upon him.

"But what have you to fear?" he asked, bending slowly towards her with an intense look in his eyes. "I am your friend equally with your father's, as I have already declared, and fortunately I know the intentions and the dastardly intrigues of those who are plotting his ruin."

"Then you can save him by exposing their plot?" she cried, utterly amazed at his words. "You will—will you not?" she implored breathlessly.

"I can save him—yes, I can, within twelve hours, cause the very men who now seek the downfall of the Ministry to fly in fear from Rome," he said. Then, after a pause, he added, "I know the truth."

"And you will tell it?" she urged breathlessly, advancing towards him. "My father's future, my own future, the honour of our house all depend upon you."

He had examined her father's private papers, and undoubtedly knew the truth on both sides. He had acted with the enemy, and yet he declared himself to be her friend? "You will save my father?" she implored.

With a sudden movement he took her hand in his and whispered in a quick, earnest voice into her ear—

"Yes, I will save him—on one condition. Of late, Mary, I have noticed that you have avoided me—that—that you somehow appear to shun me in suspicion and mistrust. You doubt my good intentions towards you and your family. But I will give proof of them if you will only allow me."

She felt his hot breath upon her cheek, and trembled.

"Save my father from the hands of these unscrupulous office-seekers," she panted. "His honour—his very life is to-day at stake."

"Upon two conditions, Mary," was his low, quiet answer, still holding her hand firmly in his. "That he gives his consent to our marriage, and that you are willing to become my wife."

"Your wife!" she gasped, drawing her hand away, starting back, and looking blankly at him with her magnificent eyes. "*Your wife!*"

"Yes. I love you, Mary," he cried passionately, taking her hand again, "I love you. You must have seen how for months past I have lived for you alone, yet I dared not, until to-day, reveal the truth. Say one word—only say that you will be mine—and your father shall crush those who intend to wreck and ruin him."

"You—then you make marriage the price of my father's triumph?" she faltered hoarsely, as the ghastly truth gradually dawned upon her.

"Yes," he cried, raising her inert hand to his hot lips. "Because I love you, Mary!—because I cannot live without you! Be mine. Speak the word, and I will reveal the truth and save your father from ruin."

But, realising the cleverly laid trap into which she had fallen, she stood silent and rigid, her eyes fixed upon him in an agony of blank, unutterable despair.

CHAPTER NINETEEN.
THE SACRIFICE.

The glaring afternoon had drawn to a close.

Camillo Morini, after a heavy day's work in the silence of the big old library at San Donato shaded from the sun-glare, rose, and joining Mary, went out along the hill to enjoy the *bel fresco* of the departing day. The Italian habit is to go out and wander at sundown, and when up at his villa His Excellency always made it a rule to take a stroll through the cool pine woods, generally accompanied by Mary; for his wife was not a good walker, and seldom ventured far. Therefore father and daughter, in the two hours preceding dinner, frequently made excursions on foot through the smiling vineyards and great pine forests around the magnificent old mansion.

They had skirted the mediaeval walls of the village and passed down the old cypress avenue, saluted on every side by their *contadini*, then striking off on a bypath through the wood they halted at a point known by the countryfolk as the Massa del Fate—or Fairy's Rock—where there opened suddenly before them a magnificent view—Tuscany, the paradise of Europe, in the sundown.

Surely nothing could be so beautiful as the lines of the Arno valley, the gentle inclination of the hills, and the soft fugitive outlines of the mountains which bounded them. A singular tint and most peculiar harmony united the earth, the sky, and the wide winding river. All the surfaces were blended at their extremities by means of an insensible gradation of colour, and without the possibility of ascertaining the point at which one ended or another began. It appeared ideal, possessing a beauty beyond nature; it was nevertheless the genuine light of old-world Tuscany.

The Minister of War, in his white drill suit and straw hat, a trifle negligent of attire as he always was when he was up there in that remote retreat, halted at the break in the high dark pines, gazed out upon the marvellous panorama, and inhaled a deep breath of the cool, refreshing wind that came up from the valley with the sundown.

After hours of intricate work in his darkened study he stood there to refresh himself, while Mary, in pale blue with a big straw hat, was at his side, her eyes turned away up the valley, reflecting upon some meaning words he had just uttered.

Mary often came to that lonely point on the high-up estate to enjoy the grand scene of departing day. In that hour, when the evening bells came up from the white villages dotted far below, the summits of the Apennines appeared to consist of lapis-lazuli and pale gold, while their bases and sides were enveloped in a vapour which had a tint now violet, now purple. Beautiful clouds like light chariots borne on the wind with inimitable grace that came from seaward made one easily comprehend the appearance of the Olympian deities under that mythological sky. Ancient Florence seemed to have stretched out all the purple of her Cardinals, her Signori, and her Medici, and spread it under the last steps of the God of Day.

"Well?" asked the Minister, as he watched the girl's beautiful face set full to the dying sunset and saw the far-off look in her wonderful eyes.

"I have nothing to say, father—nothing," was her quiet answer as she turned to him, and he saw that she was on the point of tears.

"Then you are content that it should be so? I mean you will permit me to give a favourable reply to the count?" he said, not without some hesitation. He had aged visibly since those quiet days in rural England, and the lines upon his pale brow gave him an expression of deep anxiety.

She sighed, and for a few moments made no response.

"Is it your wish that I should marry him?" she asked in a low, mechanical tone, her face pale, her hands trembling.

"I have no desire to place undue pressure upon you, my dear," he said, placing his hand kindly upon her shoulder. "I merely ask you what response you wish me to give. He came to me while I was sitting alone in Rome three nights ago, and requested permission to pay his court to you."

"And what response did you give?" she inquired in a voice scarcely above a whisper.

"I told him that I desired to hear your own views before giving him an answer."

She was again silent, her face turned to the darkening valley. The sundown in Italy disappears less quickly than in England, for when the tints are on the point of vanishing they suddenly break out again and illumine some other point of the horizon. Twilight succeeds twilight, and the charm of closing day is prolonged.

"And what is your wish, father?" she asked presently, still looking blankly before her; for those grey fading lights seemed to be but the reflection of her own fading life and happiness.

"Well, Mary," he said, his hand still upon her shoulder, "let me speak frankly and candidly. This morning I discussed the matter fully with your mother, and we both came to the conclusion that the count is a very eligible man. Neither of us desire you to marry if you entertain no love for him, but both in England and in Italy we have noticed for a year past that you have not been averse to his attentions, and—well, I may as well tell you quite plainly, my dear—we have been much gratified to think that the attraction has been mutual. Yet," he added, "it lies with you entirely to accept or to reject him."

"It would please you, father, if I became the Comtesse Dubard, would it not?" she asked, tears that were beyond her control springing to her eyes.

"It would please both of us," he said in a low, earnest voice. "But you, yourself must decide. That he will make you a good husband, I have no doubt. Yet, as I have already said, as your father I would be the very last to endeavour to force you to marry a man you do not love."

She did not reply. He stood gazing upon her face, and his own thoughts were sad ones. Soon, very soon, the blow might fall, and then his wife and daughter would be left alone. He was, therefore, anxious to see her married before that catastrophe, which he knew was inevitable.

When the count had sat with him that evening making his request, he recollected the strange story Mary had told him regarding the secret examination of his papers. It was curious—so curious and so utterly devoid of motive that he could see no reason in it. Yet if that Frenchman had really discovered certain things concealed behind that green-painted steel door, it was to his interest that he should become his son-in-law and so preserve the secret.

Yes, he was anxious to see his daughter married to that man to whom he had taken such a personal liking, yet he affected to leave the decision entirely in her own hands.

She spoke at last in a hard, tuneless voice, as though her youth and life were slowly dying just as surely as the day was fading.

"If it is your wish, father, that I should become his wife, you may give him an affirmative answer. But—"

And she suddenly burst into a torrent of hot tears.

"Ah no! no!" her father cried, touching her pale cheek tenderly. "No. Do not give way, dear. I have no desire that you should marry this man if you yourself do not really love him. Perhaps your mother has been mistaken, but by various signs and looks that both of us noticed in Rome and in England, we believed that you entertained for him a warm affection."

"I know that my marriage would please you," she said. "Mother gave me to understand that two months ago, therefore,"—and she paused as though she could not utter the words which were to decide her fate—"therefore I am willing to accept him."

"Ah, Mary!" he exclaimed quickly, his face brightening, for her decision aroused hope within him. "I need not tell you what happiness your words bring to me. I confess to you that I have hoped that you would give your consent, for I would rather see you the wife of the count, with wealth and position, than married to any other man I know. He loves you—of that I am convinced. Has he never told you so?"

She did not answer for a few moments. She was reflecting upon that scene in the little salon in Rome when he had revealed himself to her in his true colours.

"Yes," she answered at last in that same hard, colourless voice. "He told me so once."

He attributed her blank, despairing look to the natural emotion of the moment. It was the great crisis of her young life, for she was deciding her future. He was in ignorance of how already she had made the compact with Dubard—of how she had decided to sacrifice herself in order to save him.

Her father, in ignorance of the truth of how nobly she was acting, went on to analyse the young Frenchman's good qualities and relate to her all that he had learnt regarding him.

"His youth has been no better and no worse than that of any young man brought up in Paris," he said, "yet from the information I have gathered it seems that he has sown his wild oats long ago, and for the past couple of years he has given up racing and gambling and all such vices of youth, and has become a perfect model of what a young man should be. Men who know him in Paris speak highly of him as a man of real grit—a man with a future before him. You do not think, Mary," he went on, "that I should have welcomed him as a guest at my table if I were not sure that he was a man worthy the name of friend?"

"Ah!" she sighed, "you have, my dear father, sometimes been disappointed in your friendships, I fear. Angelo Borselli, for instance, has been your friend through many years."

"Angelo!" he exclaimed impatiently. "Yes, yes, I know. But I am speaking of Jules—of the man you have consented to marry."

A slight hardness showed at the corners of her mouth at mention of the man who had so cleverly entrapped her. She knew that escape was impossible. He could place her father in a position of triumph over his enemies, and in return claimed herself. Ah! if she could only speak the truth; if she could only take her father into her confidence, and show him the reason she so readily gave her consent to a union that was odious to her! Yet she knew that if she gave him the slightest suspicion of her self-sacrifice he would withhold his consent, and the result would be dire disaster.

She knew her father's brave, unflinching nobility of character. Rather than he would allow her to marry a man whom she hated and mistrusted, he would face ruin—even death.

And for that reason she, pale and silent, gazing into the rising mists, accepted the man who had made her father's honour the price of her own life.

"Tell the count," she said, in a voice broken by emotion, "tell him that I am ready to be his wife."

And her father, gladdened at what he, in his ignorance, believed to be a wise decision, bent to her and pressed his lips to her cheek with fatherly affection, in a vain endeavour to kiss her tears away.

They were not tears of emotion, but of a sweet and tender woman's blank despair.

CHAPTER TWENTY.

TELLS THE TRUTH.

On the following afternoon, in consequence of a telegram, the Minister of War drove into Florence, and met Vito Ricci at the club.

He seldom took the train to Florence because, on account of his position, the obsequious officials treated him with so much ceremony. He was a modest man, who at heart hated all bowing officialdom, much preferring to drive through the rich vineyards of the Arno valley to being received at the station by all the officials and having the ordinary traffic stopped on his arrival.

The Florence Club, an institution run upon English lines, is one of the most exclusive in Europe. It occupies the whole of a huge flat in the new Piazza Vittorio Emmanuele, handsomely appointed, with fine spacious rooms overlooking the busy centre of Florentine life. Its members are mostly men of the highest social standing in Italy, together with a select few of rich English and Americans, to whom membership gives the hall-mark of rank in that complex cosmopolitan world. In winter and spring its rooms are well-filled and its bridge-tables are well patronised, but in summer and autumn, when all Florence is away in the mountains or at the sea, it is deserted and handed over to the care of a couple of waiters, who scarcely see a member from one week's end to the other.

The Deputy Ricci had telegraphed that he had no time to come up to San Donato, as he could only spend three hours in Florence; therefore the club was the most convenient place where they could meet and consult undisturbed. The urgency of Ricci's message had aroused the other's apprehensions that something was amiss.

"Ah!" cried the deputy in relief as the Minister entered the small card-room where he stood impatiently awaiting him. "I began to fear that my telegram had not reached you." And the pair having shaken hands, Ricci went to the door and locked it.

Then when they crossed to the window, which gave a view of the wide-open piazza with its colossal statue in the centre, Ricci said—

"I left Rome this morning at nine, and I return by the express at six. I came here purposely to see you."

"Has something occurred?" asked His Excellency quickly, glancing at the dark face of the Piedmontese lawyer who sat in the Chamber of Deputies and made politics his living.

"Yes," was Ricci's answer in a low half-whisper. "You recollect our conversation when we met last—about the impending crisis?"

"Yes. You promised, for certain considerations, to turn the political tide in my favour."

"I have tried to do so, but have failed," said the other in a deep, serious voice.

"Failed?" gasped the Minister as, in an instant, all the light died out of his face.

"The Opposition is too strong," he explained. "Borselli has so completely won over the Socialists that he can cause them to dance to any tune he pleases."

Camillo Morini's face was blanched. Ruin was before him—ruin, utter and complete. He had trusted in Vito, feeling confidence in that adventurer's ingenuity and influence. More than once this adventurer had cleverly turned the tide of popular thought, for certain journals were always open to write what the popular deputy for Asti dictated, and of course received substantial bribes for so doing. Yet at this most crucial moment he had failed!

"I made you the payment on condition that you were successful in rendering me the service," remarked His Excellency hoarsely.

"I know, I know," was the other's response. "I have brought back the money to repay you." And he took from his leather wallet a banker's draft, which he handed to the Minister.

The tall, thin, refined-looking man stood motionless, his eyes fixed for a moment upon the slip of paper thus offered back to him. He recognised that the efforts of his secret agent, whose services had so often been invaluable, were of no avail, that his doom was sealed.

"No. Keep it, Vito," he said hoarsely, with a dry, hollow laugh, that sarcasm born of desperation. "You have earned it—keep it."

The other raised his shoulders in regret, and then, with a word of thanks, replaced the draft in his pocket.

There was a long silence. A company of *bersaglieri*, those well-set-up men with their round hats and cock's plumes, were crossing the piazza, marching to the fanfare of trumpets, and behind them came a company of the Misericordia, that mediaeval confraternity disguised in their long black gowns with slits for their eyes, passing with their ambulance on an errand of mercy.

Morini gazed upon that weird, tragic procession hurrying across the square, and within him there arose grave and morbid reflections. He had worked for Italy, had given his whole soul to the reform of the army and the perfecting of the defences of the nation he had loved so well. It was more the fault of the system than his own that he had been guilty of dishonesty. The other members of the Cabinet were equally guilty of misappropriating the national funds. They were, indeed, compelled to do so in order to keep up their position, to maintain and pay the secret agents they employed, and to bribe the men of influence from seeking to expose their thefts.

Surely poor strangled Italy under the régime of his lamented Majesty King Umberto was in very evil case!

"I have trusted in you, Vito," the Minister had said feebly, ... tongue, for the ugly truth had utterly staggered him.

"And I have done my best, your Excellency," was the other's reply. "In the Camera and out of it, I have worked unceasingly in order to try and win you back into favour, but Borselli is far too strong. He has influential friends, who believe they will obtain appointments and money if he is in office as Minister of War. Hence they are working by every means to place him in power."

"And to cause my downfall and ruin!" murmured the unhappy man, staring blankly down at the piazza, still dazzlingly white in the hot sun-glare.

The adventurer sighed. To Camillo Morini he owed everything, and was conscious of the fact. He had no words to express his regret at his failure, for he knew too well all that it meant to the man before him.

"The success of the French secret service upon the Alpine frontier is the chief capital of the Opposition," Ricci explained. "They say you have connived at it, and that Solaro was assisted by your daughter, the Signorina Mary."

"Solaro assisted by her! How?"

"They have discovered that he was her friend. They were noticed together in Rome a year ago, when they allege that she gave him certain information gathered from your papers, which, in due course, reached the French Ministry of War!"

"Impossible?" declared the Minister. "They are acquainted, I know. But my daughter would never assist a traitor. It is infamous?"

"I quite agree with you. I cannot believe the signorina guilty of any such action. Yet the truth remains that the secrets of the Tresenta are actually in the hands of France."

"I know," groaned the unhappy man. "I know, Vito. But Solaro is disgraced and imprisoned. Surely that is enough for them?"

"No. You misunderstand. They are raising the cry everywhere that Italy is in danger—that you personally are culpable."

"They will say next that I myself have sold the plans to France!" he cried bitterly.

"Ah! you know the kind of men Borselli has behind him—the most unscrupulous set of office-seekers in Italy. They will hesitate at nothing in order to arouse the public indignation against you. The fire is already kindled, and they are now fanning it into a flame. I tried to extinguish it. I offered a dozen bribes in various quarters, knowing that you would willingly pay to secure safety—but all were rejected because of Borselli's promise to them of fat emoluments in the future."

"Italy!" cried the Minister. "Oh, Italy! Must you fall into the hands of such a gang of thieves? I have done my best. Dishonesty has been forced upon me by this very man who now seeks to hound me out of office and take my place. I have been blind, Vito," he added, "utterly blind."

"Yes," sighed the other, "I fear you have. Borselli has laid his plans too well, and arranged the conspiracy with too deep a cunning, to fail. I naturally believed that he could be fought with his own weapons, but I have found myself mistaken. We must, alas! face the worst! To-morrow the Socialists are to raise the question of Tresenta in the Camera; the vote will be taken, the Government defeated, and the whole blame will fall upon yourself. Borselli's organs of the Press all have their orders to shriek and scream at you, to demand a searching inquiry regarding the disposal of certain sums set apart for the army—even to the giving of contracts to German contractors."

Morini started, and his grave face went paler.

"Then Borselli has betrayed me—he, who is equally guilty with myself?"

"To his friends who intend to obtain Government appointments at high salaries he is innocent, while you alone are guilty," Ricci pointed out. Then, sighing again, he added in a sympathetic voice,—for although a political adventurer he was nevertheless a firm personal friend of the Minister's,—"I declare to you, Camillo, I have done my very utmost. But the weak point in our armour is the Tresenta affair, and the signorina's acquaintance with the traitor Solaro. The natural conclusion, of course, is that she assisted him."

"But what do they say of his friendship for her?"

"They allege that she was in love with him, but that, being only an officer with little else but his pay, he feared to approach you to obtain your permission to pay court to her, and that she, in order that he might obtain money from the French War Intelligence Department, gave him copies of certain secret documents which were in your possession."

"But I have no plans of the Tresenta," he declared quickly.

"There are other matters of which they allege the French have gained knowledge—details of the new mobilisation scheme."

"Those papers are safely locked up at the Ministry," he answered. "Mary has no knowledge of their existence."

"If France obtained copies of them, would they be of service to her?"

"Of course. They would reveal our vulnerable points, and would show where she might strike us in order to destroy the concentration of our troops upon the frontier. Those papers are the most important of any we possess. The commanders of the various military districts have their secret orders, but they would be useless without the key to the complete scheme, which is kept safely from prying eyes in the Ministry. The French have surely not obtained a copy of that!" he gasped.

"It seems that they have—through your daughter, it is alleged." Then he added, with a sigh, "They have all their facts ready to launch against you."

"Their untruths—their lies!" he cried desperately, clenching his fist. "Ah, it is cruel! It is infamous! They even go so far as to brand my daughter—my dear

Mary—as a traitress!"

And the strong man of Italy—the ruler of a European army—covered his face with his hands and sobbed aloud.

Vito Ricci had failed, yet was it any wonder that Morini's enemies sought to attack his honour by making false and ignominious allegations against his daughter?

The unhappy man looked into the future of ruin, disgrace, perhaps prosecution by those very men who had been his friends, and saw but one way open from that shame—death.

And yet was not such a thought irreligious and cowardly? If they intended to attack his daughter, was it not his duty to defend her and vindicate her good name?

Ricci, unscrupulous as he had been through years of political life, sometimes holding by his intrigues the very fate of Italy in his hands, stood by in silence, his chin sunk upon his breast, for he knew too well that the ill-judged man to whom he was indebted for so much was to be made the scapegoat of the corrupt Ministry—he knew that the man before him was doomed, and yet he was utterly powerless to save him, even though he was prepared to go to any length to attain that end.

Then, a moment later, when Camillo Morini thought of that degraded officer, silent and suffering in the gloom of his prison, his mouth hardened, he held his breath, and his jaws became hard set. He remembered how that accused man had broken his sword before him and cast the pieces at his feet as guage of his innocence.

Yet the die was cast. To-day he, Camillo Morini, was Italian Minister of War, and the trusted adviser of his sovereign, King Umberto. But to-morrow—to-morrow? Ah! would that the morrow could not come.

CHAPTER TWENTY ONE.
THE EAR OF THE MINISTER.

After luncheon Camillo Morini left his wife, Mary, and the three young English girls, Anna and Eva Fry and Violet Walters, and retired as usual to his study. He had been silent and thoughtful at table, and his wife, ignorant of the crisis, attributed it to worry over state affairs, as was so often the case. A Minister's life is never a happy one, and always full of grave responsibilities.

Her Excellency had seen her husband, to whom she was so devoted, age before his time, and in the years gone by she had greatly assisted him by her wise counsels and womanly help.

He looked at her in silence from where he sat at the head of the table, and sighed bitterly to himself. If he told her all, the shock would be too great for her. It might, indeed, have serious consequences. Therefore he was compelled to keep his secret from everyone save Mary.

The long green sun-shutters were closed, and the great, high, old frescoed room in which he sat alone was in half-darkness. He had told the liveried servant Francesco that he did not wish to be disturbed, and on entering had locked the door behind him. It was a dull, depressing room at any time, for the ponderous cases of old vellum-bound books breathed an atmosphere of a glorious but forgotten past. Gerino's frescoed angels looked down upon him from the ceiling, and the ponderous beams still bore traces of bright colouring and faded gilt. Closed against the stifling heat outside, only a few rays of light struck across the big writing-table where His Excellency was sitting dejectedly, his head buried in his hands. From without came the monotonous hum of the insects and the harsh chirp of the cicale, the only live things astir under the burning Tuscan sun.

His wife and the girls had gone to their rooms for the siesta, previous to driving over to Montelupo to visit the Marchioness Altieri, and he was alone with his bitter grief and blank despair.

Little sleep had come to his eyes for the past week. Last night he had spent the hours under the steely sky, first down in the valley and then away over the mountains until he reached a point high up on a barren summit, where he sank down upon a heap of stones and watched the breaking of day over the Apennines. His thoughts were always of what Vito had revealed to him, and of his failure.

His return to the house had passed unnoticed, and after a wash he had taken his coffee and entered that room with a firm and desperate resolve. The whole

morning he had occupied in placing his papers in order, arranging them carefully, tying them in bundles, and scribbling certain instructions upon each, with the

He had worked on in grim silence, sighing sometimes and laughing bitterly
to himself at others. More than once he murmured Mary's name or that of his beloved wife, while nearly the whole time his kind eyes were filled with tears.

At luncheon he had motioned Francesco to give him a liqueur-glass of cognac
with his coffee, a most unusual proceeding, for he was a very abstemious man,
and now he sat motionless, his fingers in his grey hair, staring thoughtfully at the
blotting-pad before him.

For fully half an hour he remained in that position, often murmuring to himself. He was reflecting upon all the bitterness of the past. He, the man whose name
was one to conjure with in Italy, was at that moment without one single friend to
give him help or sympathy.

Suddenly the silence of the room was broken by the whir-r of the telephone
bell—the private line that connected him direct with his secretary at the Ministry
at Rome three hundred miles away.

Quickly he rose, walked to the corner where the instrument was placed, and
responded.

"The Onorevole Ricci desires to speak with your Excellency in private," announced the voice which he recognised as one of his private secretaries.

"Va bene!" was the Minister's anxious response.

Vito had, before they parted at the club, arranged to telephone to him in case
of necessity.

"Are you there?" inquired the voice of the deputy for Asti.

"Yes. What is it?" asked the Minister, as through the instrument he distinctly
heard the snap of the padded door of the telephone cabinet in the Ministry, which
was now closed against listeners.

"It is as I thought," Ricci said in a slow, distinct voice. "I have been active ever
since my return, and it is just as I believed. Last night at the club, Lapi, Marchesi,
Prosperi, and Montebruno were playing bridge together, and when they had
finished at half-past two I joined them, and from their conversation learned that
Montebruno is to bring forward the question of the French frontier in the Camera.
This morning I saw Borselli and that young Frenchman Dubard walking together
in the Corso. They were talking earnestly, and it seemed as though the count was
telling Angelo something which surprised him. I stopped and spoke to them, but
they appeared to betray some uneasiness at meeting me. What do you know about
the Frenchman?"

"Nothing to his detriment," was the Minister's reply. "It is at present a secret,
but he has asked me for Mary's hand."

"Then don't give it."

"Why?"

"Because I don't like his intimate friendship with Borselli."

"It was I who first introduced them. They met at dinner at my table," Morini said, surprised at his spy's warning. "What do you suspect?"

"I have no suspicions," was the reply. "Only if he is an intimate friend of yours, as he seems to be if he is to marry the signorina, it is strange that he should at this moment be so constantly in Borselli's company. I hear that nowadays the pair are inseparable. They walked to the Ministry, and were closeted together for over an hour. This has struck me as very curious, especially as I have just heard from a secret socialistic source that the question is to be asked by Montebruno in the Camera at five o'clock this afternoon."

"This afternoon?" gasped His Excellency, his countenance in an instant white to the lips. "Then they really mean to ask the question?"

"Yes. I understand that the Opposition have made a sudden resolve, and that they intend to strike the blow against the Government immediately. To-morrow, unfortunately, all Italy will be aflame. I only regret that I am powerless to prevent it. I miscalculated my influence—I admit it."

"Then I must face the worst, Vito!" remarked the unhappy man in a low, desperate voice, starting at his own whispered words as they seemed to ring through the lofty, old-world room.

"The instant I heard their intentions I made investigations, and found that nearly every Socialist deputy is in Rome ready to shriek that the safety of the kingdom is at stake. Our friend Borselli has indeed laid his plans very cleverly. But what puzzles me most is the reason Dubard is associating himself so closely with your enemy if he intends to marry your daughter! He surely cannot anticipate becoming your son-in-law and at the same time conspire to cause your downfall! To me it is a mystery, and that is why I urge you to be wary. That man has some hidden motive—depend upon it."

Morini glanced mechanically across at that big green-painted steel door of the safe, and recollected Mary's curious story of what she had witnessed.

"But he is very fond of Mary, and as I have given my consent to their marriage and my daughter has accepted him, he can surely have no motive in acting contrary to my interests."

"He is your enemy, I repeat," declared Vito Ricci. "I have made inquiries, and the results all point to one conclusion, namely, that he is acting with Angelo; and, moreover, I have been told on the best authority that certain of the charges to be made against you are based upon information supplied by him."

"I can't believe it."

"Be patient, and you will soon see whether the facts I have gathered are true. The question is to be put at five o'clock. I will telephone to you the result as soon as it occurs. I am going down to the Chamber at once, and will do my very utmost; but, as you can see, against such overwhelming opposition I am utterly powerless.

If we could prevent Montebruno from putting the fatal question we might gain time and perhaps succeed, but how can we prevent Borselli carrying out his inge-

adventurers of the Socialist party?"

"Try! Try!" urged Camillo in a wild, desperate voice. "Try, Vito—for the sake of my poor wife and daughter."

"Remain firm," came back the voice of the deputy. "Be patient, and watch the result of the attempt to wreck the Government."

"You are hopeless. I recognise it in your voice!" wailed the desperate man. "I know too well that all the blame and opprobrium must fall upon me. They intend, as you have already told me, that I shall be the scapegoat, and that Angelo shall take my portfolio."

The deputy returned no answer. What, indeed, could he say? His Excellency, who was a shrewd, far-seeing man, spoke the truth.

"Ah, I know!" cried the Minister. "The plot is complete. For me, the future is hopeless. Yet I am more than mystified at what you tell me regarding Dubard. Try and discover his motive. Do not fail me in this, Vito, I beg of you. My poor daughter's future depends on that."

"Trust me, my dear friend," was the response. "Spinola is awaiting me outside, and we are going down to Montecitorio together. Have courage, and after five o'clock I will ring you up again. Addio!"

And a moment later the tiny bell rang, which showed that the communication had been cut off.

Then Camillo Morini, after glancing at his watch and finding that it was already three o'clock, stood immovable, his dark eyes staring across the silent room like a man in a dream.

"Courage! Courage!" he repeated to himself hoarsely, with a bitter laugh. "Courage—and for a man who has no to-morrow!"

In two short hours that voice from the Eternal City would, he knew, sound his doom.

"I am ready?" he laughed to himself. "I am quite ready. They think to place all the blame upon me, to hound me down and charge me with having sold Italy into the hands of her enemies?" And from his vest-pocket he took tenderly a tiny glass tube containing three small pink tabloids, and held it in the ray of light to satisfy himself that they were still there under the plug of cotton wool.

Then, as he replaced the tube in his pocket and slowly paced the room, his thoughts wandered to what Ricci had said regarding the man whom he had given leave to marry his daughter Mary.

"He has suspicions—but of what?" he asked, speaking to himself in a voice scarcely above a whisper. "That he should be friendly with the man who has so suddenly turned my enemy is certainly curious. But he surely cannot be seeking my ruin if he is to marry dear Mary?"

His eye caught the shining brass knobs of the safe door, and he halted before it. If Dubard had really examined those papers he might be aware of the truth! The very thought caused him to hold his breath. But next instant, when he reflected upon the morrow, his countenance relaxed into a bitter smile.

CHAPTER TWENTY TWO.
CONCERNS A MAN'S DUTY.

The man whose brilliant career had ended, longed to open the safe and to see whether certain papers it contained had really been disturbed. But even if he possessed the key which he had flung into the Arno on that memorable night, it could not be opened on account of the piece of wire which prevented the lever from working. The truth was therefore withheld from him.

Sometimes he regarded Mary's story as ridiculous, while at others he wondered whether Dubard had really opened the safe in order to investigate. He had been inclined to think that Mary, watching through the keyhole as she had done, had not been able to see distinctly, and that in her limited range of vision had imagined that the safe was being tampered with. Ricci's words on the telephone were, however, ominous. Apparently Dubard was in some mysterious way taking part in that vile and despicable plot which sought to brand Mary as a traitress equally with himself.

He turned from the safe and again flung himself into his writing-chair, where he remained a long time with his arms folded, staring straight in front of him.

At last he stirred himself, reached down a sheet of notepaper, and commenced to write rapidly a letter commencing, "My dear wife." Briefly and to the point, he explained that he had fallen the victim of circumstances, although he had done his best for his king and country, and prayed for her forgiveness.

The next letter he wrote was upon the big official paper headed "Ministro della Guerra: Divisione prima," and with tears in his eyes and hand trembling with emotion he penned his resignation to his sovereign. He sought to make neither explanation nor excuse.

"I have been your Majesty's obedient and trusted servant and the servant of the Italian nation for twenty-one years," he wrote, "and during my term of office as Minister of War my endeavour has been to improve the condition of the army and place it upon a level with those of other nations. Your Majesty has been pleased to signify your gracious pleasure at my efforts, and that, in itself, has been for me my highest reward. Circumstances which I could not foresee have, however, so conspired against me and mine that I am unable to remain longer in office, and therefore beg of your Majesty to relieve me of the portfolio I have so long held. I have enjoyed your Majesty's marks of favour through many years, and I only beg most humbly to express a fervent hope that justice may be done to me, for, if so, it will be proved that I have never abused either my sovereign's confidence nor disgraced the honour of the Italian people. I pen this resignation with deep and heartfelt regret—the regret of a man whose life has been for his country, and who is taking leave of an office he was proud to hold, and of a high and gratifying position in his sovereign's gracious esteem."

He read and re-read the words he had penned with such difficulty. Such was the ignominious end of his brilliant ministerial career! The resignation would go direct into the hands of His Majesty, yet before it could reach the Quirinale he would have escaped his enemies.

The third note he wrote was to Mary, a long and tender letter, in which he sought her forgiveness and declared himself innocent of the grave offences with which his enemies were charging him.

"I admit that I have had faults, that I have misappropriated the public money under dire necessity, in order to sustain my position as Minister. Yet it is an open secret that every member of the Cabinet has done the same. I am no better and no worse than the others. But as regards the sale of our military secrets to France, I am as innocent as I believe you to be. They may attack you, but do not heed their charges. Marry, be happy, and when you recollect your father, remember him only as one who has been more sinned against than sinning; one who has been the victim of a foul conspiracy, ruined and broken by the false and exaggerated charges of adventurers, but also one who, having given his life for his king and his country, has also forgiven his enemies. My estates will be sold—confiscated, probably—and you and your mother will be comparatively poor. Yet you will, at least, have your husband Jules to guard and protect you even though your father has left you. I need not speak of my regrets—for they are but vain ones. My reputation has been undermined, and I have fallen. I must face the inevitable, and do so with courage, and in the knowledge that you, Mary, my daughter, will forgive me. There are charges—base, false charges—which I cannot refute. Why should I give my enemies satisfaction by facing them? I cannot hope for justice either at their hands in a court of law or of the people themselves, on account of the widespread intrigue to secure my downfall. It is therefore best to turn my back upon them in contempt, and bid you, my beloved child, farewell."

And as his thin, unsteady hand penned those final words in Italian, the hot tears dropped, blurring the writing and blistering the paper—the tears of a man bidding adieu to the one he most cherished—nay, to life.

Having folded the paper and addressed the envelope with the simple words, "To my daughter Mary," he took from his finger a curious old Etruscan ring he wore, an ornament that had been found years ago during the excavations of the amphitheatre at Fiesole, and imprinting a kiss upon it, enclosed it in the envelope for her.

Then he glanced anxiously at his watch. Soon the dread news would be spoken into his ear. He sighed again, his face white and hard set, his pale lips trembling.

He leaned back in his padded chair, and all the past came before him in rapid review. Now he saw clearly how Angelo Borselli had, through all those years, been his cringing underling and for what object. The cunning Under-Secretary had squeezed secret commissions out of everyone for their mutual pecuniary benefit, yet at the same time he was always careful to incriminate the man whose

Mary had never liked him. A dozen times had she openly expressed her suspicion and distrust. But he had been blind—blind to everything. He was a man with, few vices himself, and never recognised them in others. Had his wife enjoyed good health she would nowadays have been his helpmate. But, unfortunately, owing to a carriage accident at Vichy five years before, her nerves were unstrung, and she was nearly always under medical treatment.

But there were mysteries connected with the curious conspiracy that had arisen against him—mysteries which he could not solve.

Had he acted rightly in suggesting to Mary that she should marry Jules Dubard? That point sorely troubled him. Ricci's words over the telephone caused him to reflect deeply. His devotion to his daughter was complete, and he had suggested marriage with that man because he was an honourable gentleman of means, and had, during their acquaintance, rendered him certain valuable services in Paris. He looked upon Dubard as a friend of the family, and therefore had been much gratified when he had asked for Mary's hand. Now, however, in those moments of despair as he reviewed the past, he recollected his daughter's calm dignity when he had approached the subject, and how she had accepted the man with an inert disregard, as though she had only done so to obey his wish.

And this man was in active association with his bitterest enemy!

He remembered how at Orton, when the pair had met beneath his roof, they had betrayed no desire for each other's company. Indeed, Borselli had dropped a plain hint that Dubard's presence was unwelcome. And yet at the moment of the crisis they had become warm friends!

Was it possible that the man who only a few days before had asked for Mary as his wife could actually be plotting against him in secret? The idea seemed too absurd, and he dismissed it. Dubard had already shown himself as his friend, and with that open generosity that had caused his downfall, he declined to prejudge him until he received absolute proof. He was shrewd and far-seeing concerning affairs of state, but to his own interests he was often utterly indifferent.

He rose again, and for half an hour he paced up and down the marble floor of the long darkened room. The carriage-bells sounded outside, and as the noise of wheels died away he knew that his wife and the girls had gone out visiting.

"Mary! Mary!" he cried aloud to himself. "Have I done right? If not, forgive me!"

Of a sudden he thought of what Vito had told him in the club on the previous day regarding the startling allegation that his daughter had furnished information to the man now degraded and imprisoned as a traitor. Why had she begged for his release? That very fact in itself went far to prove that the allegation had some foundation in fact. He saw how his enemies, not content with attacking him, intended to denounce her as a traitress.

She had declared that Felice Solaro was innocent. Yet if his last decree as Minister of War was one of clemency, releasing the accused man, his action would surely be misconstrued into one of connivance at the betrayal of the secrets of that high-up Alpine fortress.

Was Solaro really guilty after all? At times he was convinced of it, because the proofs had been so plain, and the evidence of that young woman Nodari had been borne out by witnesses. Sometimes, however, he doubted. And if there was doubt, should not the accused be given the benefit of it? Ought not his last act to be one of fearless clemency?

Slowly he walked to the window and then back again.

"Yes. He shall have the benefit of the doubt," he murmured, recollecting how the man had defiantly broken his sword before him. "It shall not be said that Camillo Morini did an injustice even to shield himself. My enemies will regard my action as proof of my guilt, and they are welcome to do so," he added in a blank, hoarse voice. "My last action shall at least be one of justice."

And reseating himself at his table, he took out a big sheet of official paper, upon which he wrote—

"It is hereby ordered that Felice Solaro, ex-captain of the 6th Alpine Regiment, convicted of treason, degraded, dismissed from the army of Italy, and imprisoned at the military prison of Turin, shall be immediately released and reinstated in his former rank, with pay to date from his arrest, as he is found not guilty of the false charges brought against him.

"The governor of the military prison at Turin and General Arturo Valentini commanding the forces on the Alpine frontier are ordered to execute this decree given under my hand this first day of October in the year one thousand nine hundred and one."

Then, beneath, he signed that name that was magical with everything concerning the defences of Italy: "Camillo Morini, Il Ministro della Guerra," after which he placed the document in an envelope and directed it to the prison governor.

He drew a deep breath. At risk of being branded as one who sold Italy's secrets to the French War Office, he had extended to the accused man a clemency which he might not deserve. Nevertheless, he felt convinced that he had acted with justice, and hoped that after all his enemies would not denounce Mary as Solaro's accomplice.

The allegation was, to him, a mystery. It was true that she had met the good-looking young captain in society, for he recollected perfectly well how, about eighteen months before, at a ball given by the Princess Capellari in Rome, he had noticed them dancing together. But Mary, being a great favourite, was much sought after by her male acquaintances, and he had never regarded the young Alpine captain as anything more than her mere acquaintance.

He, however, could not disguise from himself the fact that she had had access to those carefully guarded papers which constituted the complete scheme by which the millions of Italy's armed men were to be mobilised in case of war.

In order to preserve greater secrecy, he had employed her in his study in the palace in Rome to copy certain portions of the secret scheme relative to the army of

commanding in case of necessity. He preferred her assistance in this rather than to employ one of the secretaries, for his confidence in her was complete. It was therefore amazing that this should actually be known to those who were seeking his ruin. They charged her with gaining knowledge of the whole scheme—which, indeed, she might easily have done—and with having afterwards handed a copy of it to Felice Solaro.

Such an imputation upon his daughter's honour was infamous. That was Italy's reward for all he had done for her!

He glanced at his watch again, and saw that it was already five o'clock, the fatal hour when that thin-faced adventurer, Paolo Montebruno—an advocate, of course, as well as a Socialist deputy—was to rise and launch his bombshell into the Chamber!

He held his breath, and as he sat staring before him fixedly in desperation and despair, he pictured to himself the scene at Montecitorio at that moment. He knew well that huge, semicircular Camera, and he had often sat listening to Montebruno shrieking in that quick, impetuous, high-pitched voice which inflamed the members of his wild-haired party. Yes! he knew well what hard invectives he would use when, as the mouthpiece of Angelo Borselli, he poured forth his terrible charges against the Minister of War.

In that silent room, now darker as the sun declined, the man whose doom was sealed conjured up to himself the staggering sensation which would be caused by those allegations that he, the trusted adviser of his sovereign, had foully betrayed his country. Already he was speaking, without doubt, and already the wires were flashing the astounding charges to every corner of Italy. In a few brief hours those irresponsible journals inspired and subsidised by Borselli would be full of the sensation, screaming that Italy had been betrayed, and demanding a prosecution.

He knew, from what Ricci had told him, that the charges could not fail to set all Italy aflame. The plot against him had been too cleverly prepared. The hour had passed. The Camera were already staggered at the magnitude and seriousness of the charges. He was already hounded down as a thief and a traitor.

His nervous hand went to his vest-pocket, and drawing forth the small glass tube, he gazed upon it with a bitter smile of satisfaction.

Of a sudden the telephone bell rang sharply behind him, causing him to start. The voice from across those high misty mountains would speak his doom.

For a few moments the despairing man sat motionless, bent forward upon the table staring at the tube, then rising slowly, he staggered across to the instrument, took the receiver in his trembling fingers, and mechanically placed it to his ear.

CHAPTER TWENTY THREE.
THE PLOT.

On that same hot afternoon, while His Excellency was pacing the library in the high-up old villa in the Apennines, Dubard alighted from a cab in the Via Salaria, in Rome, and entered a fine modern mansion, the home of Angelo Borselli, Under-Secretary for War. He was conducted to a small sitting-room, where, in the dim light of the closed sun-shutters, the arch-schemer was taking his siesta in a long wicker lounge-chair, half dozing, and yet revolving within his brain every detail of his ingenious plan to oust the Minister from office and to replace him.

"Why, my dear Jules!" he cried in surprise as the young Frenchman entered. "I thought you had gone up to San Donato in order to be near your charmer when the blow fell."

"No," responded Dubard in a rather hard voice. "I am still here—in Rome." Then after a brief pause he looked the sallow man straight in the face and added, "The question must not be asked in the Chamber. The blow must not be struck—do you understand?"

"What do you mean?" cried Borselli, starting to his feet. "What has happened? I see by your face that something has occurred."

"It has," was the other's answer. "Montebruno must be stopped."

"Why?"

"Because to seek to overthrow Morini at this moment is against our interests."

"Oh!" laughed the other. "So you have just discovered that fact, have you? It is against your interest, of course, because you intend to marry his daughter; but not against mine."

"I tell you that no revelation must be attempted," said Dubard firmly.

"But why do you say this? What is there to prevent the question being put and the Ministry criticised?"

"It is unwise. It would be a serious blunder on your part."

"And yet you have assisted me! My dear Jules, I don't really understand you! Do you not recollect what we arranged in London when our reconciliation took place? Have you forgotten what we agreed only the day before yesterday?"

"I have forgotten nothing. I only speak plainly, and say that by making the revelations at the present moment you will imperil your own position."

"No. I shall become Minister on Morini's downfall. All is arranged. I am not the man to pick the chestnuts out of the fire for others—you surely know that?"

"......... in the matter of certain secret commissions? Did you not rather unfortunately arrange matters and act as the go-between?"

"Of course. But I shall be careful enough that my own interest in the matter does not appear. The Minister of Justice is no friend of Morini," he added, with a grin upon his thin, hard features.

"Montebruno must be stopped," declared Dubard determinedly after a pause. "Let us telephone to him to come here."

"He is already down at the Camera," said the Under-Secretary, glancing at the little French timepiece on the mantelshelf. "The question is to be put at five, and it is already half-past four."

"But it shall not be put!" cried the young man.

"Who will prevent it?" inquired Borselli, looking at him defiantly.

"I will," he said sternly. "Let us be quite plain and outspoken, my dear Angelo. I tell you that you shall not imperil the future by this premature action. Morini knows of the conspiracy against him, and is prepared."

"Well—and if he is? What then?"

"He may seek to defend himself in a manner of which you little dream."

Borselli regarded his companion suspiciously, for he saw that he was in possession of some information which he was keeping to himself.

"You know something," he said, fixing his dark eyes upon Dubard. "What is it?"

"I only know that it would be most injudicious to make any revelations, or to stir up the public indignation at the present moment," was the response. "There is no time to lose. You must telephone at once to Montebruno and stop him."

"Impossible. The whole matter is arranged. All the Socialist deputies are in their places awaiting the bolt to be launched."

"Then let them wait. It shall not be launched to-day," replied Dubard in a clear, distinct voice.

"But it shall?" exclaimed Borselli. "It has taken me nearly three years to complete preparations for this *coup*, and I do not intend to abandon it merely because you hint mysteriously that it is premature. I speak quite candidly upon this point."

"And I speak equally candidly when I tell you that Montebruno must not put the question to the Chamber. There are reasons—serious reasons."

He said nothing of his compact with Mary or of his demand of His Excellency for her hand.

"And what are they, pray?"

"Well,"—and he hesitated. "Well, if the *coup* is made at the present moment you will merely imperil yourself, that is all I can say. Morini will retaliate, and charge you with certain things which will place you in a very awkward position."

A silence fell between the two men. Borselli was reflecting upon a certain agreement at which they had arrived when in London.

"I really can't understand you, Jules," he exclaimed at last. "You have rendered us the most valuable assistance until the present moment, and now, when all is prepared, you suddenly withdraw and make mysterious hints that our efforts may result in serious consequences. What do you mean?"

"I mean that the revelations are premature."

"But tell me the truth, once and for all. Are you still on our side, or has the girl's beauty appealed to you, and you now intend to save her father? I know what a soft, impressionable heart you have—like all your race."

"I am still united with you," the Frenchman declared quickly. "It is because of that I give you warning." Borselli's dark eyes were fixed upon the other's with a look of quick shrewdness. He was a man whose mind, when once made up, was not easily turned from its purpose.

"And your warning I shall certainly not heed," he said slowly. "You know my intentions, and I shall carry them out to-day to the letter."

"You shall not?" the other exclaimed defiantly.

"Oh! and who will prevent it?" asked the Under-Secretary.

"I will. You shall not seek your own ruin blindly like this!"

Dubard very cleverly endeavoured to convince his companion of his own interest in the conspiracy against Morini, while Borselli, of course, had no knowledge of his compact with Mary. Nevertheless, he saw plainly that the Frenchman's sudden withdrawal from the affair was due to some hidden motive, and he refused to be turned from his object. To him the overthrow of Morini meant wealth and power, and he had no intention of relinquishing his efforts just at the moment when the reins of office were within his grasp. All was prepared. The revelations were to be made, and charges of misappropriation and treason hurled at the unfortunate Minister; charges which would, on the morrow, be taken up by the subsidised Press and exaggerated and distorted into a public scandal which no statesman, however popular, could withstand. The plot had cost him three years of clever scheming, during which time he had acted as Morini's humble underling, expressing profound thanks for any small benefits, but secretly hating and despising him, and yet always seeking to worm himself further into his confidence. And Dubard wished him to abandon it all at the very hour when success was assured! No. He flatly refused. And he told his companion so in plain, forcible language.

The other, however, merely shrugged his narrow shoulders and was silent, allowing the Under-Secretary to upbraid him without offering a word in self-defence. Then, when Borselli paused to gain breath, he said—

"I merely repeat what I have said—the question must not be put."

"I say it shall be put?" cried the other fiercely.

Dubard was silent again and quite cool, only the slight flush upon his high cheeks told that a fierce anger consumed him.

"If it is put, it will be at your own risk," he exclaimed at last, placing his fore-finger on the table to emphasise his words. "Remember there are many who would gloat over the downfall of Angelo Borselli."

"And there are more who would like to see me Minister of War."

"You will never obtain office if you carry out the scheme you have arranged," Dubard declared. "I think up to the present I have shown myself your friend, for without me you surely could not have done what you have. You have many times admitted that. Why, therefore, do you not take my advice?"

"Because, my dear Jules, you have suddenly turned round and are now cham-pioning Morini."

"No, you mistake me. I am merely warning you in our mutual interests. Mori-ni will retaliate—and if he does—!" And again he shrugged his shoulders signifi-cantly.

"Well, and if he does? What can he do?"

"He can make some ugly revelations, you know."

"I have no fear of anything he may allege," laughed the other. "He cannot establish his innocence."

"Then you will not listen to reason and postpone the public sensation you have arranged for this afternoon?"

"No," replied Angelo. "I will not."

"Then, if you intend to imperil both of us by acting so injudiciously, I, for one, do not intend to suffer."

"What do you mean?"

"Simply this. If you are determined not to interfere, and to allow the question to be put and the stream of allegations to pour forth from the Socialists, I shall, in order to save myself, place myself on the side of Morini."

"Of course, my dear Jules. You are always on the side which pays you best," sneered the other.

"And in your company," remarked the Frenchman quite coolly, adding in a firm voice, "I wish you to give me a line to Montebruno now, this moment, and I will take it to him in the Camera—a word to him to postpone the question."

"I shall do nothing of the sort. I do not intend to sacrifice my future because of your sentimentalities. You are defending Morini."

"Yes," he cried. "I will defend him! I tell you again, and very clearly, that if Montebruno speaks in the Camera to-day you will be relieved of office."

"Oh, how's that?"

"I am speaking plainly," Dubard said, with knit brows.

"Time does not admit of more words, otherwise Montebruno will rise and put the question. I therefore tell you that if you do not give me the letter I require at once, I shall make a clean breast of the whole affair." And he glanced at his watch as he spoke.

"You!" gasped Borselli quickly, staring at the speaker. "Ah yes! I was a fool to have trusted you after all. I recognised it when too late. You have turned in Morini's favour."

"I have my own interests to serve as well as yours," Dubard remarked quite frankly. "It is to my interest that the question is postponed."

"And it is to mine that it should be put."

"But you will not allow Montebruno to proceed, and risk your own position. Remember that in this affair my interests at the moment are not the same as yours."

"And you actually declare that you will tell the truth if Montebruno speaks?" said Borselli hoarsely, realising how completely the man before him held his future in his hands.

"I do," was the response. "You surely know me well enough! In such moments as these I do not trifle. Give me the letter! It is already a quarter to five, and I have only just time to drive to the Camera and place it in Montebruno's hand."

"But I can't understand your motive," exclaimed Borselli, realising that his companion meant what he said. "Remember what we agreed that night in London."

"Perfectly. While our interests are similar, I am your friend; but where they divide, I am friend of myself alone. Come, Angelo, we cannot afford to waste further words—the letter, just two lines, or exposure of the truth. The latter would, I think," he laughed, "be even a greater sensation to the public than the allegations against the Minister."

CHAPTER TWENTY FOUR.

IN THE CHAMBER OF DEPUTIES.

The man who had laid such an elaborate plot against His Excellency stood hesitating and confounded. He had never dreamed that Dubard, upon whom he had relied so implicitly, would be seized with this sudden caprice to defend Morini. Mary might have persuaded him to adopt this course, he reflected, yet he knew Jules too well as a man in whose heart there did not exist a single spark of either respect or true affection for the opposite sex.

"Come," exclaimed the elegant Frenchman, with a look of determination on his pallid countenance. "Write the note quickly, or it will be too late. Recollect, if Montebruno speaks, I shall tell the truth."

"And betray me?"

"Of necessity."

Then Angelo Borselli, seeing that all his elaborate preparations for a *coup* were checkmated by the very man who had rendered him such valuable help, threw himself into a chair, and muttering some hard words, scribbled three lines to the man, his puppet, who was to hurl those terrible charges against the Minister of War.

"Good," exclaimed Dubard airily, as he took the letter and thrust it into his pocket. "You have done well to save your own reputation, my dear Angelo. It would not be wise for the public to know everything, would it? Excuse me running away so quickly, but I have only just time to drive down to the Camera." And snatching up his hat he rushed out, leaving the Under-Secretary standing in the centre of the room, silent in disappointment and chagrin.

Meanwhile, in the Chamber the excitement among the Socialist group had gradually increased as the hands of the big clock moved on towards the hour of five. They watched Montebruno seated in his place armed with many formidable documents, and saw how he was preparing himself for one of those oratorical efforts for which he was so famous. He was a thin, black-bearded man with small dark eyes and aquiline features—a man who had made the law a stepping-stone to politics like so many of his *confrères*. Time after time he fidgeted, changed his position, stroked his beard thoughtfully, and re-examined his papers, every action being watched anxiously by his party, among whom it was whispered that he was to put some sensational question—but of what character was to them a mystery.

The hand of the big clock pointed to the hour of five, and the Chamber was occupied with other business. Vito Ricci, sitting in his place almost opposite Montebruno in the great horseshoe chamber, waited breathlessly, well knowing that the words which would fall from his lips would seal the doom of that man waiting so patiently in his library in the far-off Apennines.

The tension of those moments of expectancy was terrible.

The clock marked five, ten, fifteen minutes past the hour, when, of a sudden, the voluble Socialist rose, and began by expressing regret at being compelled to take up the time of the Chamber upon a most important and very pressing matter. He had just arrived at that point, holding the whole Camera in attention by his clever oratory, when a prominent member of his own party pulled his coat-tails and handed him a letter. This he tore open mechanically while still speaking, but on glancing at the contents, he hesitated and stopped short in utter confusion.

"Go on! Go on!" urged his party wildly, eager to hear what allegations he was about to make against the Government.

But regaining his self-possession in a moment, he turned to them, and with a smile said—

"Gentlemen, I have just learned, and very fortunately perhaps, that I have been somewhat misinformed regarding certain matters to which I intended directing the attention of the Camera, and therefore I will no longer occupy your time."

And he sat down abruptly, whereat those in opposition jeered at him, and even the Socialists themselves rose and went out in disgust, disappointed at relinquishing what was promised to be a staggering blow against the Government. With them went Vito Ricci, who, ten minutes later, was in the Ministry of War describing the curious scene to Camillo Morini over the telephone.

The words he spoke put fresh life and hope into the despairing Minister. He breathed again when he heard how he had been saved almost by a miracle. Then he walked to his table, and the letters he had written he carried to the fireplace and there lit them with a wax vesta and watched them consume—all save the order for Solaro's release and reinstatement.

He held the latter in his hand for a long time thinking deeply. But at last the temptation grew too strong within him, for slowly, and with seeming reluctance, he opened it, applied a match, destroying it as he had done the others, and as he watched it burn to black tinder he murmured to himself—

"No! I dare not release him. If I did they might suspect—suspect. And yet Mary declares that he is innocent! What, I wonder, can she know?"

New life had been created within him, new hope, new aspirations. A moment before he had looked upon that tiny tube with its fatal tabloids as the only means by which he could escape his enemies, but now he laughed to himself as he placed it in a drawer of the writing-table—laughed at his own cowardice.

He never dreamed that he had been saved by Mary's self-sacrifice. The incident, as related by Ricci over the telephone, was curious and mysterious. The letter handed to the man who had risen to denounce him had evidently contained something which prevented him making the charges, but what it was he could not imagine.

unravel and report.

When his wife and the girls returned, they found him idling on the terrace beneath the pretty arbour from which spread that glorious view of the Arno valley up to Florence. He was a changed man from an hour before—that hour when he had come face to face with ruin and death. By the mysterious turn which events had taken a new life had suddenly opened to him. The blow they intended to aim at him had apparently been abandoned, even though all preparations had been made. The reason was an utter enigma.

He laughed merrily with Mary and the English girls as they came along the terrace where he was sitting idly smoking a cigar, inquiring where they had been and how they had found the lady they had visited.

All three began to chatter, as was their wont, while Her Excellency, fatigued after the drive, entered the house to rest before dinner. She, however, did not fail to notice her husband's unusual good-humour, for of late he had been thoughtful and depressed, silent and moody when in her presence, and apparently full of serious state affairs.

The instant Mary saw her father's countenance she read the truth. She had left the villa well knowing—through Dubard, who had sent her word in secret—that the blow was to be dealt that afternoon. She knew all that her father was suffering, and she feared the worst, even though she had made that compact with the man she suspected and despised. She had dreaded to return lest some hideous tragedy should have occurred, and all the time she was absent she had reproached herself that she had not remained at his side to support and encourage him in face of the threatened peril.

But the danger was over. He had no doubt received word over the telephone, for he was his own old self again, and began chaffing Violet Walters, the blue-eyed daughter of the London barrister, regarding a young lieutenant of the *bersaglieri*, an aristocrat of Florence, who had dined with them on the previous evening, and towards whom she had been very much attracted.

"It is really too bad!" declared the English girl, blushing to her eyes. "You declare that I'm in love with every good-looking man, and I'm sure I'm not."

"We Italians always find English girls very charming," His Excellency said, smiling. "That is why I married an Englishwoman myself," whereat the two Fry girls, pale-faced and insipid, tittered to themselves.

"Really it was most disgraceful of Violet to flirt with young Capponi as she did last night!" exclaimed Mary mischievously, upholding her father's view.

"I did not!" protested the barrister's daughter. "You know I didn't, Mary!"

"He'll be proposing next Monday when he comes again to dinner, and you'll be the Marchesa Capponi," Mary said, spreading out her skirts and bowing with mock obeisance.

Her father, full of good-humour now that the terror of those anxious hours had passed, rose, and placing his hand kindly on Violet's shoulder, assured her that his words were not meant to be taken seriously; for he saw the girl's indignation was rising, and that she resented being accused of flirtation before the two daughters of the Genoese merchant.

They all gossiped together for some time, until presently Mary went forth, as usual, to accompany her father on his evening stroll through the pine woods.

When alone, His Excellency was the first to speak, explaining to her all that Vito Ricci had related over the telephone.

"Then the crisis is prevented," she remarked, in a strange, mechanical voice, he thought. He had expected her to betray surprise and joy, but, on the contrary, she received the information of his escape with an inertness which surprised him. "It must have been the letter handed to the Socialist deputy," she added.

"Without doubt," he remarked. "But how annoyed and disappointed Angelo must be at the failure of his scheme just at the very moment when his triumph was assured."

"I expect so," his daughter said, walking slowly at his side, her eyes fixed upon the ground. Her father had been saved at the cost of her own happiness, her own life. But would that man adhere to his compact? she wondered. Was the crisis only postponed until after her marriage—until after she had given herself to him in exchange for her father's life? She knew too well that he would never face exposure; she knew, alas! that, like many before him, he would rather take his own life than bear the brunt of those scurrilous and unscrupulous attacks. He had more than once told her so—not directly, of course, but in language that was unmistakable.

She had had no confidence in Dubard since the night when he had examined the safe in the library. He would, she felt assured, play her false. His ingenuity was unparalleled, and he was, moreover, a friend of her father's bitterest enemy. Therefore, what had she to hope from him? The attack upon the Minister and his methods was only postponed in order to lure her and her father into a sense of security. What was to prevent the allegation being made after she had given herself to him in marriage? As she walked there in the evening light beneath the high dark pines she fully realised the insecurity of the position. In the end the man Borselli must triumph, and she, with her father, would be equally a victim.

What her father had told her of the incident in the Chamber that afternoon revealed the truth. Dubard had, by his clever scheming, succeeded in postponing the blow until after she had become his wife. She knew well his intimate friendship with Angelo Borselli, and felt assured that it was in the interests of the Under-Secretary that he had opened that safe which His Excellency had believed to be closed so effectively to everyone.

"You will seek to retaliate, will you not?" she asked her father suddenly. "You will surely not allow Borselli another opportunity of conspiring against you! He should be removed from office upon some pretext or other."

Her father smiled at her words, and replied—

"It would be easy to retaliate, my dear, but it would be unwise.

"Why? If he remains in office, he may to-morrow, or on some occasion when you least expect it, level a blow that might crush you?"

"I know! I know!" he groaned. "I am not safe by any means. Until Vito discovers what has really occurred I must remain patiently inactive."

"But why not remove Borselli from office? You could surely do that! It is your duty to yourself to do so!"

"Ah! You do not know everything, Mary," answered her father very gravely. "To attempt his dismissal at the present moment would be a most injudicious course. By making charges against him I should also implicate myself. If I spoke a single word to his detriment, it would be suicidal. I should be seeking my own downfall."

"Then, to speak plainly, you are unable to dismiss him?" she said in a low, distinct voice, looking her father straight in the face with a glance of reproach. "You are entirely in that man's hands?"

His Excellency, grave and thoughtful again, nodded in the affirmative, sighed heavily, and then admitted—

"You know the truth, my dear. My secrets are, unfortunately, his?"

And she echoed his sigh with her white lips compressed. She foresaw, alas! that for her there was no hope of escape from that hideous compact she had been compelled to make. She had given herself as the price of her father's honour, the price of his very life, to a man whom she could neither trust nor love—a man who, when it suited his own interests, would break his bond without the slightest compunction, and allow the crushing blow to fall upon her house—a blow that must be fatal to her beloved father, who stood there so grave and thoughtful at her side.

She contemplated the future, but saw in it only a grey, limitless sea of blank despair.

CHAPTER TWENTY FIVE.

BILLY GRENFELL IS PHILOSOPHIC.

"Then we must break up the home, I suppose?"

"I suppose so, Billy, much as I regret it. But a fellow has to take advantage of the main chance in his life, you know, and this is mine?" declared George Macbean, leaning back in his padded chair at the breakfast-table in their high-up old room in Fig Tree Court, Temple.

"I should think so! An appointment in the Italian Ministry of War at such a salary isn't an offer that comes to every man, and you'd be a fool if you didn't accept it. You must have some high official friend whom you've never told me about—eh?" And William Grenfell, barrister-at-law, known as "Billy" to his intimates, with whom Macbean shared chambers, took up his friend's letter and re-read it, asking, "What's the signature? These foreigners sign their names in such an abominable manner that nobody can ever read them."

"Angelo Borselli, the Under-Secretary. I met him in the summer, while I was staying with my uncle near Rugby."

"And he offers you a billet like this? By Jove, you're lucky!" And the big, burly, clean-shaven fellow of about thirty-five, one of the ever-increasing briefless brigade, rose and looked out across the quiet courtyard. "You'll throw over that pompous ass Morgan-Mason, won't you? I wonder how you stood the cad so long."

"Necessity, my dear fellow. It has been writing letters for Morgan-Mason or starve—I preferred the former," remarked Macbean, with a smile.

The old panelled sitting-room, with its well-filled bookcase, its pipe-rack, its threadbare carpet, and its greasy, leather-covered chairs, worn but comfortable, differed but little from any other chambers in that old-world colony of bachelors. Macbean and Grenfell had had diggings together and employed the same laundress for the past three years, the former spruce and smart, mixing with the West End world in which his employer moved, while the latter was a thorough-going Bohemian, eccentric in many ways, unsuccessful, yet nevertheless a man brimming over with cleverness. They had been fast friends ten years before, and when opportunity had offered to share chambers they had eagerly embraced it.

Billy never had a brief. He idled in the Courts with a dummy brief before him in order to impress the public, but his slender income was mostly derived from contributions to certain critical reviews, who took his "stuff" and paid him badly for it.

George Macbean, though he could so ill afford it, bore the major portion of the

that had been Billy's, and what a good, generous fellow he really was at heart.

Through those three years they had lived together no wry word had ever aris-en between them, but this letter which Macbean had received caused them both to ponder.

Grenfell was a man of even temper and full of good-humour. He bubbled over with high spirits, even in the face of actual adversity, while over at the Courts he was recognised as a wit of no mean order. But thought of the breaking up of their little home and their separation filled him with deepest regret.

Macbean realised all that his friend felt, and said simply—

"I'm very sorry to go, Billy. You know that. But what can I do? I must escape my present soul-killing drudgery. You don't know of half the insults I've had to swallow from Morgan-Mason because I happen to be the son of a gentleman."

"I know, old chap; I know well. Of course you must accept this appointment," said the other in a tone of quiet sadness. "I can shift for myself—or at least I hope so."

"To leave you is the only regret I have in leaving England, Billy," declared Macbean, taking his friend's hand and grasping it firmly.

But the big fellow, with his eyes fixed before him across the square, remained sad and silent.

The letter had come to George as a complete surprise, reviving within his mind pleasant memories of Orton, of the Minister Morini who had lived incognito, of Borselli, and of Mary most of all. He would, if he accepted, meet them again, and become on friendly terms with the most powerful men in Italy. The offer seemed almost too good to be real. Had it been the first of April he would have suspect-ed fooling. But he read the big official letter headed "Under-Secretary for War—Rome" offering him the appointment, and saw that no fraud had been attempted.

Both men filled their pipes mechanically, lit them from the same match, as was their habit, and smoked in silence. Both were too full of regret for mere words. They understood each other, and neither was surprised at the other's heavy thought. Their friendship had been a very close and pleasant one, but in future their lives lay apart. Grenfell regarded it philosophically with a little smile, as was his wont whenever things went wrong with him, while Macbean pondered deeply as to what the future had in store for him.

Before his eyes rose a vision of a lithe and dainty figure in a white dress on the tennis-lawn at Orton, that woman who was so delightfully cosmopolitan, with the slight roll of the r's when she spoke that betrayed her foreign birth—the woman whom rumour had engaged to the young French count upon whom the honest village folk looked with considerable suspicion.

"You'll be glad to leave the service of that hog-merchant," Billy remarked at last, for want of something better to say, "and I congratulate you upon your escape from him. What you've told me in the past is sufficient to show that he only regards you as a kind of superior valet. Had I been you I should have kicked the fellow long ago."

"The pauper may not kick the millionaire, my dear old chap," said Macbean, smiling, — "or at least, if he does he kicks against the pricks."

"I can't make out how some men get on," remarked Grenfell between the whiffs of his huge pipe. "Why, it seems only the other day that Morgan-Mason had a shop in the Brompton Road, and used to make big splashes with advertisements in the cheap papers. I remember my people used to buy their butter there. An editor I know used to laugh over the puff paragraphs he sent out about himself. He's made his money and become a great man all in ten years or so."

"My dear Billy, money makes money," remarked his friend, with a dry laugh. "Society worships wealth nowadays. Such men as Morgan-Mason have coarsened and cheapened the very *entourage* of Court and State. Let the moneyed creature be ever so vulgar, so illiterate, so vicious, it matters naught. Money-bags are the sole credentials necessary to gain admission to the most exclusive of houses, the House, even to Buckingham Palace itself. Men like Morgan-Mason smile at the poverty of the peerage, and with their wealth buy up heritage, title, and acceptance. The borrower is always servant to the lender, and hence our friend has many obsequious servants in what people call smart society."

"And more's the pity! Society must be rotten!" declared Billy emphatically. "I don't know what we're coming to nowadays. I should think that the post of secretary to such an arrant cad must be about the worst office a gentleman can hold. I'd rather earn half-crowns writing paragraphs for the evening papers myself."

"Yes," Macbean admitted, with a sigh, "I shall be very glad to leave his service. I only regret on your account."

"Oh, don't mind me. I'm a failure, dear boy, like lots of others!" Grenfell declared. "There are dozens in the Temple like myself, chronically hard up and without prospect of success. I congratulate you with all my heart upon your stroke of good fortune. You've waited long enough for your chance, and it has now come to you just when you least expected it. Death and fortune always come unexpectedly: to all of us the former, and to a few of us the latter. But," he added, "this Italian politician — Bore-something — must have taken a violent fancy to you."

"On the contrary, I only met him once or twice," responded Macbean. "That's what puzzles me. I don't see what object he has in offering me the appointment."

"I do. They want an English secretary who knows Italian well. You'll just fill the post. Foreign Governments make no mistakes in the men they choose, depend upon it. They don't put Jacks-in-office like we do. Didn't you tell me once that you met the Italian Minister of War? Perhaps he had a hand in your appointment."

"Possibly so," Macbean admitted, recollecting that well-remembered day when he had greeted His Excellency on the lawn at Orton and the statesman had at once recognised him.

"Well, however it has been arranged, it is a jolly good lift for you, old man," declared Billy, smoking vigorously. "You should take a leaf out of Morgan-Ma-

most hide-bound of bureaucrats, for your own advantage. If you do, you'll get on in the world. It's the only way nowadays, depend upon it. New men, new methods. All the old traditions of life, all the dignity and delicacy and pride of birth, have gone by the board in these days of brainy smartness and pushful go. Life's book to-day, old fellow, is full of disgraced and blotted leaves."

George sighed. He was used to Billy's plainly expressed philosophy. His criticisms were always full of a grim humour, and he was never tired of denouncing the degenerates of the present in comparison with bygone days. He was a Bohemian, and prided himself on that fact. He entertained a most supreme and withering contempt for modern place-hunters and for the many wind-bags in his own profession who got on because of their family influence or by the fortunate circumstance of being in a celebrated case. He declared always that no man at the bar came forward by sheer merit nowadays, and that all depended upon either luck or influence. Not, however, that he ever begrudged a man his success. On the contrary, he liked to see the advancement of his friends, and even though downhearted and filled with poignant regret at being compelled to part with George Macbean, yet he honestly wished him all the good fortune a true friend could wish.

Mrs Bridges, the shuffling old laundress, whose chief weakness was "a drop o' something," who constantly spoke of her "poor husband," and whose tears were ever flowing, cleared away the remains of their breakfast, and the two men spent the whole morning together smoking and contemplating the future.

"I suppose they'll put you into a gorgeous uniform and a sword when you get to Rome," laughed Grenfell presently. "You'll send me a photo, won't you?" And his big face beamed with good-humour.

"Secretaries don't wear uniforms," was the other's response.

"No, but you'll soon rise to be something else," the barrister assured him. "A fellow isn't singled out by a foreign Government like you are unless he gets something worth having in a year or two! They'll appreciate you more than our friend the provision-dealer has done. I shan't forget the way the fellow spoke to me when I called upon you that morning. He couldn't have treated a footman worse than you and me. I felt like addressing the Court for the defence."

"Well, it's all over now," laughed his friend. "This evening I shall give him notice to leave his service, and I admit frankly that I shall do so with the greatest pleasure."

"I should think so, indeed," Billy remarked. "And don't forget to tell him our private opinion of such persons as himself. He may be interested to know what a mere man-in-the-street thinks of a moneyed dealer in butter and bacon. By Jove! if I only had the chance I should make a few critical remarks that he would not easily forget."

"I quite believe it!" exclaimed George merrily. "But now I'm leaving him we can afford to let bygones be bygones. I only pity the poor devil who becomes my successor."

And both men again lapsed into a thoughtful silence, George's mind being filled with recollections of those warm summer days of tea-drinking and tennis when he was guest of his uncle, the Reverend Basil Sinclair, at Thornby.

What, he wondered, could have induced that tall, sallow-faced foreigner, the Italian Under-Secretary for War, to offer him such a lucrative appointment? He had only met him once, for a few moments, when the Minister's wife had introduced them in an interval of tennis on the lawn at Orton.

There was a motive in it. But what it was he could not discern.

CHAPTER TWENTY SIX.
A MILLIONAIRE'S TACTICS.

Mr Morgan-Mason, the Member for South-West Norfolk, sat alone in his gorgeous gilt and white dining-room with the remains of dessert spread before him. A coarse-faced, elderly man with grey side-whiskers, a wide expanse of glossy shirt-front, and a well-cut dinner coat, he was twisting his wineglass between his fingers while a smile played about his lips. His obese figure, with shoulders slightly rounded, a bull neck, and gross, flabby features, gave one the impression that he lived for himself alone, that his life was a selfish, idle one.

His house in town and his place in the country were the typical abodes of a *nouveau riche*. His motors, his yacht, and his racehorses were the very best that money could command, and yet with all his display of wealth he still carried the tenets of the counting-house into his private life. He gave "fifty-guinea-a-head" dinners at the Carlton, it was true, but his entertainments were not on a large scale. He lent the aristocracy money, and allowed them to entertain him in return. He considered it an honour to be made use of by the hard-up earl or by the peeress whose debts at bridge were beyond her means. A knighthood had been offered him, but he had politely declined, letting it be distinctly known to the Prime Minister that nothing less than a peerage would be acceptable; and this had actually been half promised! He was the equal, nay, the superior, of those holders of once-exclusive titles who left their cards upon him and who shot his grouse; for, as a recent writer has declared, the god Mammon is to-day gradually drawing into its foetid embrace all the rank and beauty and nobility that once made England the glorious land she is.

He had taken a telegram from his pocket, and re-read it—a message from a woman bearing one of the noblest titles in the English peerage, asking audaciously for a loan, and inviting him up to her country-house in Durham, where an exclusive party was being entertained. He smiled with gratification, for the sovereign was among her ladyship's guests.

He touched the bell, and in answer the butler entered. "Tell Macbean to come here," he ordered, without looking up. "And give me a liqueur. I don't want coffee to-night."

The elderly, grave-faced servant served his master obsequiously, and noiselessly disappeared.

A few minutes later there came a light rap at the door and George Macbean entered.

"Just reply to this wire," the millionaire said, handing it to his secretary. "Tell her ladyship that I'll leave King's Cross at eleven to-morrow, and that what she mentions will be all right. You need not mention the word loan; she'll understand. I can't dictate to-night, as I'm going to the club. Be here at seven in the morning, and I'll reply to letters while I'm dressing."

Macbean took the telegram and hesitated.

"Well? What are you waiting there for? Haven't you had your dinner—eh?"

"Yes, I have had my dinner, Mr Morgan-Mason," was the young man's quick reply, his anger rising. "I wish to speak a word to you."

"Well, what's the matter? Work too hard? If so, you can take a month's notice and go. Lots more like you to be got," added the man with the fat, flabby face.

"The work is not too hard," was Macbean's response, speaking quite calmly. "I only wish to say that I intend leaving you, having accepted a Government appointment."

"A Government appointment?" echoed the millionaire. "Has Balfour given you a seat in the Cabinet, or are you going to be a doorkeeper or something of that sort down at the House?"

"Neither. My future is my own affair."

"Well, I wish you good luck in it," sneered his employer. "I'll see that the next secretary I get isn't a gentleman. Airs and graces don't suit me, my boy. I see too much of 'em in Mayfair. I prefer the people of the Mile End Road myself. I was born there, you know, and I'm proud of it."

"Shall I send the telegram from the Strand office?" asked Macbean, disregarding the vulgarian's remarks. "It is Sunday night, remember."

"Send it from where you like," was the man's reply. And then, as the secretary turned to leave, he called him back, saying in a rather more conciliatory tone—

"You haven't told me what kind of appointment you've accepted. Whatever it is, you can thank my influence for it. They know that I wouldn't employ a man who isn't up to the mark."

"I thank you for your appreciation," Macbean said, for it was the first kindly word that he had ever received from the millionaire during all the time he had been in his service.

"Oh, I don't mean that you are any better than five hundred others in my employ," the other returned. "I've got a hundred shop-managers who would serve me equally well at half the wages I pay you. I've all along considered that you don't earn what you get."

"In that case, then, I am very pleased to be able to relieve you of my services, and to take them where they will be at last appreciated."

"Do you mean to be insolent?"

"I have no such intention," replied Macbean, still quite cool, although his hands were trembling with suppressed anger. "The Italian Government will pay me well for my work, and will not hurl insults at me on every possible occasion

humble servant, but after despatching this telegram I shall, I am glad to inform you, no longer be yours to command."

"The Italian Government!" exclaimed the millionaire, utterly surprised. "In what department are you to be employed?"

"In the Ministry of War."

"What!—in the office of that man we saw regarding the Abyssinian contracts?—Morini his name was, wasn't it?"

"No. In the office of the Under-Secretary, Borselli."

"I suppose you made it right with them when I took you with me to Rome—made good use of your ability to speak the lingo—eh?"

"I had then no intention of entering the Italian service," was his reply. "The offer has come to me quite spontaneously."

Morgan-Mason was silent, twisting his glass before him and thinking deeply. The name Borselli recalled something—an ugly affair that he would have fain forgotten.

"I thought you had secured an appointment in one of the English Government offices," he said at last, with a sudden change of tactics. "Why go abroad? Why not remain with me? I'll give you an increase of fifty pounds a year. You know my ways, and I hate strangers about me."

"I much regret that I cannot accept your offer," replied George. "I have already accepted the appointment, which is at a salary very considerably in advance of that you have been paying me."

"But I'll pay you the same as they offer. You are better off in England. How much do they intend to give you?"

"I am too fond of Italy to refuse a chance of going out there," Macbean replied. "I spent some years in Pisa in my youth, and have always longed to return and live in the warmth and sunshine."

A brief silence fell.

Presently, after reflection, the Member of Parliament exclaimed, in a tone more pleasant than he had ever used before—

"Let me speak candidly, Macbean. I would first ask you to forget the words I uttered a few moments ago. I am full of business, you know, and am often out of temper with everything. I was out of temper just now. Well, you want to leave me and go to Italy, while I desire you to remain. Tell me plainly what salary you will accept and continue in my service."

"I am as perfectly frank as you are," George replied. "No inducement you could offer would keep me in England."

Mr Morgan-Mason bit his lip. He never expected this refusal from the clever man whom he had treated as an underling. It was his habit to purchase any service with his money, and this rebuff on the part of a mere servant filled him with chagrin—he who so easily bought the smiles of a duchess or the introduction of a marquis into the royal circle itself.

He did not intend that Macbean should enter the service of Angelo Borselli. He had suspicion—a strong suspicion—and for that reason desired to keep the pair apart. His mind was instantly active in an attempt to devise some scheme by which his own ends could be attained. But if his secretary flatly refused to remain?

"I think you are a consummate fool to your own interests," remarked his employer. "Foreign Governments when they employ an Englishman only work him for their own ends, and throw him aside like a sucked orange."

"English employers often do the same," answered Macbean meaningly.

The millionaire was full of grave reflections, and in order to obtain time to form some plan, he ordered Macbean to despatch the telegram and return.

An hour later, when George entered the splendidly appointed study wherein his employer was lounging, the latter rose, lit a cigar, and turning to him in the dim light—for they were standing beyond the zone of the green-shaded writing-lamp upon the table—said—

"I wish very much, Macbean, that you would listen to reason, and refuse the appointment these Italians offer you. You know as well as I do the insecurity of Governments in Italy; how the man in power to-day may be disgraced to-morrow, and how every few years a clean sweep is made of all officials in the ministries. You have told me that yourself. Recollect the eye-opener into Italian methods we had when we saw the Minister of War regarding the contracts for Abyssinia. I wonder that you, honest man as you are, actually contemplate associating yourself with such a corrupt officialdom." The arrogant moneyed man was clever enough to appeal to Macbean's honour, knowing well that his words must cause him to reflect.

"I shall only be an obscure secretary—an employee. Such men have no opportunity of accepting bribes or of pilfering. Theft is only a virtue in the higher grade."

"Well, since you've been out I've very carefully considered the whole matter. I should be extremely sorry to lose you. You have served me well, although I have shown no appreciation—I never do. When a man does his best, I am silent. But I am prepared to behave handsomely if you will remain. Your salary shall be raised to five hundred a year. That's handsome enough for you, isn't it?"

Macbean slowly shook his head, and declared that no monetary inducement would be availing. He intended to go to Italy at all hazards.

The millionaire stroked his whiskers, for he was nonplussed. Yet he was shrewd, and gifted with a wonderful foresight. If Macbean really intended to go to Rome, then some other means must be found by which to ingratiate himself with the man he had so long ill-treated and despised. There might come a day when Macbean would arise against him, and for that day he must certainly be prepared.

He flung himself into his big morocco arm-chair and motioned George to the seat at the writing-table, having first ascertained that the door was closed. Then, with a few explicit words of regret that the young man preferred service abroad, he said in a low, earnest voice—confidential for the first time in his life—

"If you go to Rome it is for the purpose of improving your position—of making money. Now, I am desirous of obtaining certain information, for which I am prepared to pay very handsomely, and at the Ministry of War you can, if you go cautiously to work, obtain it."

"You mean some military secret?" remarked Macbean, looking quickly at his master. "I certainly shall never betray my employers."

"No, no, not at all," protested the arrogant man before him, with a dry laugh. "It is a secret which I desire to learn—one for which I will willingly pay you ten thousand pounds in cash, if you can give me proof of the truth—but it is not a military one. You need have no fear that I am asking you to act the traitor to your employers." The two men regarded each other fixedly. Each was suspicious of double-dealing. The millionaire was searching to discover whether the sum named was sufficiently tempting to induce his secretary to act as his spy, while the latter, scanning the large eyes of the other, endeavoured to read the motive of the mysterious offer.

"You can earn ten thousand pounds easily if you are only wary and act with careful discretion," went on the millionaire, seeing that Macbean had become interested. "It only requires a little tact, a few judicious inquiries, and the examination of a few official documents. To the latter you will no doubt have access, and if so it will be easy enough."

"And what is it?" asked George Macbean after a brief pause, shifting in his chair as he spoke. "What is it you desire to know?"

"The truth regarding the exact circumstances of the death of poor Sazarac."

The other held his breath.

"I desire to avenge his death," went on the millionaire quietly, looking straight into the face of the astonished man, "and I intend to do so. He was my friend, you know. Discover the truth, and I will willingly pay you the sum I have named—ten thousand pounds." George Macbean sat before his employer utterly bewildered, stupefied.

CHAPTER TWENTY SEVEN.
VITO IS INQUISITIVE.

Three months had gone by.

The winter season in Florence had commenced in real earnest, and the streets of the grey old city were agog with the crowd of wealthy foreigners who migrate there for blue sky and sunshine. The Via Tornabuoni was bright with smart toilettes, the Lung Arno was crowded with handsome equipages, the Cascine was full of life at the fashionable hour of four, while Vieusseux's and the Floreal tea-shop overflowed, and there was gay laughter and cosmopolitan chatter everywhere.

Florence had awakened from her summer siesta beneath the glare and heat, and with her streets still sun-blanched she had put on that air of irresponsibility which is always so attractive to the leisured foreigner. Florentine hostesses were already beginning to receive, and the mass of small and jealous cliques, which calls itself English society, had started their five o'clock and teacup scandals.

The Englishman who visits Florence to inspect her art treasures and to bask in the sunshine of the Lung Arno or the heights of Fiesole is entirely ignorant of its curious complex society—of the blood pride of the Florentines, or of the narrow-minded prejudices of those would-be cosmopolitan Britons, mostly with double-barrelled names, who are residents. Probably there is no circle in all the world so select and so conservative as the society of the aristocratic Florentines. The majority of the princes, marquises, or counts are on the verge of bankruptcy, be it said; nevertheless, they still retain all their pride of race, and neither man nor woman is judged by his pocket. Those huge, ponderous cinquecento palaces, with their gloomy cortiles and their closely barred windows, may have been stripped of their pictures, their sculptures, and their antique furniture long ago, yet at the receptions given in those bare skeletons of ancestral homes no one comments upon the pinch of poverty that is so painfully displayed.

Your Florentine aristocrat makes a brave show to the world and to the little English cliques around him. He has a grand carriage with his arms and coronet boldly emblazoned on every panel, he drives fine horses, he has his clothes made in London, and his wife's dresses come from the Rue de la Paix; he gambles at the circolo, and he lounges picturesquely at Giacosa's or Doney's. And yet in his great palace, the doors of which are rigorously closed, he lives frugally in a few huge, barely furnished rooms, and is scarcely able to make both ends meet.

The American invasion has, however, commenced to break down even this barrier of caste, for several men of the bluest Florentine blood have, of necessity, married American wives, in order to save themselves from ruin, and have been loudly condemned for so doing.

of Count Jules Dubard with Mary Morini, daughter of the popular War Minister. By reason of her mother's health, they had remained on at the villa all the autumn; for neither had any desire for the wild gaieties and entertaining which residence in Rome entailed upon them, and preferred the quiet life of their ancient hillside home.

Daily through the streets of Florence Mary and Dubard flashed in the Minister's motor-brougham, hither and thither, paying calls or shopping, being greeted and congratulated on every hand. Her father's official position had given Mary the *entrée* to the most exclusive set, and in Florence she was always as popular as she was in the court circle at the Quirinale. She dressed usually in cream flannel, with a large black hat and a huge ostrich boa; while Dubard, smiling and elegant, was ever at her side in the smart conveyance which rushed everywhere with loud trumpeting.

Her family, in ignorance of the tragedy of her young life, were delighted with the engagement, and on every hand had she received heartiest good wishes. For a girl to marry an Englishman or Frenchman is considered the height of *chic* in Italy, and Mary's social prestige was increased a hundredfold by her prospect of becoming a French countess. The young pair became the most striking and popular figures in the best Florentine society, while the English sets all vainly struggled to get them to their houses. Madame Morini being too unwell to go out at night, Mary was usually chaperoned by the old Princess Piola, a well-known society leader; and solely in order to please her mother, Mary went to all the functions to which she was bidden.

The Minister's wife, however, had never entertained any great affection for the English set in Florence. She had once been an English governess herself, and having known them all well through twenty years, had become thoroughly disgusted with their petty bickerings and constant scandal-mongering. Strange that the English on the Continent always divide into a quantity of small cliques. The French, the Germans, even the Scots, all join harmoniously and patriotically in a continental tour; but, as the Italians are so fond of saying, "the English is a good but strange nation."

With the exception of the British Consul-General's wife, who was an old friend of her mother's, Mary visited no other English house.

"The Italian law of caste is bad enough, my dear," her mother had said to her one day, "but the English backbiting is infinitely worse."

And so, with the man she was engaged to marry, she was seen night after night at those huge old mediaeval palaces, often dimly lit on account of the penury of their owners, and where the refreshments frequently consisted of home-made lemonade and tarts from the pastrycook's.

One night at a dance at the great Cusani Palace on the Lung Arno, where the old Marchioness Cusani was entertaining her friends, she found herself chatting with Vito Ricci, the deputy, who, wearing on the lapel of his coat the dark green ribbon and white cross of the Order of Saints Maurice and Lazarus, had bowed low over her hand and murmured his congratulations.

The great salon, with its polished floor, faded gilding, and crumbling frescoes, was of the ornate style of three centuries before, but over everything was a faded and neglected aspect. Those empty niches in the wall had once contained statues by Donatello, Niccolo Pisano, and Montorsoli, all of which had been sold and exported from Italy to America years ago; while the two large panels painted white had each contained a Raphael, long since disposed of to the National Gallery in London. And although the supper consisted of sandwiches from Doney's, and in lieu of champagne sweet Asti at two-francs-fifty the bottle, yet the nobility of Florence far preferred gathering there to being patronised by the wealthy Americans or English.

The music was good, and Ricci invited Mary to the waltz which at that moment was just commencing. She had known her father's secret agent ever since she had been a child; therefore, nothing loth, she gave him the favour he requested. Both were excellent dancers. Ricci went into society of necessity, in order to keep in touch with the trend of affairs, and was equally well known in Rome as in Florence, in Turin, or in Naples. His sponsor had been Morini himself, and he was one of the very few of the rank and file of the Camera who moved actually in the best sets.

"I have wanted to meet you for quite a long time, Miss Mary," he said in Italian, after they had finished dancing and were strolling through one of the high old ante-rooms, where two or three cavalry officers were lounging with their partners. At dances in Italy a hostess is always careful to have a sprinkling of the military on account both of the brilliant uniforms and of the fact that they are all dancing men. "I suppose, however," he added, bending to her and speaking in a low tone that could not be overheard, "I suppose that, now you are to marry Jules, any question that concerns him is debarred—eh?"

"What do you mean?" she inquired, looking at him quickly with her fine dark eyes.

"I mean that I hesitate to put a question to you lest you should be offended."

"It all depends upon the nature of the question," she answered, as they turned into a long, dim corridor, where they found themselves alone.

"Well," he said, "as you are aware, I am your father's friend, and have been so through many years. Recently there was a—well, a crisis, which was averted in a very unexpected and mysterious manner."

"I know," she remarked, turning rather pale. She wore turquoise blue that night, a beautiful gown of Paquin's which suited her admirably. "My father has told me everything. You made every effort to wreck the Socialist conspiracy—and you were fortunately successful. I return you my very warmest thanks. You saved my father."

"No; you are quite mistaken. I did not. The questions were abandoned for some mysterious motive which I am still endeavouring to discover. It is in pursuance of an inquiry that I am now approaching you. Do you follow me?"

"Perfectly."

"As far as I can gather, your father's enemies have only postponed their blow. It may fall at any time, therefore we must be prepared for it. Montebruno received orders in secret to postpone his attack, and there must have been a reason for this. Perhaps the time was not yet ripe—perhaps the Socialists feared a retaliation which might crush them. In any case, we must get at the truth, and thus be forearmed."

"And how can I assist you?" she asked, knowing the bitter truth of her self-sacrifice, but determined to keep her secret to herself.

"By being frank with me."

"Well?"

"You are to marry Jules Dubard?"

"Yes."

"At your father's instigation?"

She was silent, and her cheeks turned slightly paler. Their long acquaintance gave him the right to put such a question to her, yet within her heart she resented it. Why should this secret agent, this man who was an adventurer, although so useful in her father's service, seek to learn the truth?

"My father gave his consent to our marriage," she replied simply.

"I know that. He has already told me so. I speak plainly, and say that I am desiring to get at the truth."

"The truth of what? I don't understand you."

"The truth regarding certain circumstances which are exceedingly curious. I have been for three months in active pursuit of knowledge, and in my inquiries have discovered some very strange things. Remember, I am working in the interests of your father, and anything you may say to me is in strict confidence. We have known each other for a long time, Miss Mary," he added—"indeed, ever since you wore short frocks and used to flirt with me in the salon at San Donato. Do you recollect it?"

She laughed as a slight blush suffused her cheeks at recollection of her girlhood days before she went to school at Broadstairs. She recollected how in those youthful days she had admired Vito Ricci, the well-dressed, debonair deputy who was her father's closest friend.

"I remember," she admitted, laughing.

"Then let us speak in confidence," he went on, deeply in earnest. "You were acquainted with Felice Solaro, captain in the 6th Alpine Regiment, who fell in love with you?"

She nodded, with eyes open in surprise.

"He declared his love, and you refused him. Your father, who suspected that the young captain had had the audacity to court you, was furious, and forbade you to receive him. But you saw him in secret one day to bid him farewell as he was ordered to a garrison on the French frontier. Your father being absent, you received him, at his own suggestion, in the library of the palace in Rome. While you were talking with him you heard some visitors approaching, and you rushed out, locking him in the library, pretending that your father had taken the key. He remained there in secret for over two hours, until you could escape from the callers, release him, and let him out in secret. Is that so?"

She blushed to the roots of her hair at recollection of that youthful escapade, and admitted that all he had alleged was the truth.

"And that man is now in prison, charged with having sold military secrets to France—a copy of a confidential document which was in a drawer in your father's writing-table."

She stood staring at him, utterly speechless.

"But that is not the charge against him," she hastened to declare. "He is believed to have sold the plans of the Tresenta fortress."

"That is so, but there is also the graver charge—the copying of that document which was in your father's keeping, and one of the most secret and important concerning our army."

"But he is innocent?" she exclaimed. "I know he is innocent, Signor Ricci. He is the victim of a woman named Nodari, at Bologna, who gave perjured evidence against him."

"I know the whole facts. I have read the depositions given at the secret court-martial, but I have no means of judging whether he is innocent or guilty. One fact, however, I desire to learn, and it is this. Has the count ever mentioned to you the captain's name, or has he ever admitted acquaintance with him?"

"Never to my knowledge," was her frank answer. "Felice Solaro once declared his love for me, and therefore, in order not to arouse the count's jealousy, I have never referred to him."

"Naturally. But the fact is all the more curious that the allegation of Solaro's sale of the copy of the secret document to France—the copy of that obtained from your father's writing-table—was actually made by the count."

"By the count?" she cried. "Then it was actually upon his evidence that poor Felice has been degraded and condemned?"

"Exactly. But the motive is utterly incomprehensible, for it would really seem as though the captain was actually guilty of the treasonable offence."

Mary was silent as they paced down the long, deserted corridor. Then at last she turned slowly to her companion, and in a strange, hoarse voice said—

"Yes, it is incomprehensible why an innocent man should be made to suffer, unless—unless my father and the count have acted in accord to secure poor Felice's ruin and disgrace."

No words escaped her. She only shrugged her white shoulders. Yet the man at her side saw in her fine dark eyes the light of unshed tears. But even he did not suspect the truth.

CHAPTER TWENTY EIGHT.
"WAS SAZARAC YOUR FRIEND?"

It was a bright morning in Rome.

"You will recollect, Miss Mary, that when I congratulated you at Orton upon your engagement to Dubard, you declared that you had no thought of any such thing," exclaimed George Macbean, with a smile. "I suppose I may now be permitted to repeat my congratulations?"

"If you wish," was the girl's mechanical reply. "And I thank you very much," she added, her face quite serious.

They were standing together one morning in one of the smaller reception-rooms of her father's palace. He had called on the Minister on official business, and they had met quite accidentally in the great mediaeval courtyard, where the plashing of the old marble fountain broke the quiet, playing on as it had done for nearly four hundred years; that courtyard that was so full of stirring memories of the long past ages, and the stones of which had echoed to the tramp of the armed retainers of the great prince whose ancestral home it once was.

Since his arrival in Rome two months ago fortune had certainly smiled upon George Macbean General Borselli had given him a lucrative appointment in the Ministry at a salary which enabled him to rent a comfortable little bachelor apartment in the Via Sistina. The work was very different from the drudgery from Morgan-Mason's correspondence, and he had quickly found that his position at once gave him the *entrée* to the official society of the Italian capital. The Under-Secretary was kindness itself, and he soon found that his office was one of those sinecures with fat emoluments which are found more or less in every Government department.

For three weeks or so after his arrival he had no occasion to meet His Excellency the Minister, but when he one day entered Morini's private cabinet, he took the opportunity of thanking him for the appointment. The Minister thereupon, as though suddenly recollecting their previous acquaintanceship, made a number of inquiries as to what office he was filling in the Ministry and the nature of his work, the outcome of which was that within six weeks of his arrival in the Eternal City he found himself appointed private secretary to the Minister himself.

This displeased Borselli, he thought; for when he informed him of the Minister's order, he remained silent and his sallow face assumed an expression of distinct disapproval. The general had not expected that Morini would take the young man into his service, or he would probably have hesitated to call him from London. Nevertheless, the Under-Secretary was too clever to openly exhibit any

bowing to every decree of his superior, even though in his heart he was ever plotting against him. And so George Macbean had become one of His Excellency's private secretaries, and very soon enjoyed a good deal of the confidence of his principal.

Hitherto, however, his work lying always at the Ministry, he had never had occasion to go to the palace. From the first moment of his arrival in Rome his mind had been full of recollections of Mary. He had seen her driving on the Pincio on the bright winter afternoons; he had passed her in the Corso, and had seen her, exquisitely gowned, seated with her mother in a box at the Constanzi. But she had never once noticed him, and on that morning, when he had been compelled to call at the palace to receive instructions from his chief, who was unwell, they had come suddenly face to face for the first time.

The meeting gave them mutual satisfaction. There was no doubt upon that point. She had looked hard at him ere she recognised him, for, like all the corridors in those mediaeval palaces, it was not very light, and she would have passed him without acknowledgment had he not uttered her name.

While standing there in that painted room with the tarnished gold furniture and mosaic floor, so different from the country drawing-room at Orton, with its bright chintzes and flowers, he had briefly told her of the unexpected offer that had reached him in England, of his acceptance, and of his ultimate appointment to be one of her father's private secretaries.

"Only fancy!" she laughed. "The world is really very small, is it not? I never thought, when we played tennis together at your uncle's tournament at Thornby, that you would be given an office in the Ministry of War. But I remember now how well you spoke Italian, and that you told me how fond you were of Italy."

"I owe all my good fortune to your father, Miss Morini. Believe me, it has lifted me out of a world of drudgery and insult—for, as I think I told you, I have been secretary to a Member of Parliament named Morgan-Mason."

"Ah! of course!" she exclaimed quickly, regarding him with a curious, fixed look. "You were secretary to Mr Morgan-Mason."

"Yes. Do you know him?"

"Not personally," she faltered, with some confusion. "I—well, I've heard of him. Some English friends of mine know him very well, and through them I have heard of the fellow's pompous egotism."

"Then you can well understand how very deeply I thank your father for his kindnesses towards me." And then he spoke of her engagement, about which everyone in Rome was at that moment talking.

He noticed her disinclination to speak of the man whom she was to marry—that man whom he knew so well.

"The count is in Paris," she answered briefly, when he inquired about him. "Have you not met him yet? I recollect when in England he was very anxious to meet you."

"No. I have not seen him to congratulate him upon his good fortune," replied George, with a touch of bitterness; "but no doubt he will soon return, and we shall come across each other."

"He is due back in a week in order to go to the royal reception at the Quirinale on the nineteenth," she said. "When I write to-morrow I will tell him that you are now in Rome."

"No," exclaimed Macbean quickly. "Don't tell him. I like giving old friends pleasant surprises. When he returns I will call on him unexpectedly."

His was a good excuse, and he was gratified to see that she accepted it. It would, he knew, never do for her to write and inform her lover of his presence in Rome. If she did, he certainly would not dare to return to the Eternal City. George had resolved to conceal his presence from the Frenchman and to carefully watch his movements. Therefore he induced the Minister's daughter to make no mention of him.

He found her somewhat more wan and pale than she had been in England. She seemed preoccupied, *distraite*, with a touch of sadness in her deep, liquid eyes that was scarcely in keeping with the passion and ecstasy of an engagement. She was not her old self, bright, lighthearted, and careless, as she had been in those summer days in England. Something had occurred, but what it was he had no means of ascertaining.

The one thought that held him spellbound was the reflection that she was actually to marry Jules Dubard.

She was about to sacrifice herself, and yet he dare not tell her the terrible truth. He stood gazing into her great brown eyes, speechless before that calm and wondrous beauty that had for months arisen constantly before his eyes amid the whirl of London life. Yes, he loved her—he had fallen to worship at her shrine ever since those warm afternoons when they had played tennis on the level English lawns, and now this re-encounter had awakened within him all the wild passion of his yearning heart.

During those days in Rome he had heard much of her, for she was popular everywhere, a reigning beauty in the gay, exclusive circle which surrounded the royal throne, and one of the most courted of all the unmarried girls in the capital. The season was at its height, therefore she was seen everywhere, mostly in company with Dubard. If the truth were told, however, it was much against her own inclination. She was in no mood for gaiety. All the life and gaiety had been crushed from her heart, and she only attended the various functions because it was her duty towards her father to do so. Many a sleepless night she spent in prayer and in tears.

Long ago she had become nauseated by all the glare and glitter, the chatter and music of those gilded salons where smart Rome amused themselves each evening. Whenever she could, she made excuses to stay at home in the quiet and silence of her own room; but as it was part of her father's statecraft that she should ⋯⋯⋯⋯⋯⋯⋯⋯⋯⋯⋯⋯⋯⋯⋯⋯⋯ cent gowns with a sigh, dance when her heart was leaden, and smile even though she was bursting with grief.

Yet she rigorously kept the secret of her self-sacrifice, and none suspected that the young French *élégant* had compelled her to accept him as husband. Indeed, Dubard was already very popular in Rome. He was possessed of means, belonged to the most exclusive Italian club, and drove a smart phaeton and pair each afternoon, frequently with Mary at his side.

The men and women who were Dubard's friends were among the highest in society, yet none knew the truth save Borselli and George Macbean, neither of whom dare, for their own sakes, utter one single word in denunciation.

"You told me at Orton that the count was an old friend, Mr Macbean," exclaimed Mary, after a brief pause. She had met his gaze unflinchingly, and then lowered her eyes to the ground. She looked fresh and neat in her plain black tailor-made gown, for she was dressed ready to go out for her morning walk in the Corso.

"Yes. We met several years ago," was Macbean's reply.

"Where?"

"In London."

"You must have been close friends," she remarked, "for he has on several occasions asked whether I had heard of you."

George smiled, for his reflections were bitter ones. "Yes," he said, "I knew him quite well; but we drifted apart, as friends so often do."

"Then you will, of course, be glad to meet him again."

"For one reason, very glad. Because I want to inquire of him what has become of one who was our mutual friend, and who mysteriously disappeared—a very curious affair."

"Was it a man?" asked Mary, suddenly interested.

"Yes—a French army officer—a General Felix Sazarac."

"Sazarac!" she gasped, with open mouth and cheeks suddenly blanched as the name recalled to her the strange conversation between Borselli and her father. "Was Sazarac your friend?"

CHAPTER TWENTY NINE.
AROUND THE THRONE.

Mary, accompanied by the faithful Teresa, a stout, middle-aged woman in black, who had seen fifteen years of service in the family, went out along the Corso, at that hour crowded by the Roman idlers and foreign visitors.

The bright air of the spring morning was refreshing after the dull gloom of the great old Antinori palace, and all Rome was full of life, movement, and gaiety. Carnival had passed, and the Pasqua was fast approaching, that time when the Roman season is its gayest and when the hotels are full of wealthy foreigners from the north.

The court receptions and balls had brought the Italian aristocracy from the various cities, and the ambassadors were mostly at their posts because of the weekly diplomatic receptions.

As Mary went along the Corso to an artists' colour shop, in order to purchase some tubes for the painting which occupied her spare time, she was saluted on every hand, for she was well-known and popular everywhere. Her beauty was remarked wherever she went.

She bowed and smiled her acknowledgments, but, alas! only mechanically. She really did not recognise any of those men who raised their hats, the smart officers who drew their heels together and saluted, or the well-dressed women who nodded to her. Truth to tell, she was thinking of the man with whom she had so suddenly come face to face, the straight, athletic man who had spoken so openly and so frankly about himself when they had stood upon that green, level tennis-lawn at Orton. The recollection of him had almost faded from her memory until only half an hour ago, and now she found herself reflecting deeply, wondering whether he had really schemed to enter her father's service, and, if so, with what motive.

He had acknowledged himself to be a friend of Dubard, the man she held in such suspicion and distrust, and yet there was something so frank and honest in his manner that it held her mystified. As she walked along that narrow, crowded thoroughfare in the heart of Rome, memories of those idle summer days in England arose vividly before her, of the rural tennis tournament at Thornby, of the village flower-show held in the old-world rectory garden, and of George Macbean's visit to Orton.

Teresa spoke to her, but she heeded not. Her mind was filled with thoughts of the pleasant past when her life was free and she was unfettered. Now, however, that compact she had made to secure her father's freedom had crushed all light ... ... she became more inert and melancholy.

Her delicacy, grace, and simplicity were astonishing when one viewed that irresponsible and artificial world of modern *chic* in which she lived. Her character, indeed, resolved itself into the very elements of womanhood. She was beautiful, modest, and tender, so perfectly unsophisticated, so delicately refined that she was peerless among all others in that vain, silly, out-dressing set, where religion was only the cant of the popular confessor and the scandal of a promenade through Saint Peter's or San Giovanni, the brilliant glittering crowd who formed the court circle of modern Italy around King Umberto's throne.

She had sprung up into beauty in that far-off modest school that faced the grey English Channel at Broadstairs, and on making her bow before her sovereign she had instantly created a sensation and a vogue for herself that still continued, one which, was fostered by the Minister and his wife, although at heart she hated all the hollow shams and scandalous gossip. True, she had had her little flirtations the same as other girls, yet she had never caught from society one imitated or artificial grace. She preferred the society of her father or her mother to that of girl friends; for most of the latter of her own world she found giddy and empty-headed, generally boasting of conquests they had made among men, and ridiculing them as fools.

She tolerated society only under sheer compulsion. Through these three wild years of whirling excitement she had fortunately retained her woman's heart, for it was unalterable and inalienable, as part of her being. And it was because of that she had now sacrificed herself to become the wife of Jules Dubard.

Oh, the tragedy of it all! No single person was there in whom to confide, or of whom to seek advice. The bitter truth was forced upon her more and more each day. The compact with the man whose artificiality and mannerisms she held in such abhorrence she was bound to keep, for did she not hold her beloved father's future in her hands?

Of a sudden, when she was half-way up the Corso towards the Porta del Popolo, she heard the musical sounds of harness bells as a fine landau and pair swept up behind her.

Every man's head was uncovered and every woman bowed, for there flashed by Umberto the Good and his Queen Margherita, both worshipped by the people, and on every hand there rose the cry, "Viva il Re! Viva la Regina!"

Mary bowed with the rest, and Her Majesty, quick to notice her, gave her a nod of recognition and gracious smile; for, as the world of Rome knew quite well, she was one of those behind the throne, a personal friend of the queen, who was never tired of admiring the wondrous beauty of the Minister's daughter.

The royal pair passed on at a gallop up the Corso, and Mary sighed to herself as the carriage disappeared. It recalled to her that she was compelled to attend the state ball at the Quirinale that night, much as she hated all those glittering official functions. Her dress, a marvellous creation in yellow, had arrived from Paris the day before; but when Teresa had taken it from its long box and shaken out the magnificent skirt, she had scarcely glanced at it. She wore those gorgeous gowns which were so admired at court only because it gratified her father. Personally, she delighted in a short, tailor-made skirt and a blouse like those she could wear at Orton. The vagaries of the *mode* never interested her in the least. Paquin had her model, and made her dresses as he liked. She simply wore them, annoyed at those long and difficult trains he gave her—that was all.

The gay world around the throne believed that she studied the fashions and wore those costly gowns because she delighted in them. But such was not a fact. Her tastes were of the simplest, and her ideal always was a life in the rural quiet of Orton Court, with an occasional shopping visit to London as a dissipation. The very atmosphere of Rome, with its false appearances, its bartering of a girl's bright youth, loveliness, and purity for titles, its gambling and its drug habits, stifled her. She loathed it all, and longed to enjoy life's good gifts in rural England. Yet, alas! such an ideal was to her but a dream. It was her fate to be drawn into that maelstrom where each man and woman must be seen, must be known, and must be notorious in some way or other, no matter how.

And because she was born in the official world, she was bound, for her father's sake, to act her part in it.

Through all that day she reflected upon the words which the young Englishman had uttered regarding Sazarac—that unusual name she had once overheard spoken, and which she recollected so well. She remarked how her father had distinctly betrayed fear at mention of it, and therefore the reason had ever since been a puzzling mystery to her.

For months she had wondered at what Borselli meant when he had threatened her father. The latter had reproached him of his intention to betray him, whereupon the Under-Secretary had said—

"I am in earnest. You act as I have suggested—or you take the consequences!"

That in itself showed plainly that the Sicilian still held power over her father on account of what had been mentioned between them as "the Sazarac affair."

After luncheon she casually mentioned to her father her meeting with George Macbean, whereupon he said—

"Oh, I quite thought I had told you of his appointment. I wanted an English secretary, and he was the very man to fill the post. You recollect that he visited us once or twice at Orton, but I had previously met him when he came to interpret for his employer Morgan-Mason regarding an army contract for Abyssinia."

"Did you offer him the appointment?" she asked.

"No; Angelo did. He apparently knew of him."

His Excellency's reply surprised Mary. Why, she wondered, had her father's enemy appointed the young Englishman to a post in order to transfer him to her father's cabinet as private secretary? She was suspicious of Borselli, and discerned in this some hidden motive.

And yet was it [illegible] friend, while Dubard himself was in the secrets of Angelo Borselli! The more she pondered over the problem the more bewildering did it become.

At midnight she alighted with her mother from the brougham in the great courtyard of the Quirinale, and gathering up her train, passed through the long flower-decked corridors, up the great staircase of marble and porphyry, where stood the tall, statuesque guards, and on into the magnificent Hall of the Ambassadors, where the guests at the court ball were assembling.

As she let down her train and entered the magnificent salon with its gilt ceiling and myriad electric lights her appearance caused a murmur of approbation as every eye was turned upon her. The assembly was perhaps the most brilliant of any that could be gathered in any European capital. The men were in uniforms of every colour, with the crosses and ribbons of the various orders of chivalry. The ambassadors and their staffs were all there, from the Chinese representatives in their national dress to the cunning old gentleman from St. Petersburg in his white uniform tunic with the blue ribbon of St. Andrew at his throat. Lord Elton, the British Ambassador, a dark-bearded, elderly man, wearing the star of Knight Commander of the Bath, came forward to greet the War Minister's wife and daughter, and there came up also to salute the ambassador Morini himself in his gorgeous uniform with the cerise and white ribbon of the Order of the Crown of Italy and the green and white cross of Saints Maurice and Lazarus, as well as a number of minor foreign orders across his breast.

In uniform Camillo Morini always looked his best, tall, refined, distinguished, a man who would be marked out anywhere as a leader among men. He was pale and haggard, however, having risen from his bed to come there and be seen because it was policy—always policy.

Around on every side were high Italian officers in their gala uniform with golden epaulettes, women dressed exquisitely, and aged diplomatists and politicians bent beneath the weight of their gold-laced coats and many decorations. The room was a bewildering blaze of colour, diamonds gleaming in the tiaras of the women and in the crosses of the men, while on every hand was the loud, excited chatter of the gay, laughing crowd bidden there by royal command.

Lord Elton was chatting in English with Mary and her mother, explaining that only yesterday he had returned from London, where he had been on leave, when of a sudden three loud, distinct knocks were heard, and in an instant there was silence. Then, a moment later, at the farther end of the apartment two long white doors were thrown open by the royal flunkeys bearing white wands in their hands, and through them flowed the crowd into the magnificent ballroom, one of the finest both in proportions and in decoration of any palace in the world. And here and in the suite of huge gilded reception-rooms beyond the gay court of Italy commenced its revels as the splendid orchestra in the balcony struck up the first dance upon the programme.

From the ballroom there opened out through the open doors a vista of magnificent salons unequalled in grandeur even in that city of ancient palaces, and the elderly folk who did not care for dancing strolled away, greeting their friends at every step, and forming little groups for gossip.

Mary, who had quickly become separated from her mother, found herself, almost before she was aware of it, in the arms of her friend Captain Fred Houghton, the British naval attaché, dancing over the magnificent floor and receiving his compliments, while in a corner of the room, apart from the others, stood Angelo Borselli in his general's uniform, watching her with a strange smile upon his thin lips.

And all around was in progress that drama of intrigue, of statecraft and duplicity, of diplomacy, of unscrupulous scheming for office and power which is inseparable from the vicinity of every European throne.

In that gold and white room, while the orchestra played waltz-music, the prosperity of the gallant Italian nation often trembled in the balance, for those polished floors formed the stage whereon some of the strangest of modern dramas were enacted.

CHAPTER THIRTY.
THE PATH OF THE TEMPTER.

An hour had passed, and Mary, against her inclination, had danced with various partners, and had heard around her comments regarding her personal beauty and her dress such as always reached her ears on such occasions. Everyone courted and flattered her, for in that gay court circle she was one of its reigning queens. Yet the hot air stifled her; the mingled perfumes of flowers and chiffons nauseated her. She hated it all, and was longing to get away back to the solitude of her own room, where, after old Teresa had brushed her hair, she might sit in her big easy-chair and think.

Blasé of life before her time, she was disappointed, world-weary, and heart-broken, although as yet only in her early womanhood. She had been dancing with the young Prince de Sarsina, a well-known figure in Roman society, and he had led her to a seat beside the old Duchess de Rovigor, when, in the lull of the music, those mysterious knocks were again repeated, and at the farther end of the ballroom there stood the black-habited royal chamberlain.

There was silence at once. Then the royal official announced in Italian in a loud, ringing voice—

"His Majesty the King!"

And at the same moment a pair of long gilt and blue doors were flung open, and into the room there advanced the sovereign, a well-set-up, pleasant-faced figure with white moustache, before whom all bowed low three times in obeisance as he strode with regal gait into the centre of the enormous ballroom. In his splendid uniform outrivalling all, and wearing the grand crosses of the Crown of Italy, Maurice and Lazarus, and Savoy orders of which he was master, his figure presented a fitting centre to that brilliant assembly; and soon, when the obeisances were made and he had saluted in return, he moved away in conversation with Morini, who, as all were aware, was one of his most intimate friends.

Then, when the queen, wearing her wonderful pearls, entered with the same ceremony, together with the Crown Prince and Princess of Naples, the orchestra struck up again and the revelry continued notwithstanding the presence of the sovereigns, who mixed freely with their guests and laughed and talked with them.

Presently, as Mary on the arm of a partner was passing near to where Her Majesty was sitting upon the raised daïs at the end of the room, the queen suddenly beckoned to her, whereupon she left the man who was her escort, curtseyed as etiquette demanded, and approached the royal presence.

"I only heard the news the day before yesterday on our return from Berlin," exclaimed Her Majesty in English, with a kindly smile as the girl came up to her. "But of course your engagement scarcely comes as a surprise. Let me congratulate you. You must present the count to me at the first opportunity. Is he now in Rome?"

"No, Madame," was the girl's blushing reply. "But I thank your Majesty for your kind thought of me."

"I wish you every happiness, my dear," declared the queen, for Mary was an especial favourite with her. "Perhaps I may be able to attend your wedding. When will it be?"

"In June, Madame."

"Very well. Give me good notice of the date, and I'll see if I can come." And then she dismissed the Minister's daughter by turning to speak with one of her ladies-in-waiting who had returned from executing some commission upon which her royal mistress had sent her.

What irony, thought the girl, as she curtseyed and left the royal the trap into which she had fallen!

Through those high-roofed, magnificent chambers, with their wonderful friezes, priceless paintings, and gilt furniture, she wandered on, acknowledging greetings on every hand, yet only mechanically, for her thoughts were far away from that scene of royal revelry. The atmosphere held her asphyxiated, the music jarred upon her ears, and the gossip she heard on every side was for her devoid of all interest.

One face alone arose before her amid that glittering throng, the face of the Englishman she had met so unexpectedly that morning—George Macbean.

And why? She asked herself that question, and yet to it could give no direct response. His frank honesty of countenance and his muscular English form attracted her, but when the suggestion crossed her mind that she loved him, she laughed such an idea to scorn. They were comparative strangers, and she prided herself on being one who had never fallen into the error of affection at first sight as so many other girls did. Her character, it was true, was too well balanced for that.

Yet the truth remained that all her thoughts that day had been of him.

Both the Baron Riboulet, the French Ambassador, and old Prince Demidoff had grasped her hand and paid their compliments, while the princess managed to whisper in French, "I never saw you looking so well as to-night, my dear. That gown suits you admirably, and is by far the most striking here. One cannot wonder at Count Dubard's choice. He has always been known in Paris as a connoisseur of beauty, you know," and Her Excellency the Princess showed her yellow teeth in a broad grin at what she meant as humour.

Wherever Mary went, half a dozen of the younger men followed in her train like bees about their queen. She laughed with them, made humorous remarks, and

chatted to them with that air of bright, irresponsible gaiety by which she so cleverly concealed the heavy burden of grief and disappointment that filled her heart. In

Morini, hence at such functions as these they liked to be seen in her company,
laughing or dancing with her.

The young Duke di Forano, who had recently returned from Paris, where he
had acted as first secretary of the Italian Embassy, had taken her in to supper in
the huge winter garden where the tiny tables were set beneath the palms, and
they had been waited upon by the royal servants. In the dim light of the Chinese
lanterns the duke, an old friend, had taken her hand in his; but she had withdrawn
it in indignation, saying—

"You have no right to do that, now that I am engaged."

"Ah yes! of course," he exclaimed, with a word of apology, at once interested.
"I heard something about it in Paris, but quite forgot. Jules Dubard is the lucky
fellow—isn't he?"

She nodded.

And as she looked into his dark, well-cut features in the half-light she fancied
she discerned a curious look, half of pity and half of surprise.

"I hope you'll be happy," he remarked in a hard voice. "I always thought you
would marry Solaro—poor devil! Do you remember him?"

"Remember!" she echoed. "Yes; I recollect everything. You may well say 'poor
devil.' He has been convicted of being a traitor—of selling army secrets to France."

"I know—I know," answered her companion quickly. "We had all the papers
concerning the charges through the Embassy, and I am aware of all the facts. My
own idea is that he's innocent, yet how can it be proved? He was betrayed by some
heartless woman in Bologna, it seems. She made all sorts of charges against him."

"She lied!" cried Mary quickly. "He is innocent. I know he is, and some day I
hope to be able to prove it."

"Ah, I wish I could help you!" was his fervent declaration. "He was my friend,
you know. Perhaps the real truth may be known some day, but until then we can
only wait, and he must bear his unjust punishment."

"But it is a crying scandal that he should have been degraded when he is innocent!" declared the daughter of the Minister of War.

"Your father, no doubt, ordered the most searching inquiry. It is strange that,
if he is really innocent, his innocence has not been proved."

"You are quite right," she said. "That very fact is always puzzling me."

"There may be some reason why he has been consigned to prison," remarked
the diplomatist, thoughtfully twisting his champagne-glass by the stem, "some
reason of State, of which we are ignorant."

"But my father would never willingly be party to such an injustice."

"Probably not; but what seems possible is that Solaro is held in prison by some power greater than your father's—the power of your father's enemies."

She thought deeply over those strange words of his. It almost seemed as though he were actually in possession of the truth, and yet feared to reveal it to her!

Presently they rose again, and returned to where the cotillon had commenced. She did not take part in it, because her heart was too full for such frivolities. The young diplomatist had left her at a seat, when almost immediately her father's enemy, Angelo Borselli, approached, and bowed low over her hand.

She knew well how he had endeavoured to ruin and disgrace her father, and how he intended to hold the office of Minister himself; yet, owing to the instructions His Excellency had given her, she treated him with that clever diplomacy which is innate in woman. In common with her father, she never allowed him to discern that she entertained the slightest antipathy towards him, and treated him with calm dignity as she had always done.

Borselli, in ignorance that the Minister was aware of all the ramifications of his shrewd scheming, still affected the same friendship for Morini and his family, and affected it with a marvellous verisimilitude of truth. One of the cleverest political schemers in Europe, he was unrivalled even by Vito Ricci, who in the past had performed marvels of political duplicity. Yet Mary's tact was a match for him.

Only three days ago she and her father had dined at his big new mansion in the Via Salaria, and neither man had betrayed any antagonism towards the other. It is often so in this modern world of ours. Men who inwardly hate each other are outwardly the best of friends. Neither Morini nor Mary had any trust in him, however, for both knew too well that he intended by some clever *coup* one day to deal the blow and triumph as usurper. Yet both, while wary and silent, masked their true feelings of suspicion beneath the cloak of indifference and friendliness.

Having taken a seat beside her, he began to gossip pleasantly, while his dark eyes were darting quick glances everywhere, when suddenly he asked—

"Is not Jules here? I thought he was commanded here to-night."

"No. To the next ball. He is in Paris," she said simply, without desire to discuss the man to whom she had engaged herself.

"And you do not regret his absence—eh?" remarked the Sicilian in a low voice, bringing his sallow, sinister face nearer to hers.

"I do not understand you," she exclaimed, drawing herself up with some hauteur. "What is your insinuation?"

"Nothing," was his low response. "You need not be offended, for I do not mean it in that sense. I merely notice how you are enjoying yourself this evening during his absence, and the conclusion is but natural." And his face relaxed into a smile.

"Well," she declared, as across her fair face fell a shadow of quick annoyance, "I consider, general, your remark entirely uncalled for." And she rose stiffly to leave him.

But he only smiled again, a strange, crafty smile, that rendered his thin, sallow face the more forbidding, as he answered in a low voice, speaking almost into her ear, and fixing his eyes on hers—

"I may surely be forgiven as an old friend if I approach the truth in confidence, signora. You have accepted that man's offer of marriage, but you have done so under direct compulsion. You desire to escape from your compact. You see I am aware of the whole truth. Well, there is one way by which you may escape. But recollect that what I tell you is in the strictest secrecy and confidence from your father—from everyone. I speak as your friend. There is a way by which you can avoid making this loveless alliance which is naturally distasteful to you—a way by which, if you choose to adopt it, you may save yourself!"

She faced the man, her brown eyes meeting his in speechless surprise and wonder at his enigmatical words.

What could he mean?

CHAPTER THIRTY ONE.

IN WHICH A DOUBLE GAME IS PLAYED.

"I do not quite follow you, general," faltered Mary after a brief pause, regarding him with a puzzled air.

"Then let us find a quiet corner where we can be alone, and I will explain," said Borselli, rising and offering the girl his arm. Both were well acquainted with all the ramifications of the splendid state apartments, the ante-chambers, the winter garden, and the corridors, therefore he led her through the Throne Room to a small apartment at the rear of the Hall of the Princess, an elegant little room hung with pale green silk and the gilt furniture of which bore embroidered on the backs of the chairs the royal crown with the black eagle and white cross of Savoy.

So cleverly did Angelo Borselli conceal his schemes and his hatreds that through years he had deceived so shrewd and far-seeing a man as his chief Morini. His insinuating address and rather handsome exterior rendered him, if not welcome in Roman society, at least tolerated, more especially as through him recommendations could be made to Morini, whose word was law on every point concerning the army of Italy. A certain degree of suspicion and some feeling of awe attended him, though it was rather in his absence than his presence, for his ready wit and fluent conversation were not calculated to inspire other than agreeable thoughts.

It was only as he cast himself into a chair at her side, hesitating how to put the matter before her, that in the glance of his dark, sparkling, deeply set eyes might have been detected a sinister motive and a searching and eager expression at variance with the frank and joyous manner of a moment before.

That glance betrayed the depth of the man's cunning.

"You have no love for Dubard," he remarked slowly. "I have watched, and I have seen it plainly. Yet you are engaged to him because he has compelled you to accept him as your husband. He holds a certain power over you—when he orders you dare not disobey! Am I not correct?" he asked, looking straight into her brown, wide-open eyes.

She nodded in the affirmative, and a slight sigh escaped her. She was suspicious of him, but did not recognise the trend of his argument.

"Then let us advance a step further," he said, in the same quiet, serious manner. "It is but natural you desire to escape from him. He is repugnant to you; perhaps you loathe him, and yet you wear a mask of pretended happiness! Surely you cannot take up life beside a husband whom you secretly despise! You are a woman who desires to love and be loved, a woman who should marry a man worthy your

genuine solicitude for her future.

His attitude was full of mystery. The sudden interest which he—her father's bitterest enemy—betrayed on her behalf was inexplicable.

"Well," she faltered at last, "and if I really desire to break off my engagement with the count? What course do you suggest?"

"You must break your engagement, signorina," he exclaimed quickly. "For several weeks I have desired to speak plainly and frankly to you, but I feared that certain distorted facts having perhaps come to your ears, you might treat me as your enemy rather than your friend. But to-night, finding you alone, I resolved to speak, and, if possible, to save you from sacrificing yourself to a man so unworthy of you."

"But I always thought he was your friend!" she exclaimed in surprise, looking straight at the man before her and toying with her big feathered fan.

"We are friends. We have been guests together under your father's roof in England, you will remember," he admitted. "Yet I entertain too much respect for your father and his family to stand by and see you become the victim of such a man as Jules Dubard."

"You are his friend, and yet you speak evil of him behind his back!" she remarked.

"No, I do not speak evil in the least. You misunderstand my motive. It is in the interests of your own well-being and future happiness. We must not allow that man to force you into an odious union. He is clever, but you must outwit him. Your duty to yourself is to do so."

"But how can I?" she asked, with a desperation in her voice that came involuntarily, but which revealed to Borselli her eagerness to escape from the web which Dubard had weaved about her.

The future of that beautiful girl, the most admired of all that brilliant throng at court, was the future of Italy. Angelo Borselli knew it, and recognised what an important part that handsome daughter of the Minister was destined to play.

"There is one way—only one way," he answered, bending towards her, speaking confidentially, and keeping his deep-set eyes fixed upon hers. "The man Dubard has very cleverly succeeded in forcing you to accept him as husband. But you must escape from your present peril by revealing the truth."

"The truth of what?"

"The truth of that man's motives."

"But they are all a mystery. How can I ascertain the truth?"

"There is one man who knows—one man who, if he chose to speak, could at once give you freedom."

"But who is he?" she inquired eagerly.

"Felice Solaro—your friend."

"Solaro!" she gasped. "But he is in prison in Turin, condemned for fifteen years for treason!"

"For an offence of which he is not guilty," declared the Under-Secretary quickly.

"Ah! And that is your opinion, as mine, general!" she cried eagerly. "I know he is innocent."

"Then secure his release. Persuade your father to sign a decree reversing the finding of the court-martial, and he, in turn, can save you from falling victim to this man to whom you are giving yourself in marriage."

Angelo Borselli met her piercing glance unmoved. She seemed to be trying to divine the schemer's secret thoughts.

"You will do this—for your own sake," he whispered earnestly. "It is unjust that the poor captain should be kept in prison for a crime of which he is innocent."

"But if you know that he is not guilty, why have you not already used your own influence as Under-Secretary to secure his release?" she asked, with distinct suspicion, a thousand uneasy thoughts agitating her bosom.

"Because I am powerless. It is only His Excellency, your father, who can sign decrees," was his reply, adding, "I have more than once directed his attention to the act of gross injustice, but his reply has in each case been the same—namely, that he had examined the evidence, and that he could discover no doubt about the captain's culpability in selling the secrets of Tresenta and of our mobilisation scheme for the protection of the French frontier. Both secrets actually reached the Intelligence Department of the French Ministry of War, for that has been proved beyond doubt by our secret agents in Paris; and, further, they passed through the hands of a lady friend of Solaro's—Filoména Nodari."

"Where is that woman now? Still in Bologna?"

"No, I think not," was his reply, without, however, telling her how he had taken the woman into his service and sent her to England. "I learned a short time ago that she had left, and gone abroad."

"It was through her false evidence that Felice was convicted. She told foul untruths concerning him," his companion cried angrily.

"I know. Perhaps it is owing to fear of the truth being exposed that she has left Bologna. But in any case, it is only common justice that poor Solaro should be released. He has never had a chance of a proper appeal—your father refused it to him."

"But why? Has my father any reason why the poor fellow should be kept in prison?"

Angelo Borselli raised his shoulders and exhibited his palms in a gesture more forcible than mere words.

"And if he has, then how can I hope to succeed in turning his favour towards the accused man?"

"Try. Do your utmost, signorina," he urged, with perhaps more eagerness than was really warrantable in such circumstances. "Appeal to your father's sense of justice, to his honour, to his reputation as one always ready to redress wrongs. You, as his daughter, can accomplish everything if you wish—even the freedom of Felice Solaro."

"And if I do?"

"Then he will speak the truth, and you need have no fear of the man who has so cleverly entrapped you into this engagement. When the truth is out he will at once relinquish his claim to your hand."

She hesitated. She was wondering whether the crafty statesman who had risen by her father's favours was really aware of the secret compact she had made with Dubard; whether he knew that she had given her hand to him in exchange for his protection of her father's honour.

Jules had seen her a few days after the curious scene in the Chamber of Deputies. He had come to her to receive the payment he had demanded in the shape of a formal engagement of marriage. But he had told her nothing concerning the manner in which he had managed to avert the crisis, and she only knew the story of the letter to Montebruno through Vito Ricci, her father's spy. She was unaware of Jules' visit to the man now before her, or of his threat to make revelations if the fatal question were asked in the Chamber.

Women of Mary Morini's type rise to higher heights of sacrifice and, when determined, act with a courage rare among men. She is herself in a thousand ways men never dare to be, and a fine woman is worth a hundred of the finest men.

"But if you are really speaking in my own interests as my friend, general, why cannot you furnish me with the weapon by which I can defend myself from him?" she suggested at last.

"For two reasons. First, your parents, ignorant of the real facts, are delighted at the prospect of your marriage; secondly, Solaro alone holds the truth. He can speak and prove his facts."

"Regarding what?"

"Regarding Jules Dubard."

"Regarding the man whom you still allege is your friend? Really, general, the manner in which you exhibit friendship towards others is a rather curious one, if this is an example of it?"

He was unprepared for such a remark from her. But it showed him, nevertheless, how frank and fearless she had become.

"I merely offer you my advice, signorina," he answered, shifting slightly in his chair and settling his sword. "It is surely a thousand pities that you should become the victim of a man of Dubard's stamp when, by a little clever manoeuvring, you may not only do an act of justice by freeing poor Solaro, but also free yourself from the engagement into which you have entered against your will."

"But you tell me that my father has already refused to release the captain?" she remarked, regarding him with a puzzled air. "If this is so, then what can I do further?"

"Persuade him. You alone can induce him to act as you desire. Recollect that upon that man's liberty your own future depends."

The Sicilian, careful student of the human character as he was, knew well that a generous, magnanimous woman, like the one before him, is more ingenious and confident in well-doing than any man. He had carefully watched her, and by means of his secret agents knew that she entertained no love for the man to whom she had become engaged. Therefore, with his unequalled cunning, he had devised a fresh means of making his *coup* and attaining his end in spite of Jules Dubard.

He watched her beautiful countenance, and saw that his words had created an impression. A grave injustice had been done in degrading and imprisoning the handsome young captain who had once admired her so, and he knew that she would seek to remedy it. He had given her a strong and direct motive for securing Solaro's release—her own liberty.

"Very well," she sighed at last. "I thank you, general, for speaking to me so frankly. I will see what I can do in order to obtain a pardon for him. But if I do, will you promise to assist me in the matter which concerns me personally?"

"I promise you that Solaro shall tell the truth; that on the day following his release you shall be placed in a position to defy this man who believes that you have fallen his victim. Do you agree?"

She was silent for a moment, still distrustful of the man who had so narrowly encompassed her father's downfall. Yet she recollected that the face of politics changes quickly, and in a low voice and with sudden resolution answered—

"I do."

He stretched forth his white gloved hand, and without further word she took it in pledge of good faith. She had in her desperation made terms with the enemy, and as the Under-Secretary rose to escort her back through the gay assembly in the state-rooms, a faint, good-humoured smile flitted across his sallow features.

He felt confident that his craft and cunning must succeed—that she would obtain Solaro's release, and then the triumph for which he had so long and patiently waited would be his.

True, the fate of men's lives and nations' destinies was often juggled with in those great gilded halls where the air was heavy with perfume, the ear charmed with delightful music, and the eye dazzled by the glitter of that brilliant court, every member of which, man or woman, schemed, struggled, and intrigued to satisfy their own vices or their own ambitions.

CHAPTER THIRTY TWO.
THE BIRTH OF LOVE.

George and Mary met frequently in the days that followed. His Excellency was still suffering from an attack of that prostrating malady Roman fever, and George, as his private secretary, was daily in attendance upon him.

Morini liked the young man for his honest English sturdiness of character, his diligent application to his duties, and his enthusiasm for all that was beneficial to the army. He had quickly picked up his duties, and already the Minister of War found his assistance indispensable.

He worked a good deal in the big old library of the palace, wherein the Minister's daughter and wife often entered to salute him and sometimes to give him an invitation to remain to luncheon, when the conversation would generally be upon English matters in general and things at Orton and Thornby in particular. Both mother and daughter delighted in their English home, and always regretted leaving it for that fevered existence they were compelled to lead continually in the Italian capital.

Mary was already engaged, otherwise neither Morini nor his wife would probably have allowed the two young people to be thrown so constantly into each other's society. Thus, however, the bond of friendship gradually became strengthened between them, he loving her fondly in secret, while she regarded him as a man in whom she might one day confide. She had no friend in whom she could trust, save her father. Amid her thousand acquaintances in that brilliant world around the throne there was not one who would not betray her confidence at the moment any profit might be made out of it. Therefore she kept herself to herself, and mixed with them only as etiquette or her father's policy demanded.

George Macbean was, on his part, filled with wonder. She was actually to marry Jules Dubard—that man of all men!

Surely her parents were in ignorance of who and what the fellow had been; surely by his clever cunning and shrewd manoeuvring he had misled even the sharp-eyed Minister himself, and induced him to give his consent to his daughter's marriage.

He pitied Mary—pitied her from the bottom of his heart. He knew that there must be some secret which she held and would not divulge; for if not, why should she regard her forthcoming marriage with such a lack of enthusiasm—why, indeed, should she purposely abstain from discussing Dubard? He closely watched her, and recognised how she had sadly changed since those bright days at Orton. Upon her brow was now a settled expression of deep thought and sadness, and when she thought herself unobserved a low sigh would sometimes escape, her, as though her thoughts were bitter ones.

Was it possible that she suspected the truth concerning Jules Dubard? Was it even possible that she was marrying him under compulsion?

In the silence of his own apartment he sat for hours, smoking his English pipe and wondering, while the babel of sounds of the foreign city came up from the street below. How strange were the ways of the world, how bitter the ironies of life! He loved her—ah yes! He loved her with all the passion of his soul, with all the deep and earnest devotion of which an honest man is capable. Yet, poor as he was, merely her father's underling, how could he ever hope to gain her hand? No, he sighed day after day, it was hopeless—utterly hopeless. Hers was to be a marriage of convenience—she was to wed Dubard, and become a countess.

But if he only dared to speak! He might save her—but at what cost? His own disgrace and ruin.

And he bit his lip to the blood.

Fortune had lifted him out of the drudgery of Morgan-Mason's service and brought him there to Rome, to a position of confidence envied by ten thousand others. Could he possibly sacrifice his future, his very life, just as it had suddenly opened up to him?

And he pondered on, meeting her, talking with her, and each hour falling deeper under the spell of her marvellous grace and beauty.

Mary, on her part, was full of thought. A frightful gulf was opened before her; she could not fly from its brink; she was goaded onwards though she saw it yawning beneath her feet.

While sitting alone with her father in his room one evening she approached the subject of Felice Solaro; but he instantly poured forth such a flood of invectives upon the condemned man that she was compelled to at once change the subject. To her it seemed that for some unaccountable reason he was prejudiced against the imprisoned man, and anything she might say in his favour only served to condemn him the more.

On looking back upon the past, she found that she had regarded love as a matter of everyday occurrence. She heard of it, saw it wherever she moved; every man who approached her either felt or feigned it; and so accustomed was she to homage and devotion that its absence alone attracted her attention. She had considered it part of her state—and yet of the real nature of true affection she had been perfectly unconscious.

She had more than once imagined herself in love, as in the case of Felice Solaro, mistaking gratified vanity for a deeper emotion—had felt pleasure in the presence of its object, and regret in absence; but that was a pastime and no more—until now.

But now! She held within her heart a deep secret—the secret of her love.

And this rendered her future all the more serious—her marriage all the more a fearful undertaking. She had no escape from her fate, she must marry a man who at least was indifferent to her. Could she ever suffer herself to be decked for this unpromising bridal, this union with a man who at heart was the enemy of her family and whom she hated?

One evening she again met George Macbean. He had returned from Naples, where he had executed a commission given him by the Minister, and had reported to his chief his visit to the commandant of the military district. He afterwards sat with Mary and her mother in one of the smaller reception-rooms of the ponderous old mansion. Mary, who was in a black dinner-dress slightly *décolleté*, took up her mandoline—the instrument of which he was so fond—and sang the old Tuscan song, in which, with his heart so overburdened, he discerned a hidden meaning—

> "Io questa notte in sogno l'ho veduto,
> Era vestito tutto di broccato;
> Le piume sul berretto di velluto,
> Ed una spada d'oro aveva allato.
> E poi m'ha detto con un bel sorriso.
> Io non posso piu star da te diviso!
> Da te diviso non ci posso stare,
> E torno per mai piu non ti lasciare!"

These words sank as iron into his soul. Did she, he wondered, really reciprocate his concealed and unexpressed feelings? Ah no, it was impossible—all impossible.

And when she had laid aside her instrument, he commenced to describe to them the grand review of troops which he had witnessed outside Naples that morning, and how the general staff had treated him as an honoured guest.

"Ah!" sighed Madame Morini. "If we were to tell the truth, Mr Macbean, both Mary and I are tired of the very sight of uniforms and the sound of military music. Wherever my husband goes in Italy a review is always included in the programme, and we have to endure the heat and the dust of the march past. Once, when I was first married, I delighted in all the glitter and display of armed forces, but nowadays I long and ever long for retirement at dear old Orton."

"And so do I," declared her daughter quickly. "When I was at school in England I used to look forward to the day when I would be presented at the Quirinale and enter Roman society. But oh, the weariness of it all! I have already become sick of its glare, its uncharitableness, and its intrigues. England—yes—give me dear England, or else the quiet of San Donato. You have never been there yet, Mr Macbean," she added, looking into his face. "When you do go, you will find it more quiet and more beautiful than Orton."

"I have no doubt," he said. "If it is in the Arno valley, I know how beautiful the country is there, having passed up and down from Pisa many times. Those are photographs of it in madame's boudoir—are they not?"

"Oh yes. Ah! then you've noticed them," she exclaimed. "It is a delightful old place, is it not?" His eyes were fixed upon hers, and he read in their dark depths the burden of sorrow that was there. Dubard was due back in Rome, but he had not returned, nor had she mentioned the reason. He wished to meet him—to observe what effect his presence would have upon that man who had robbed him of all the happiness of life.

The chiming of the little French clock reminded him that it was the hour to take his leave, therefore he rose, grasped the hands of the grave, kind-faced Englishwoman and her daughter, and went forth into the old-world street, striding blindly on towards his own rooms.

"Really a delightful fellow," remarked her mother when the door had closed behind him. "His English manners are refreshing after those of all the apeish young fools whom we are compelled for the sake of policy to entertain. But," she added, with a laugh, suddenly recollecting, "I ought not to say that, my dear, now that you are to marry a Frenchman. I married an Italian, and as far as my choice of a husband has gone, I am thankful to say I have never regretted it—even though our natures and our religions are different."

"I will never become a Catholic—never!" declared Mary decisively. "I do not, and I shall never, believe in the confessional."

"Nor do I," responded her mother. "But there is no need for you to change your religion. The count has already told me that he has no such desire. By the way, he was due back the day before yesterday. Why has he not returned?"

"I heard from him yesterday. He has gone down to the Pyrenees—on business connected with the estate, he says;" and then, after some further gossip regarding a charity bazaar at the German Embassy, at which they were to hold a stall on the morrow, the unhappy girl rose, and with uneven steps went along the gloomy, echoing corridors to her own room.

Teresa brushed her long brown tresses as she sat before her long mirror looking at the reflection of her pale face and wondering if the young Englishman guessed the truth. Then as soon as possible she dismissed her faithful serving-woman, and still sat in her chair, her mind occupied by a thousand thoughts which chased each other in quick succession.

One thought, in spite of all her efforts, she was unable to banish; it returned again and again, and would intrude in spite of her struggles to suppress it—the image of George Macbean, the man who had so suddenly become her friend.

The night wore on, and in the silence of her pretty chamber she wept for some time, abandoning herself to melancholy fancies; at length, reproaching herself for thus permitting sorrow to usurp the place of that resignation which the pure faith she had adopted ought to inspire, she threw herself upon her knees and offered to Heaven the homage of an afflicted and innocent heart.

As she rose from her knees the church bells of Rome were chiming one. She shuddered at the solemn stroke, for every hour seemed to bring her nearer the terrible self-sacrifice which she was compelled to make for her father's sake. Her fears had risen almost to distraction, and she had wept and prayed alternately in all the agonies of anxiety.

The truth that had now forced itself upon her held her aghast, immovable. She loved George Macbean. Yes, she murmured his name aloud, and her words sounded weird and distinct in the silence of the night.

Yet if she withdrew from her unholy agreement with the man who had forced her to give her promise, then the hounds of destruction would be let loose upon her house.

And her father? She had discovered in the drawer of his carved writing-table at San Donato that tiny tube of innocent-looking tabloids; and though she kept the secret to herself, she had guessed his intention.

Could she deliberately allow him to sacrifice his life when there was still a means open whereby to save him?

She sank again upon her knees by the bedside, and greyed long for Divine help and deliverance.

CHAPTER THIRTY THREE.
MRS FITZROY'S GOVERNESS.

Mrs Charles Fitzroy was delighted with her new Italian governess.

She had contemplated engaging a Frenchwoman or a Swiss to teach little Bertha, but most fortunately, General Borselli, whom she had met during a season spent with her husband in Rome, came to her aid and recommended the daughter of the deceased Colonel Nodari. She came, and her slight, rather tall figure in neat black, her well-cut, handsome features, and her plainly dressed hair, almost black, had attracted her mistress from the first. She was refined, unobtrusive, merry-eyed, and just the kind of bright companion and governess she required for her child. She noticed that although her dresses were well made there were tokens, in more ways than one, that since her father's death she and her mother had fallen upon evil days.

Fitzroy himself liked her. There was something interesting in her quaint broken English and in her foreign gestures that commended itself to him in preference to the angular blue-stocking Miss Gardener, who had recently left his wife's service. So "Mademoiselle," as they called her in preference to the rather ugly word "Signorina," quickly became as one of the family, and within a week of her arrival she met that pompous millionaire of eggs and bacon, Mr Morgan-Mason.

The latter became as much attracted by her as were the others, but she exerted no effort to captivate or to gain admiration, merely acting her part modestly as became the humble governess in a wealthy family. Nevertheless she recollected the general's instructions, and more than once, in the secrecy of her room, wrote to that address in Genoa reporting her progress.

Mrs Charles Fitzroy, a pretty and rather extravagant woman, still on the right side of forty, moved in a very good set, and entertained a good deal at her house in Brook Street. Her husband was a magnate in the city, and the fact that Morgan-Mason was her brother gave her the *entrée* to houses which would have otherwise been closed to her. Fitzroy, a rather short, grey-bearded man with a florid countenance, had risen from a clerk's stool to be what he was, and differed in little particular from thousands of well-off city men who live in the West End and enter the anteroom of society.

Nevertheless, through the influence of the white-waistcoated Member for South-West Norfolk, a good many well-known people dined at Brook Street from time to time, while to Morgan-Mason's smart gatherings at his house or his dinners at the Carlton his sister and her husband were always invited.

It was pleasant enough to mix with such people as surrounded her employers, but, truth to tell, Filoména Nodari quickly found the post of governess monoto-

character as a paid menial; secondly, she hated children; thirdly, Bertha was a spoilt child, with no leaning towards lessons; and fourthly, the small bare school-room at the top of the house was a gloomy place in which to spend those bright spring days. Still, she never complained. She was well paid by the Minister of War, and with a woman's love of intrigue, she had set herself to carefully accomplish the difficult task which Borselli had given her.

She was fortunate, inasmuch as Mrs Fitzroy treated her with such consideration. Indeed, sometimes when there were no visitors, she would invite her in to lunch with her, when they would generally talk French, a language with which her mistress was well acquainted.

So well did she act her part that the governess was quickly voted a treasure, and as Bertha was a particular favourite of her Uncle Morgan-Mason, the latter became gradually interested in her. Sometimes, indeed, he would come up to the schoolroom while lessons were in progress with an excuse to leave a packet of sweetmeats for his niece; but Filoména, with her woman's shrewd intuition, knew that he came to have a little chat with her.

He was inquisitive—always inquisitive.

One day as he sat with Bertha upon his knee in the schoolroom he asked about her parentage.

"You are a native of Bologna—where the sausages come from?" he laughed.

Perhaps he sold that comestible at his many shops, she reflected, but she answered in her broken English—

"Yes. But just as none of straw hats are made in Leghorn, so there are none of Bologna sausages made in Bologna."

"You must be already tired of life here in London after your beautiful Italy?" he remarked.

"Ah! non," she assured him. "I like your London—what leetle I have seen of it. But that is not very much. I take Bertha for one walk in the park, or down to what you call Kensington, every day. And many times we ascend to the roof of an omnibus. But omnibuses are so puzzling," she added, with a laugh. "You never know where one goes. We always ascend and seet there till we come to the end of the voyage. But we make some amusing errors many times. Only the day before to-day we ascended on a 'bus outside the Gallery Nationale, where are the fountains, paid twenty centimes—I mean two pennies—*eh bien*! the next street-corner past a church they turned us off—the omnibus went no farther!"

The millionaire laughed aloud, saying—

"It must have been a Royal Oak or Cricklewood 'bus coming home. They go no farther than Charing Cross."

"But oh!" she continued, "we go many time a long, long way—out into the country—away from London. Once we went on and on till I thought we would never arrest—right on till we came to a small town down by the river—Tweet-ham—Tweek-ham—the conductor called it, or something like that. Your English names are so very difficult. There was an island in the river, and an old church close by."

"Twickenham! You mean Twickenham!" he exclaimed. "Fancy your going so far on an omnibus! Your adventures, mademoiselle, must have been amusing."

"Ah yes. But poor madame! We did not return till seven of the clock, and she was fearing something had happened."

"Naturally," he said. "But let me give you a word of advice, mademoiselle. Be very careful where you go. London is not at all safe for a foreign lady like yourself, more especially if her face is as attractive as yours."

"Oh!" she laughed. "Mine has no attraction, surely. And I tell you, m'sieur, that I am not in the least afraid."

He had expected her to be impressed by his flattery, but she was not. On the contrary, she passed his remark as though it had never been uttered, and continued to relate to him her impressions of London and London life, some of which were distinctly humorous, for the streets of our metropolis always strike the foreigner as full of quaint incongruities, from the balancing of the hansom cab to the kilt of the Highland soldier.

He found her conversation amusing and interesting. She was somehow different from the wide circle of women of his acquaintance, those society dames who borrowed his money, ate his dinners, and gave tone to his entertainments. And this was exactly how she desired to impress him.

As the weeks went on, the society swallows returned from wintering in the South, and the London season began in earnest. The millionaire, a frequent visitor at his sister's house, often met the pleasant-faced governess, who very cleverly succeeded in increasing her popularity until she was well-known to Mrs Fitzroy's lady friends, and declared by them all to be "a perfect treasure."

None knew, however, save little Bertha—who feared to speak lest mademoiselle should punish her—of a rather curious incident which occurred one morning as she was sitting with her charge in Kensington Gardens. A tall, dark-faced, middle-aged man with black moustache, well-dressed in frock coat and silk hat, a fine diamond pin in his scarf, approached, raised his hat, uttered some mysterious words in Italian, and then took a seat at her side.

At first mademoiselle regarded the stranger with distrust, until he drew a paper from his pocket and allowed her to read it. Then, apparently satisfied, she listened to all he told her. But as it was in Italian, the child could not understand. She only noticed that mademoiselle turned rather pale, and seemed to be expressing deep regret.

The dark-faced man spoke slowly and calmly, while, on her part, she shrugged her shoulders and showed her palms, and responded with quick volubility, while the child sat at her side regarding the stranger in open-eyed wonder.

Presently, after a long argument, the man took from his pocket a small tin box of matches which he gave to her. Without examining it, she transferred it quickly

hat, and strode away towards Queen's Gate, swinging his cane airily as he walked.

"Who was that?" inquired the child after he had gone. "What did he give you, mademoiselle?"

"Nothing that concerns you, dearest," was her governess's reply. "Remember you must say nothing of that m'sieur—nothing, you recollect. You must never mention him to your mother or to anyone, because if you do I shall punish you very severely, and I shall never, never take you out with me again. You understand—eh?"

The child's face fell, and her eyes were fixed straight before her as she answered, "Very well, mademoiselle. I won't say anything."

"That's a good girl," her governess responded. "Some day you shall have a watch like your uncle's if you are very good," she added, for Bertha was very fond of watches, and especially of Morgan-Mason's gold repeater. She liked to hear it chime upon its musical bell.

One afternoon a few days later Filoména watched from her window the millionaire descend from his motor and enter the house. First she hurried into the schoolroom, where Bertha was sitting with the maid, and then she leisurely descended to the drawing-room, where she found Mrs Fitzroy and her brother talking together.

"Oh, m'sieur," laughed the governess, "Mademoiselle Bertha saw you arrive, and has sent me to ask a favour."

"A favour!" he exclaimed. "Of course, I always grant the young lady's requests when she asks nicely."

"Mademoiselle wants to know if you will let her hear your watch. Since you showed it to her a fortnight ago she has allowed me no peace. So I promised I would come and ask of you."

"Certainly," was the millionaire's reply, taking his repeater and the gold albert from his pocket. "You know how to make it strike. I showed you the other day," he laughed as he handed it to her.

"I will be ve-ry careful of it, m'sieur, and will bring it back when mademoiselle is satisfied. She desires greatly one like it."

"Some day I'll give her one, when she's older," laughed Morgan-Mason good-humouredly.

And then, when the door had closed behind her, his sister remarked—

"Mademoiselle is most devoted to Bertha. So very different to Miss Gardener. She humours her in every way, and at the same time is a very good teacher. It is really wonderful how the child is improving."

"I quite agree, Maud. She's an excellent girl—and I hope you pay her well. She deserves it."

And then they fell to discussing plans for a big dinner-party at the Carlton on the following Friday.

Meanwhile, mademoiselle ran upstairs with the watch in her hand, first to her own room, where she remained five minutes or so, and then took it to the school-room, where she delighted her little pupil by making the watch strike.

"Make it go again, mademoiselle," exclaimed little Bertha, delighted at being allowed to hold it in her hand. And again and again the governess pressed the ring and caused it to chime, until at last she was compelled to take it forcibly from the child's hand and carry it back again to the grey-whiskered man in the drawing-room, returning a word of thanks as she handed it back to him.

That same evening, after her charge had been put to bed, and during Mrs Fitzroy's absence at Lady Claridge's dance, she went out and dropped into the pillar-box at the corner of Grosvenor Square a small packet in a strong linen-lined envelope addressed to "Giuseppe Gallo, Esq., care of H. Bird, Newsagent, 386 Westminster Bridge Road, S.E."

And then she returned to the little sitting-room set apart for her, and smiled confidently to herself as she settled to read the *Tribuna*, which her mother sent her regularly each day.

A week later the household at Brook Street was thrown into a state of agitation and surprise when the vulgarian dashed round in a cab and informed his sister of a most audacious entry made by thieves into his splendid flat at Queen Anne's Mansions, and how they had turned it topsy-turvy. He had, it appeared, been absent, speaking for a parliamentary candidate up at Leicester, and his valet had slept in the flat alone, the other servants being on holiday, when during the night burglars had entered by a window from some leads adjoining, and had opened everything, even to his safe, and had apparently made a minute examination of every private paper he possessed.

He had missed nothing, except a few cigars; but what puzzled the detectives most was the manner in which safe, writing-table, and two chests of drawers, which he always kept locked, had been opened. Either the thieves possessed all the keys—and this did not appear possible, as they were all in the trusted valet's room—or else they possessed a master-key to everything, the same as that which the Member of Parliament wore upon his watch-chain.

The millionaire was furious. He even spoke to the Home Secretary about it when he met him in the lobby of the House. But the manner in which the safe had been opened was a complete mystery—a mystery to all except to mademoiselle.

The vulgarian little suspected, when he so innocently lent his watch to his niece, that the handsome governess had taken an impression in wax of the small master-key upon the other end of his chain, or that she had that very same evening posted the wax impression in the tin matchbox to the clever secret agent of the Italian War Office—the man who with two colleagues had come over from Paris specially, who had met Mademoiselle in Kensington Gardens, and who was known at the newsagent's in the Westminster Bridge Road as Giuseppe Gallo, a civil engineer, seeking employment.

CHAPTER THIRTY FOUR.
IN CONFIDENCE.

General Arturo Valentini, commanding the Italian forces on the Alpine frontier of France, sprang nimbly from an open cab, and helped out his companion—a young lady in deep mourning, with her long crape veil down, as is the custom in Italy.

The sentries at the big arched gateway of the military prison of Turin, recognising the commanding officer, stood at the salute, and in response, the short, dapper little man in his uniform and row of ribbons on his breast raised his hand to his peaked cap quickly in acknowledgment, and passed at once into the great bare courtyard surrounded by the high, white, inartistic outer offices of the prison.

The soldiers off duty, who were lounging and gossiping, quickly drew themselves up to attention as he crossed the courtyard to the office of the governor, walking with his firm military gait and spurs clinking, and his sword trailing over the stones. He was one of the smartest and best soldiers Italy possessed, a man who had shown an iron nerve in those turbulent days of the struggle for unity, a man of rigid discipline and yet of kindly heart. The loss of his only son in the reverses in Abyssinia two years before had left him without kith or kin, and although he commanded a military district as large as England, and was also in possession of a private income, he led a simple life at his headquarters there in Turin, going into society as little as possible, and ever working to improve the condition of his command. His district was the most important of any in Italy, for in case of hostilities it would be the first point attacked; and as triumph usually lies with those who strike the first blow, it was his object to enter France effectively and on the instant, if the dogs of war were ever let loose.

With this end in view, he was untiring in his efforts to perfect the defences of those many valleys and Alpine passes by which the enemy might gain admittance if not perfectly secure. In both summer and winter his troops were ever manoeuvring in those high misty mountains, skirmishing, throwing bridges over the deep gorges, and executing evolutions always in secret, always fearing that the French might learn their intentions in case of war.

That enormous army on the Italian frontier which one never sees, those regiments upon regiments which dwell far up in the remote heights of the Alps, away from the civilisation of the towns, are kept a mystery by the Ministry of War. They are there, ever ready, one knows, but where all the hidden fortresses are situated, or where the death-dealing mines are laid, are secrets which only the War Office and the commander know.

And it is those secrets which French spies are ever endeavouring to discover. Indeed, one of General Valentini's chief anxieties was the ingenuity displayed by the emissaries of France, who crossed the frontier in all kinds of disguises in the endeavour to learn the military secrets. Not a year went past but two or three of these spies were arrested and condemned—and, be it said, the same state of things existed on French territory, where the secret service of Italy, the men from the bureau at headquarters there in Turin, boldly took their liberty in their hands and went forth to gain the secrets of their friends in the opposite valleys.

It required an officer of clear foresight, great tact, and wide experience to control such a command, and in Arturo Valentini, the short, stout, red-faced little man, Italy certainly had one in whom she could repose the most absolute confidence.

In the office of the prison governor the pair stood for a few minutes, until the dark-bearded, spectacled official entered, saluted the commander, invited both him and his companion to seats, and settled himself at his table.

"I wish to have an interview with Felice Solaro," the general explained. "He is still here, I suppose?"

"Until Thursday next, when he is to be transferred to Gorgona."

"To Gorgona!" exclaimed the general in surprise; for the name of that lonely penal island in the Mediterranean opposite Leghorn was sufficient to cause him to shudder. "Then it is fortunate we came to-day," he added.

"But," hesitated the grave-faced man, looking inquiringly at his company, "but of course this lady cannot see him. It is against the regulations, you know, general. No prisoner can be seen by anyone except yourself, save by order of the Minister of War."

"I know," was the old officer's reply. "But this lady happens to be the daughter of the Minister Morini." Whereupon the governor bowed politely at the figure, whose face he could not well distinguish through her veil.

"You therefore need have no hesitation in allowing the interview," added the general. "If you wish, I'll sign an order for it now."

"No, certainly not. If the lady is the Minister's daughter, it is of course different."

"But this fact is confidential, recollect. It must not appear in any report that she has visited here."

The governor nodded. It was not the first time that ladies, high born and well-dressed some of them, had, on presenting orders from Camillo Morini, had interviews with officers and men undergoing imprisonment for various offences.

Solaro's crime was, however, the most serious of that of any prisoner who had been incarcerated there since he had held the post of governor—the unpardonable crime of treason, of selling his country into the hands of its enemy! He only knew that the court-martial had found the charges proved, and therefore he was guilty.

It surprised him that the daughter of the Minister should wish to see the man condemned of such an offence, but he made no comment. He only touched his bell and gave instructions for the prisoner Solaro to be brought from his cell to the *parlatorio*, or speaking-room.

"You of course wish, general, to see the prisoner in private," remarked the governor, when the chief warder had gone.

"If you please," responded the old officer, in his sharp habit of speech.

"Then I will not accompany you. But I may tell you that the prisoner has become much changed since his sentence. He declares his innocence, and sits pondering all day in idleness."

The general sighed, without replying. They discussed the matter until the chief warder returning they rose and followed him out across the courtyard, through a small iron-bound door before which a sentry stood at the salute, into the inner courtyard of the prison itself, the small, dismal, bare stone place which formed the exercise-yard, while all around were the small, barred, high-up windows of the cells.

They passed through a door, and walking along a short corridor entered a small room divided in half by long iron bars from floor to ceiling, like the cage of some ferocious animal in captivity. Behind those bars stood the bent, pale-faced figure of Felice Solaro, different indeed from the straight, well-set-up man who had stood before the Minister of War and defiantly broken his sword across his knee. Dressed in an ill-made suit of coarse canvas, the beard he had grown gave him an unkempt and neglected appearance, the aspect of one in whom all hope was dead.

On recognising his visitors, he sprang forward to the bars.

"Ah! my general?" he cried. "How good of you to come to me!" And he put out his thin white hand through the iron cage to greet the man who had stood his friend and endeavoured to get his verdict reversed. Then, as the gallant old officer took his hand, he turned inquiringly towards the figure in black.

She threw her long veil aside, and when he saw her face revealed he gasped—

"Signorina Mary! You—you have come here—*to see me!*"

Tears rose to her eyes and almost blinded her. Recollections of the past crowded upon her in that moment, and her heart was overburdened by pity for him.

"The signorina has done her best to induce her father to sign the order for your release, captain, but, alas!"—And the general sighed without concluding his sentence.

"The Minister refuses!" said the unfortunate man behind the bars. "And yet I tell you I am innocent—innocent."

"I believe you are, captain. If I did not, I should not interest myself on your behalf. But, unfortunately, the powers in Rome are greater than mine. They are sending you out to Gorgona, it seems."

"To Gorgona!" he gasped hoarsely, all the light dying from his pale, emaciated face. "Ah! then they mean to drive me mad by solitary confinement. My enemies

"But have courage, Felice," exclaimed Mary, speaking to him for the first time and taking his thin hand. "Surely one day you will have justice done to you. I cannot understand why my father so steadily refuses to release you."

"Because he fears to do so," declared the condemned man. "I am victim of a foul intrigue in which that woman Filoména was one who conspired against me."

"And yet you loved her," remarked the girl reproachfully.

"Ah! I believe I did. I know that to you I ought not to mention her, signorina. But forgive me. Do you recollect that night in Rome—at the ball at the Colonna Palace—when I asked you a question?"

"I do," she responded, now very pale. "I was younger, and did not know my own mind then. I thought—I thought I loved you. It was our flirtation that has brought you to this. I am to blame for everything."

"No, no," he declared. "It is I who committed the indiscretion of falling in love with you when I knew that I, a poor captain, could never hope to marry the daughter of the Minister of War."

She sighed, and tears welled again in her dark brown eyes. The general at her side was no woman's man, but even he became affected at this meeting.

"They allege that you sold to France a copy of the mobilisation scheme," she went on. "They say that I purposely locked you in my father's library at Rome for three hours in order that you might have access to the secret documents which were in a drawer in his writing-table."

The prisoner, smiling bitterly, answered—

"Let them allege whatever it pleases them; they cannot make my unjust punishment greater than it is. You yourself know that the charge is an unjust one—and my general knows that I would never betray Italy!"

"But to whom do you attribute this ingenious plot by which you have been made the scapegoat of someone else's offence?" asked Mary, looking straight into his deep-sunken eyes. "That the plans of the Tresenta as well as the copy of the mobilisation scheme have reached the French Intelligence Department is proved beyond doubt. Our secret service in Paris has ascertained that."

"I have enemies—bitter ones," he answered in a strange tone, his eyes fixed upon her. "They fear me, and have taken this course in order to close my mouth—in order to prevent me making certain revelations that would effect their ruin."

"But who are they?" she demanded. "The general has brought me here on purpose to put this question to you. If we are aware of all the facts, we may be able, after all, to rescue you from the horrors of Gorgona."

The pale-faced man shook his unkempt head sorrowfully, his lips pressed together, his eyes upon hers.

"No. You can never secure my release," he declared, with despair. "They dare not give me my liberty for their own sakes. Jules Dubard and that Englishman George Macbean will take good care that I never come forth to denounce them."

"George Macbean?" she gasped open-mouthed, all the colour fading from her cheeks. "Do you know him? Is he actually one of those who is responsible for this?"

For answer, the man behind the bars clenched his teeth and nodded in the affirmative.

CHAPTER THIRTY FIVE.
THE CAPTAIN IS OUTSPOKEN.

"But tell me," cried Mary, utterly amazed at the unhappy man's startling allegations, "do you actually declare that Dubard and Mr Macbean have conspired in order to throw the opprobrium upon you?"

"I do," he answered in a low, hard tone. "I am convinced of it. Macbean is an Englishman living in London—secretary to an English deputy named Morgan-Mason."

"He is a friend of mine," she remarked quietly. "I know him quite well."

"Then do not trust him," Solaro urged. "He is the—" But he hesitated, as though fearing to make any direct charge against one who was her friend.

"The what?" she inquired eagerly.

For a few moments he remained silent.

"He is the man who, with Dubard, was the cause of my downfall," he responded, although from his hesitating tone she felt assured that those words were not what he had first intended to utter.

"And Dubard?" she asked, her face now very grave.

"What use is it to discuss either of them?" he said bitterly. "I am their victim—that is all."

"But with what motive?" she asked, bewildered at this revelation. "What connection can Mr Macbean possibly have with these false scandalous charges against you?"

"Ah! the motive is more than I can tell," he declared. "I can only surmise it."

"But there surely must be some motive!" she remarked, at the same time recollecting what she had learnt, that the information furnished by Dubard formed the basis of the charges intended to be levelled by the Socialists against her father.

"I have never had an opportunity of ascertaining it," he said. "I would, however, desire to warn you most strongly against that man Macbean."

Mary remained silent. What he had said puzzled and mystified her. His words were not prompted by motives of jealousy. That was impossible, for he was unaware of Macbean's presence in Rome. As far as she knew, the two men had never been acquainted—the one an officer in garrison in the Alps, and the other living in far-off London. She endeavoured to induce him to speak more plainly, but it was evident that her acknowledgment that Macbean was her friend prevented him from opening his mind concerning him.

All her sympathies being with the imprisoned man, she felt a distinct suspicion arising within her concerning the young Englishman.—She wondered whether after all he had really schemed to obtain an appointment in the Ministry; if his present position was only in furtherance of some sinister object?

She spoke of Dubard, but the prisoner was equally silent concerning him.

"What I can tell you about either of them amounts to nothing without proof, and without my liberty I cannot obtain that. They know it!" he said angrily. "They know that while I am here, in prison, my lips are sealed!"

"But it is infamous!" exclaimed the red-faced old general. "If you were the victim of a plot laid by these two fellows, whoever they are, the matter ought to be sifted to the bottom. I don't believe you are guilty, Solaro! I told His Excellency the Minister so!"

"Ah, my dear general, you have been my best friend," declared the man now clothed in sacking in lieu of a uniform. "But your efforts must all be unavailing. They are sending me to the loneliness of Gorgona, that place where many a better man than myself has been driven insane by solitude. They know that on Gorgona I shall not live very long—indeed, they will take very good care of that."

"They—who are they?" inquired Mary quickly.

"My enemies."

"Mr Macbean and Dubard, you mean?"

"No, others—others I need not name," he responded vaguely, with a careless shrug of his shoulders.

"But if you are the victim of a plot it must have been a most elaborate one, for the mass of evidence against you seems overwhelming. What object could the conspirators have had in view? Were they friends of yours?"

"Yes—once. Their object was probably not of their own—but that of others," he added.

His words left the impression upon her that his conviction was part of the elaborate scheme of Angelo Borselli. And yet was not that very man now urging her to secure his release!

The affair was increased in mystery a thousandfold.

"Then if Mr Macbean was only slightly known to you why should he have plotted to secure your ruin and imprisonment?" she queried in eagerness.

"As I have already said, they were both in peril as long as I was at liberty. It was to their own interests—indeed for their own safety—that I should be sent here."

"What do they fear?"

"They fear what I could reveal—the facts that I could prove if I were not held here a prisoner," he said bitterly.

"And would those facts be strange ones?"

"They would be startling—they would create a sensation throughout Italy. They would throw a new light on certain affairs connected with the Ministry of War that would come as a thunderclap upon the people."

"You defied the Minister, remember," his general remarked gravely.

"I know. I lost my head. I broke my sword and threw the pieces at his feet in defiance. I was foolish—ah! very foolish. Only I was angry at his refusal to order a revision of my trial."

"Yes," the general admitted. "You have prejudiced yourself in His Excellency's eyes, I fear. Your indignation was but natural, but it was ill-advised at that moment. The Minister Morini is not the man to brook defiance in that manner."

"But I do defy him still!" cried the desperate man, turning to the tragic figure in black. "Although he is your father, signorina, I repeat that he has done me an injustice—and that injustice is because he, like the others, fears to give me my liberty!"

"But if you were released—if I could manage to obtain for you a pardon—would you make the revelations of which you have spoken?"

For some minutes he was silent, thinking deeply, apparently reflecting upon the consequences of speaking the truth. Then he answered—

"No. I think not."

"Why not?"

"Because—well, because there are one or two facts of which I have no absolute proof."

"But you are certain of Dubard's connection with the false charges against you?"

"Positive. He arranged with Filoména Nodari for *my* betrayal."

"But why? I cannot see the motive, and yet he must have had one!"

"In his own interests, as well as those of the Englishman."

"You mean Macbean?"

"Yes—the betrayer!"

Mary's heart beat quickly. She could not grasp his meaning, yet he refused to tell her plainly the whole of the strange circumstances, apparently fearing to give her pain because she had declared herself to be a friend of the Englishman. He was, of course, in ignorance of their friendship, just as he was in ignorance of her engagement to Jules Dubard.

She was in a dilemma—a dilemma absolute and complete. What Borselli had declared—namely, that the unfortunate captain was in possession of some facts which he would prove if he regained his liberty—seemed to be the truth. Yet if she secured his liberty by pressing her father to pardon him, she would only be deliberately giving to his political enemies a weapon whereby they might hound him from office. While, further, he refused to make her a direct promise to tell the truth, or make the revelations—even if liberated.

What could she do? How could she act? His allegations held her amazed, speechless. He had declared himself to be the victim of the ingenious conspiracy formed by the Frenchman and by George Macbean—the latter, of all men! The whole affair was an enigma that was inexplicable.

That Macbean had entered into a plot against him was utterly beyond her comprehension. He was essentially a Londoner, and had surely no interest whatsoever in the Alpine defences of Italy! Dubard was certainly his friend. Had he not, indeed, told her so? He had, only a fortnight before, expressed a hope that Dubard would soon return from the Pyrenees.

And yet that broken, desperate man—the man with whom she had had that pleasant flirtation during one Roman season—had fallen their victim!

But if so, why was Borselli now anxious that he should be freed in order to make his revelations against the very man Dubard who was his intimate friend—the man who it was said had furnished the Opposition with facts—most of them false—regarding her father's political shortcomings?

She tried to reason it all out, but became the more and more utterly bewildered.

The reason of the captain's denunciation of George Macbean was a mystery. When he mentioned the Englishman's name she had noticed a flash in his deep-set eyes betokening a deadly, deep-rooted hatred. And yet it was upon this very man that all her thoughts and reflections had of late been centred.

As they were alone in that grim, gloomy room with its barred partition—the governor having granted them a private conference—she explained how the Socialists had endeavoured to make capital out of the charges against him with a view to obtaining her father's dismissal from office. She made no mention of her compact with Dubard or her engagement to him, but merely explained how at the eleventh hour, while Montebruno was on his feet in the Chamber of Deputies, the mysterious note had been placed in his hand which had had the effect of arresting the charges he was about to pour forth.

Solaro listened to her in silence while she gave a description of the scene in the Chamber, and related certain details of the conspiracy which she had learned through her father, the details gathered in secret by Vito Ricci.

"Ah?" he sighed at last, having listened open-mouthed. "It is exactly as I expected. Your father's enemies are mine. Having drawn me safely into their net, they intend to use my condemnation as proof of the insecurity of the frontier and the culpability of the Minister of War."

"But if they attack the Minister they must attack me personally?" exclaimed the general in surprise; for he had been in ignorance of the widespread intrigue to hold the Ministry of War up to public ridicule and condemnation. "As the frontier is under my command, I am personally responsible for its security?"

"Exactly," Solaro said in a somewhat quieter tone. "If His Excellency had ordered a revision of my trial, I should most certainly have been proved innocent, and that being so, the Socialists would have had no direct charge which they could level against the Ministry. But as it is, I stand here condemned, imprisoned as a traitor, and therefore my general is culpable, and above him the Minister himself."

"My father should have pardoned you long ago. It is infamous!" Mary declared, with rising anger. "By refusing your appeal for a new trial he placed himself in this position of peril!"

"Had I been released I would have given into his hands certain information by which he could have crushed the infamous intrigue against him," said the man behind the bars in a low, desperate tone. "But now it is too late for a revision of my sentence. Our enemies have triumphed. I am to be sent to Gorgona, sent to my death, while the plot against His Excellency still exists, and the *coup* will be made against him at the very moment when he feels himself the most secure." Then, watching the pale face, he added suddenly, "Forgive me, signorina, for speaking frankly like this; he is, I recollect, your father. But he has done me a grave injustice; he could have saved me—saved himself—if he had cared to do so."

"But you have said that my father fears to give you your liberty?" She remarked. "If that is so, it is fear, and not disinclination, that has prevented him granting you a pardon?"

"It is both," he declared hoarsely.

"But is there no one else who could assist you—who would expose these enemies and their plot?" she asked.

"No one," he answered. "The most elaborate preparations were made to set the trap into which I unfortunately fell. I was watched in Paris, in Bologna, in Turin—in garrison and out of it. My every movement was noted, in order that it might be misconstrued. That Frenchman who struck up an acquaintance with me in Paris, and who afterwards lent me money, was in the pay of my enemies; and from that all the damning evidence against me was constructed with an ingenuity that was fiendish. I, an innocent man, was condemned without being given any opportunity of proving my defence! Ask Dubard, or the Englishman. Ask them to tell the truth—if they dare!"

"But tell me more of Mr Macbean," she cried eagerly. "What do you allege against him?"

"I make no allegations," he answered in a low, changed voice. "I can suffer in silence. Only when you meet that man tell him that Felice Solaro, from his prison, sends him his warmest remembrances. Then watch his face—that is all. His countenance will tell you the truth."

CHAPTER THIRTY SIX.
IN THE TWILIGHT HOUR.

For Mary Morini the world was full of base intrigue and uncharitableness, of untruth and false friendship. Four years ago she had returned to Italy from that quiet school at Broadstairs to find herself plunged suddenly into a circle of society, torn by all the conflicting failings of the human heart. The world which she had believed to be so full of beauty was only a wild, stormy waste, whereon each traveller was compelled to fight and battle for reputation and for life. Already world-weary before her time, she was nauseated by the hollow shams about her, tired of the glare of those gilded salons, and appalled by the intrigues on every hand—the intrigues which had for their object her father's ruin and the sacrifice of all her love, her youth, and happiness.

Often she asked herself if there could be any element of good remaining in such a world as hers. She tried it by the test of her religious principle and found it selfish, indolent, and vain, attracting and swallowing up all who lived within the sphere of its contaminating influence. She had believed herself adapted to the exercise of her affections, that she might love, and trust, and hope to the utmost of her wishes; but, alas! hers had been a rude awakening, and the stern realities of life were to her a cruel and bitter revelation.

In her Christian meekness she constantly sought Divine guidance, even though compelled to live amid that gay whirl of Rome; for the date of her marriage was rapidly approaching, the day when the man to whom she had bartered herself in exchange for her father's life would come forward and claim her.

The season, as society knew it, was far advanced, and although her mind was filled by those grave suspicions conjured up by Solaro's allegations, she frequently met and talked with George Macbean. His duties as her father's secretary took him to the palace a great deal, and sometimes of an evening they met at various official functions to which the young Englishman had also been bidden.

Out of the very poverty and the feebleness of her life, out of sheer desperation, she became drawn towards him, and the bond of friendship became still more closely cemented, even though those suspicions ever arose within her. He was Dubard's friend—he had admitted that to her—and as Dubard's friend she mistrusted him.

She had no friend in whom she could confide, or of whom she might ask advice. She exchanged few such confidences with her mother, while she was unable to reveal to her father her secret visit to Solaro's prison for fear of his displeasure.

It was at this crisis of her young life that she felt the absolute want of a participator in her joys, a recipient of her secrets, and a soother of her sorrows, and it was

welcome to her.

Weeks had passed since her painful interview with poor Solaro. The dull burden of accumulated sorrows hung heavily upon her. She had begun afresh. She had made a fresh dedication of her heart to God. She had commenced her patient work of unravelling the mystery of the great intrigue by which to save her father, and to escape herself from the fate to which she was consigned—she had commenced the work as though it had never been undertaken before, supported by Christian faith, and ever striving not to prejudge the man whose friendship had now become so necessary to her existence.

What the unfortunate prisoner had told her, however, had opened her eyes to many plain facts, the chief of them being that Borselli had, by his suggestion that she should secure the captain's release, endeavoured to induce her to bring ruin upon her own father. For the Minister to sign a decree of pardon now was impossible. Such an action must inevitably cause his downfall; therefore it was necessary that the captain should remain in prison, although innocent.

In Rome a sudden tranquillity had fallen upon the face of that ever-changing political world around the throne. Mary, who was seen at every ball and at every official dinner, still retained her golden and exuberant youth, her joyous step, her sweet smile, and the world believed her very happy. She was to marry Jules Dubard. But at home, in the hours of loneliness in her own room, there fell upon her the grim tragedy of it all, and she shed tears, bitter tears, because she was still fettered, still unable to discover the truth.

Two years ago she had possessed all the freshness of unwearied nature, the glow of health, that life-spring of all the energies of thought and action—the power to believe as well as to hope—the earnestness of zeal unchilled by disappointment, the first awakening of joy, the clear perception of a mind unbiassed in its search of truth, the fervour of an untroubled soul. But alas! the world had now disappointed her. Like Felice Solaro, like her father, she too had fallen a victim of those unscrupulous persons whose base craft and low cunning were alike mysterious and unfathomable.

George Macbean, watching her as closely as he did, realised the gradual change in her, and was much puzzled. True, she wore the same magnificent Paris-made gowns, was as humorous and irresponsible, and laughed as gaily as she had done in those summer days in England. Yet sometimes, as they sat alone, he detected that burden of grief and sadness that oppressed her mind. Soon she was to marry Dubard, yet her attitude was by no means that of the self-satisfied bride. Ignorant of the bitter reflections within her, he was, of course, much mystified at those gloomy, despairing words that sometimes involuntarily fell from her lips. He did not know, as she so vividly realised, that the day she married Jules Dubard her beloved father would again be at the mercy of those who sought his downfall.

Her Excellency had suggested a visit to Paris for the trousseau, but this she had declined. She had no desire for the gaiety which a visit to the French capital would entail. Therefore all the dresses and *lingerie* were being made in Florence and Rome; a magnificent trousseau, which a princess of the blood might have envied, for Camillo Morini never spared any expense where his daughter was concerned.

Yet she scarcely looked at the rich and costly things as they arrived in huge boxfuls, but ordered Teresa to put them aside, sighing within herself that the world was so soon to make merry over the great tragedy of her life.

Dubard was still at Bayonne, detained on business connected with his estate. He wrote frequently, and, much against her own inclination, she was compelled to reply to his letters. More than one person in her own set remarked upon the prolonged absence of the popular young Frenchman who had become so well known in the Eternal City, but only one person guessed the true reason—and that person was George Macbean.

Late one afternoon she had been driving on the Pincio, as was her habit each day. She was alone, her mother being too unwell to go out, and just as the *passeggiata*, or fashionable promenade, was over, she passed the young Englishman walking alone. She bowed and drove on, but presently stopped her victoria, alighted, and telling the coachman that she would walk home, dismissed him.

Most of the carriages had already left that beautiful hill-garden from the terraces of which one obtains such wonderful panoramas of the ancient city, and it being nearly six o'clock, the promenaders were now mostly Cookites, the women bloused and tweed-skirted, and the men in various costumes of England, from the inevitable blue serge suit to the breeches and golf-cap of "the seaside,"—people with whom she was unacquainted. In a few moments they met, and he turned happily and walked in her direction.

"I'm cramped," she declared. "I've been in the carriage nearly three mortal hours, first paying calls with father, and then here alone. I saw you, so it was a good opportunity of getting a walk. You go to the Princess Palmieri's to-night, I suppose?"

"Yes, Her Highness has sent me a card," he answered—"thanks to your father, I suppose." As she walked beside him, in a beautiful gown of pale dove grey with a large black hat, he glanced at her admiringly and added, "I saw in to-day's *Tribuna* that the count is expected back in two or three days. Have you had news of him?"

"I received a letter yesterday—from Biarritz. He is with his aunt, who is very unwell, and is paying a dutiful visit before coming here."

In silence they walked on, passing the water-clock and descending the hill until they came to that small piazza with the stone balustrade that affords such a magnificent vista of the ancient city. Here they halted to enjoy the view, as the tourists were enjoying it. The wonderful Eternal City with its hundred towers lay below them in the calm golden mist of evening. It was a scene she had looked upon hundreds of times, yet at that moment she was attracted by the crowd of "personally conducted" who stood at the stone balustrade and gazed away in the direction of where the huge dome of St. Peter's loomed up through the haze. Like

of English tourists and hearing their comments upon things Italian—remarks that were often drily humorous. She stood at her companion's side, chatting with him while the light faded, the glorious afterglow died away, and the tourists, recollecting the hour of their respective *tables d'hôte*, descended the hill to the city. And then, when they were alone, he turned to her and, with a touch of bitterness in his voice, said—

"I suppose very soon you will leave Rome and live in Paris. Has the count made any plans?"

"We live this summer at the château," was her answer. "The winter he intends to spend on the Riviera."

"And Rome will lose you!" he exclaimed in regret. "At the Countess Bardi's last night they were discussing it, and everyone expressed sorrow that you should leave them."

She sighed deeply, and in her eyes he thought he detected the light of tears.

"For many things I shall really not be sorry to leave Rome," she answered blankly. "Only I wish I were going to live in dear old England. I have no love for Paris, and the artificiality of the Riviera I detest. It is the plague-spot of Europe. What people can really see in it beyond the attraction of gambling I never can understand. The very atmosphere is hateful to anyone with a spark of self-respect."

They were leaning on the old grey stonework, their faces turned to the darkening valley where wound the Tiber, the centre of the civilisation of all the ages, the great misty void wherein the lights were already beginning to twinkle.

Furtively he glanced at her countenance, and saw upon her white brow a look of deep, resigned despair. He loved her—this beautiful woman who was to sacrifice herself to the man who he knew had entrapped her, and yet whom he dare not denounce for fear of incriminating himself. He, who worshipped her—who loved her in truth and in silence as no man had ever loved a woman—was compelled to stand by and witness the tragedy! Night after night, when he thought of it as he paced his room, he clenched his hands in sheer despair and cried to himself in agony.

Dubard was to be her husband—Jules Dubard, the man who, knowing of his presence in Rome, feared to return to claim her as his wife!

"You are very silent, Miss Mary!" he managed to say at last, watching her pale, beautiful face set away towards the dark valley.

"I was thinking," she answered, turning slowly, facing him, and looking straight into his eyes.

"Of what?"

"Shall I tell you frankly?"

"Certainly," he said, smiling. "You are always frank with me, are you not?"

"Well, I was thinking of a man who was once my friend—a man whom I believe you have cause to remember," she replied in a meaning tone—"a man named Felice Solaro!"

"Felice Solaro!" he gasped, quickly starting back, his cheeks blanching as he repeated the name. "If Felice Solaro is a friend of yours, Miss Mary, then he has probably told you the truth—the ghastly truth?" he cried hoarsely, as his face fell. "He has revealed to you the mystery concerning General Sazarac! Tell me—tell me what allegation has he made against me?"

CHAPTER THIRTY SEVEN.
AT ORTON COURT AGAIN.

George Macbean stood at the window of the rector's little study at Thornby, gazing out across the level lawn.

Outside, the typical old-fashioned English garden, bright in the June sunlight, was a wealth of flowers, while the old house itself was embowered in honeysuckle and roses. Beyond the tall box-hedge stood the ancient church-tower, square and covered with ivy, round which the rooks were lazily circling against the blue and cloudless sky. Through the open diamond-paned window came the fragrant perfume of the flowers, with a breath of that open English air that was to him refreshing after the dust and turmoil of the Eternal City.

"Getting tired of being a cosmopolitan—eh?" laughed the big, good-humoured man, turning to him. "I thought you would."

"No. I'm not altogether tired," he answered. "But a change is beneficial to us all, you know. I suppose my wire surprised you?"

"Yes, and no. Of course I heard three weeks ago that the Morinis were returning to Orton for the wedding, and I naturally expected you to put in an appearance. What a lucky dog you are to have got such an appointment! And yet you grumble at your bread and cheese. Look at me! Two sermons, Sunday school, religious instruction, mothers' meeting, coal club—same thing each week, year in, year out—and can't afford to do the swagger and keep a curate! I never get a change, except now and then a day with the hounds or a dinner from some charitably disposed person. But what about the marriage? We all thought it was to be in Italy. He's French and she's Italian, so to be married in England they must have had no end of formalities."

"Mary is a Protestant, remember—and a Cabinet Minister can do anything—so they are to be married in Orton church," he added in a strange tone, his eyes turned towards the sunlit lawn, over which old Hayes, the groom-gardener, was running the machine.

"I ought to have called to congratulate her, but as you know I only returned last night from doing duty over at Eye. I ought to drive over after tea. Is the count there?"

"No. When we left Rome I came straight to London on some urgent private business of His Excellency's, and they remained a week in Paris, where Dubard was—to complete the trousseau, I suppose."

"It is one of Mary's whims to be married by special licence by the Canon at Orton, I've heard. Is that so?" asked Sinclair.

The young man nodded. He had no desire to discuss the tragedy, for he knew well that the marriage was a loveless one, and although his own affection had been unspoken, he was beside himself with grief and despair. He, who knew the truth, yet dare not utter one single word to save her!

For ten days he had been in London, staying at his old chambers with Billy Grenfell, and transacting business at the Italian Consulate-General connected with the formalities of the marriage, formalities which were expedited because his employer was Minister of War. Paragraphs had crept into the press, the ladies' papers had published Mary's portrait, and the marriage, because it was to take place in a village church, was called a "romantic" one.

George Macbean smiled bitterly when he recollected how much more of tragedy than romance there was in it. He adored her; for months her face had been the very sun of his existence, and in those recent weeks they had become so closely associated that even her mother had looked somewhat askance at the secretary's attentions, to which she had seemed in no way averse. A bond of sincerest sympathy had drawn them together. She was in no way given to flirtation; not even her bitterest enemies, those jealous women who were always ready to create scandal and invent untruths about her, could charge her with that. No. She had accepted George's warm, platonic friendship in the spirit it was given, at the same time ever struggling to stifle down that strange and startling allegation which Felice Solaro had made against him.

The very world seemed united against her, for even in George Macbean, the man whom she had believed to be the ideal of honesty and uprightness, she dared not put her absolute trust.

"The Court is full of visitors," George remarked a few minutes later, "so I thought I'd come here and stay. I can drive over there every day. Next week we go back to Rome again for another month, and then his Excellency returns on leave to England."

"You're cultivating quite an official air, my dear boy," exclaimed the rector, re-filling his pipe and glad to change the subject of conversation. "Your letters to me headed 'Ministry of War—First Division' are most imposing documents. I'd like to have a trot round Rome with you. I've never been farther than Boulogne—seven-and-sixpence worth of sea-sickness from Folkestone—and I don't think much of foreign parts, if that's a specimen of them."

Macbean smiled at his uncle's bluff remarks, and then fell to giving him some description of the Minister's palace in Rome, and of his position in the society of the Eternal City.

After early tea Hayes brought round the trap, and the two men drove over to Orton Court, where, on entering, there were signs everywhere for the coming event, which, now that it was known who Camillo Morini really was, created much excitement throughout the countryside. The decision that the marriage should take place in England had been quite a sudden one—but, curiously enough, it had been at Dubard's own instigation. George had gathered that fact, and it held him

The instant the rector saw Mary he recognised what a change had taken place in her. Within himself he asked whether it was due to the secret that his nephew had confessed to him. Standing in the long, old-fashioned drawing-room, with its big bowls of roses, he apologised for not calling earlier, and congratulated her; whereupon she responded in a quiet, inert voice—

"It is very kind of you, Mr Sinclair—very kind indeed. I don't know if you've had a card, it has all been done in such a rush, but you will come on Thursday, won't you?"

He accepted with pleasure, and glancing at his nephew, saw that the young man's face told its own sad tale.

"Has not the count arrived?" asked Macbean of her.

"No. I had a wire this morning. He leaves Paris to-night, so he'll be here after luncheon to-morrow."

Leaving Sinclair with Mary, George went along to the study, where he found the Minister busy with some important despatches which had just arrived by special messenger from the Italian Embassy in London, therefore he was compelled to seat himself at the table opposite and assist his chief.

So long did the correspondence take that the rector and his nephew were invited to remain to dine informally, George being placed, to his great delight, next the unhappy woman whom he so dearly loved. It was the last time he would dine with her, he told himself during the meal, and through his brain crowded memories of those happy hours spent at her side amid the brilliant glitter of the salons in Rome when, although hundreds were around him, he had only eyes for her, and her alone. And he, by that relentless fate that held him silent, was compelled to stand by and watch her noble self-sacrifice!

CHAPTER THIRTY EIGHT.
"SILENCE FOR SILENCE!"

On the following night, as eleven o'clock slowly chimed from the pointed steeple of Orton church, George Macbean was walking along the narrow path that led from the highroad to Rugby first across the wide cornfields and then through the small dark wood until he reached the river bank. Here he halted at a low stile which barred the path, and waited.

Before him ran the river grey and placid beneath the clouded moon, behind him the pitch darkness of the covert where hounds were always certain of finding a fox or two in the course of the season. The cry of a night bird, the rustling of a rat among the rushes, and the distant howl of a dog up at the village were the only sounds that broke the quiet. Not a breath of wind ruffled the surface of the deep stream, not a leaf was stirred until of a sudden there came the sound of footsteps, and the dark figure of a man loomed up against the misty grey.

"Eh bien?" inquired the man in French as he approached; for the new-comer was none other than Jules Dubard. He was staying at an hotel in Rugby, and they had met that afternoon under Morini's roof, greatly to the Frenchman's surprise. But he had managed to conceal his chagrin, to greet the secretary so that none should suspect the truth, and now, at Macbean's suggestion, had come forth to meet him alone.

The pair were once again face to face.

"And well?" George asked, speaking in the same language the Frenchman had used. "It is I who should demand the reason of your presence here, m'sieur."

"Ah, my dear friend," replied the other, "this is a meeting very fortunate for me, for it enables me to say something which I have long wanted to say."

"I have no wish to hear you. I only demand the reason you are here—a guest in the Minister's house."

"You surely know," he laughed airily. "Am I not to marry Mademoiselle Marie?"

"You have schemed to do so, I know."

"Well, well," he remarked philosophically, "we are both schemers—are we not, my dear George? In scheming, however, so very little is certain. But in this world one thing is certain—namely, that Mademoiselle Marie will become Comtesse Dubard at three o'clock on the day after to-morrow."

The two men were standing quite close to each other, and in that grey light could readily watch the expression of each other's faces.

[illegible] I have been in Rome I have not been idle. I have learned how Angelo Borselli still holds you in the hollow of his hand, and how cleverly he has made you his cat's-paw to ruin and disgrace Morini. Listen, and if I speak an untruth deny it. Ever since the Sazarac affair you and Borselli have actively conspired against Camillo Morini. The Under-Secretary, with your assistance, had arranged a political *coup*, but in order to compel Miss Mary to give her consent to this scandalous marriage, you have induced Borselli to stay his hand. You are forcing her to marry you, in order to save her father from ruin and probably from suicide, well knowing, however, what Borselli's intentions are, as soon as she is your wife and you have obtained her *dot*! You intend—"

"Look here, hound! Did you ask me to come here to insult me?" cried the Frenchman in fury, advancing a pace in a threatening manner.

"You have said you have something to say to me," was his response. "But before you say it, I wish to make plain what are my intentions."

"And what are they, pray?"

"I intend to prevent Mary Morini making this sacrifice," was his quiet, determined reply.

"You love her yourself! Friends of mine have watched you in Rome. Although I was absent, I knew quite well that you were in her father's service; but believe me, I was in no manner anxious, first because of your menial position—a mere secretary—and secondly, because of the past."

"The past!" cried Macbean. "The past! Surely you ought not to speak of the past—you, to whom the family of Morini, the father of the innocent woman you have schemed to marry, owes the peril in which he now exists. You shall never marry her!" he added angrily. "Never!"

There was a brief silence, then Dubard responded with a defiant laugh.

"You cannot prevent it, my friend."

"But I will."

"And expose yourself?"

"I shall at least expose a man who has marked down a pure and innocent woman as his victim."

Dubard laughed again, saying—

"Of course. You've fallen in love with her, and are jealous that she should become my wife!"

"I am her friend," he declared. "And I will protect her."

"And allow the charges to be made against her father."

"They will be brought whether you marry her or not—you know that quite well. I have not been private secretary to Morini without discovering the insecurity of his official position, and the deadly rivalry and crafty cunning of Angelo Borselli. Again, answer me one question—why is Felice Solaro, your friend, condemned as a traitor?"

"He doesn't concern me in the least," was the other's reply.

"But the matter concerns me," Macbean went on. "Recollect how studiously you have avoided me ever since August, when I recognised you driving over in that road yonder—when an evil fate threw me again across your path."

"You appear, then, to believe that I am in fear of you?" he said. "But let me tell you that I have no such anxiety whatsoever. Try and prevent my marriage—but recollect it will be at your own peril?"

George knew well at what his enemy had hinted—he knew too well that if he uttered one word it would bring upon him a deadly peril—that he would be hurled to ruin and disgrace. Nevertheless, he was determined to sacrifice himself rather than all that he held most dear should be snatched away from him by that man whose very existence and position was an adventure and a fraud.

But feeing the Frenchman determinedly, he said—

"The reason I invited you out here was to tell you frankly my intention, and so allow you opportunity to leave the place before the truth is known. I intend to go to-morrow to the Minister and tell him exactly the true state of affairs. He is in utter ignorance that it was you who stayed the adverse tide against him in the Chamber of Deputies—in ignorance that you made that vile, despicable agreement with his poor unfortunate daughter. When I have spoken we shall see whether he will allow the marriage to take place."

"And when you have spoken we shall also see whether he will not hear my own story."

"I am prepared for any allegation you may make against me," responded George. "You may ruin me—you may do what you and your friends will—but you shall never marry Mary Morini!"

"I defy you!"

"Very well—we shall see."

"Tell the Minister what you choose, but remember that if you endeavour to create friction between us, I will show you no mercy," he cried between his teeth. "Until now I have been silent, but—"

"You've been silent because you know too well that you fear to speak—you fear to make any allegations against me. I know rather too much!" declared the Englishman, with confidence.

"Much or little, it does not concern me in the least," replied the foreigner. "You create unpleasantness, and *eh bien*! I do the same."

"Then you actually intend that that desperate woman, in deadly fear of her father's ruin, shall become your wife?"

"I do."

"Then I tell you, Dubard," he cried, "that I will not allow it! I will never allow

[illegible]

"The consequences!" exclaimed the Frenchman in a deep, serious voice, his teeth hard set in anger which he strove to suppress, but which nevertheless rose by reason of his quick foreign nature. "The consequences! Have you realised them all? You seem to have a short memory, my dear friend—and a short memory is often convenient. Shall I refresh it for you?" he asked, as the man before him clutched at the wooden rail of the stile for support, although striving valiantly to preserve a defiant calm. "Shall I recall to you the memory of those sunny winter days when your employer Morgan-Mason took you with him to the Villa Puget at Mentone, when he was the guest of his brother-in-law, General Felix Sazarac? Shall—"

"I know! I know!" cried the young Englishman. "I know all—why should you recall all that?"

"To refresh your memory, my dear friend," responded Dubard, with withering sarcasm. "Do you recollect how that we were friends in those days—you, Felice Solaro, and myself? Solaro and I were at the Hôtel National, and you were given a room at the villa by your employer's hostess, his elder sister, Madame Sazarac—who had married the general. Do you not remember these days, spent at Monte Carlo, or up at La Turbie, our luncheons, our dinners at the Paris, and our little games at the tables? Oh yes, you had a merry time then—we all had—even the poor general himself. And then—"

"Stop!" Macbean implored, raising both his hands. "Enough!—I know! Heavens!—as though I could ever forget!"

"But you have forgotten, it seems, or you—of all persons—would never seek to come between me and the woman I am to marry. Therefore hear me—once and for all. And when you have heard, reflect well before you adopt a course which must inevitably reflect upon yourself—nay more, which must cause your own ruin. Do you recollect how your employer Morgan-Mason had gone alone to Marseilles to meet his Indian manager who was returning to England, and how you, being alone, the general often invited you to ride with him up the Corniche road, and sometimes into the mountains? He was fond of the English because his wife was English, and he had taken a great fancy to you. Being in command of the Alpine frontier defences in France, he had often to make inspections of those high-up fortresses that guard the passes into Italy, and one day he invited you to ride with him away up to the fortress of Saint Martin Lantosque that overlooks Monte Malto."

"I will not hear you!" cried Macbean hoarsely. "Enough! Enough!"

But the Frenchman continued in the same quiet, hard, meaning tone, his voice sounding clear in the quiet of night.

"With Solaro I chanced to call at the villa just as your horses were brought round, and we stood upon the steps and saw you mount. You waved your hand triumphantly to us, and trotted away at the side of the man who held the southeast frontier of France under his command. Do you recollect, as you rode down the drive bordered by its flowering azaleas, how you turned and looked back at us, in wonder whether we suspected your intentions? Perhaps not—the truth remains the same," he added, his face now closer to that of the man against whom he was making that withering accusation. "You rode nearly twenty miles into the mountains, and were high up above the Vesubie, in a wild, solitary district devoid of any human habitation, when, it being hot, you offered your brandy-flask to the general, who was without one—for you yourself had surreptitiously taken it from his holster prior to setting out. Being thirsty, he took a long drink. Half an hour later he felt ill, and dismounted. And in an hour the poor fellow was dead!"

George Macbean stood still, gripping the moss-grown rail, glaring at his accuser, though no word escaped his lips.

"The cognac you gave to the general was never suspected by the doctors, who declared the fatality to be due to an internal malady from which he had long suffered, and which was known might cause sudden death. The gallant officer was buried with military honours in Nice, and none were aware of the truth save Solaro and I. We knew that a sum of money which the general had upon him had been stolen, and further, that the brandy you had given him you had not dared to drink yourself. In secret, we charged you with the general's murder, for the sake of the money upon him; but you defied us, and made a gallant fight to brave it out. But it was useless. Solaro declared that you had concealed the money, whereupon you offered to allow us to search your possessions, and we found a draft on the Credit Lyonnais in the flap of your writing-case. You offered to allow us to seal, before your eyes, the brandy in the bottle in your room, together with that remaining in your flask, and we sent it to be analysed by an analyst in Paris whom you yourself named. You hoped to mislead us, to disarm our suspicions by allowing us to make all the inquiries we, as friends of the general, thought fit! Ah! that was a fatal mistake, my friend! You condemned yourself. The analyst's report does not lie. I still have it here, in my pocket-book, and do you know what it says? It states that the contents of both bottle and the flask filled from it were submitted to the tests of Marsh, Reinsch, and Fresenius, and in each case the result was the same—the cognac contained sufficient of a specific irritant poison of an arsenical nature to render a single mouthful of it a fatal dose! This document," he added, touching his breast-pocket as he spoke, "proves you to be the murderer of Felix Sazarac—you poisoned him deliberately when up alone in that mountain pass, and Solaro found in your effects part of the money you stole from the dead man's pockets?"

Macbean tried to speak, but his throat contracted; he was unable. Alas! that terrible truth had been ever before him since that fatal day in spring, when his life had been fettered. Try how he would, he could not put from him the horror of those awful hours. There were, unfortunately, witnesses against him, witnesses who could prove his guilt and send him to an assassin's punishment.

"Well?" he managed to gasp at last in a low, half-frightened voice, his heart beating quickly as he half turned and faced his accuser.

"Only this," answered Jules Dubard determinedly; "silence for silence! You understand now, my friend—silence for silence!"

And then the two men parted.

The morning dawned bright and sunny—the morning of Mary's wedding day—one of those fresh, brilliant days in June when the grass-country looks its gladdest and best.

The bells were pealing merrily from the old church-tower of Orton in honour of the event, upon the lawn a large marquee had been erected, and the men down from London with the wedding breakfast were bustling everywhere, while the excitement out in the village was intense.

Morini and his wife were both happy at the match, and in the long dining-room some of the presents were displayed, including a splendid pearl collar from Her Majesty the Queen of Italy. The house was full of visitors, several of them being persons of the highest aristocracy in Italy, who had been specially invited over for the wedding, and there was gaiety everywhere.

The only person who took no part in the bustle was the bride herself, for alone in her bright little room she was upon her knees imploring the Divine aid for strength in that hour of her greatest trial.

During those past weeks, as each day brought her nearer that hateful union, she had pondered deeply, trying to devise some means by which to escape, but alas! she saw too well that refusal would only bring ruin upon her father's head; while, if she did marry Dubard, she had no security that the blow would not fall upon her family afterwards. So she had been compelled to bow to the inevitable, to make that sacrifice of her love, of her very life.

Those who had seen her in Rome lolling in her splendid carriage drawn by that perfect pair of English bays, dancing in those gilded salons, or laughing with her neighbour at dinner at one or other of the foreign embassies, had surely never dreamed that that bright, happy girl, whose engagement was discussed everywhere, had such a heavy burden of sorrow within her young heart.

Before her lay her bridal gown, a magnificent creation from the Rue de la Paix, with old lace that had once belonged to the extinct royal house of Naples. But when she gazed upon it she burst into a flood of tears, and sank again upon her knees in desperation.

Teresa came at last and tried to calm her.

"Signorina! signorina!" she exclaimed, stroking the dark hair, which, unbound, fell upon her shoulders. "Your eyes will look so red. Oh, surely you should be happy to-day!"

"Happy!" groaned the unfortunate girl bitterly, as she slowly staggered to her feet. "There is no happiness for me—none—none."

At last the pale-faced girl, summoning up all the courage she possessed, seated herself before the mirror, and having allowed Teresa to dress her hair for the bridal, proceeded, with the help of Santina, her mother's maid, her mother, and Vi Walters—who was one of the wedding guests—to put on the gown with its wonderful train and real orange-blossoms from the orangery at San Donato.

Meanwhile, however, in the study below, Camillo Morini was sitting with his enemy, Angelo Borselli, who had practically invited himself on a flying visit to the ceremony, and whom he could not well refuse without giving him a direct insult. Morini hated the man who had ever been his evil genius, but in the present circumstances dared not openly quarrel with him. Therefore he treated him with diplomatic friendliness.

They were smoking their cigars together when Dubard, elegantly dressed, entered merrily, and greeted them. Borselli had only arrived late on the previous night, therefore he had not seen him before.

"Well, my friend!" cried the Sicilian, "I congratulate you. You will have the best of wives in all the world—and the best of fathers-in-law, that I'm sure."

"Ah, I'm certain I shall," replied the bridegroom. "But what great preparations are being made!"

"Half the country will be here to the reception later on," Morini remarked, laughing.

"Where is your secretary—Macbean?" inquired Dubard.

"He is not here yet. He is staying with his uncle over at Thornby," was His Excellency's reply.

And the bridegroom smiled to himself. His words of the previous night would, he knew, have their effect.

Silence for silence!

CHAPTER THIRTY NINE.
REVELATIONS.

At that moment, however, the door suddenly opened, causing the three men to turn and glance, when, to their surprise, they saw, standing before them, the man whose name had just been mentioned. Dubard held his breath. Macbean's face was bloodless, his lips quivered, his hands were clenched, his whole countenance seemed to have altered in those moments of tension and determination, and as he closed the door behind him and advanced boldly into the room, trying to speak in a cool voice, he addressed the Minister—

"Your Excellency, the tragedy of this marriage must not take place—for your own sake, as well as for your daughter's."

In an instant the three men were upon their feet, electrified by the Englishman's startling words.

"What do you mean?" asked Morini, looking at him amazed.

"Yes," cried Dubard, stepping forward angrily. "Let us hear what this fellow means."

"You wish to hear," exclaimed Macbean, facing the Frenchman boldly. "Then listen! I allege that Miss Morini has been forced into this marriage by you—and by that man there," he added, pointing to the sallow-faced Sicilian. "If you doubt me," he said, turning to the Minister of War, "ask her yourself. This man Dubard made a promise to her that, in exchange for her hand, he would prevent the crisis which Borselli had arranged to bring ruin and disgrace upon you. You will recollect the mysterious letter received by Montebruno when he was already upon his feet in the Chamber. That letter was sent by your enemy, Borselli, at Dubard's instigation, because your poor daughter had consented to sacrifice herself in order to save you. It is my duty to tell you this, your Excellency. You have been pleased to take me into your service, to treat me almost as a confidential friend, and it is my duty therefore to speak the truth and to save Miss Mary from falling the victim of this man?"

"Victim!" cried Dubard quickly. "What do you mean?"

"I mean that you intend to marry her, and having done so, your friend here, General Angelo Borselli, will strike his blow at His Excellency—a merciless blow, that will crush and ruin him."

"Bah!" exclaimed the Sicilian. "All this is a mere fiction! He loves your daughter himself, my dear Camillo. There is lots of gossip about it in Rome."

"During my employment in the Ministry I have kept both ears and eyes open," Macbean went on. "I know well with what devilish ingenuity you have plotted against your chief, how you have forced him deeper and deeper into financial intrigue, in order that your revelations may be the greater, and how, in order to propitiate your accomplice Dubard, you have stayed your hand until this marriage is effected."

"Basta!" cried the Sicilian. "I will not be insulted by a common employee like you!"

"Nor I!" exclaimed Dubard, his face white with passion, as he turned to Macbean. "My affairs are no concern of yours—they concern myself and the lady who is to become my wife. I am amazed that you, of all men, should dare to come forward and make these unfounded charges against us. Hitherto I have kept my silence, but as you have sought exposure I will speak the truth. Then your employer shall judge as to which of us is worthy of confidence, and which—"

"I make no plea for myself," declared George, quickly interrupting him. "I merely intervene on behalf of a broken and defenceless woman—the woman you have so cleverly entrapped."

But Dubard only laughed drily, and said—

"Very well. Let His Excellency listen to you—and afterwards to me."

"Then let me speak first," cried the Englishman desperately. "Let me tell you myself the truth of the Sazarac affair."

Borselli's face fell, and Morini's countenance changed colour in an instant. Mention of that name was sufficient to cause both men quick apprehension.

"You need not do that," the Sicilian managed to say. "But I will," Macbean went on. "You shall hear me. I know the truth is an unwelcome one, but lest others shall tell you any garbled version of it, I will be frank and fearless with you. In the winter three years ago I was taken by Mr Morgan-Mason, whose secretary I was, to stay with General Felix Sazarac, whose wife was my employer's elder sister, the younger sister having married a Mr Fitzroy. The general, who was in command of the French garrisons on the Alpine frontier, lived at the Villa Puget, at Mentone, and at the Hôtel National there was staying his friend Dubard—the man before you. We became friendly, for the general often invited Dubard to dine at the villa, and after a time there arrived in Mentone at the same hotel an acquaintance of the count's—a young Italian gentleman of means named Solaro, who was also introduced at the Villa Puget, and who also became one of our intimate friends. Curiously enough, however, the general did not seem to care for Solaro's company, yet he frequently invited me to ride out with him, and gave me good mounts from the barracks. Well," he went on, after a slight pause, "all went merrily for over two months, until one day, when Mr Morgan-Mason had gone to Marseilles, the general invited me to ride with him up into the mountains to the fortress above Saint Martin Lantosque, which he had to inspect. The morning was a bright one, with all the prospects of a blazing day, and we first rode across the plain behind Mentone, and then began to ascend the rough mountain paths into the Alps. We had ridden some fourteen miles or so, when the general suddenly exclaimed, 'That rascally servant of mine has forgotten my flask again!' 'Never mind,' I called to him. 'I have [illegible] I fill [illegible] with [illegible] and water before starting.' 'That's good!' he laughed.—'We shall want a drink before long. It's going to be a blazer to-day!' And then we toiled on and on, up the steep rough paths that wound higher and higher over the mountains. Just before midday, however, the general pulled up, removed his cap, and declaring that he was thirsty, took a long pull at the flask I handed to him."

"And then?" asked Morini almost involuntarily, as he stood listening to the story.

"I was not thirsty myself, so I put the flask back into the holster, and we rode on again, laughing together and enjoying the glorious panorama at our feet. Half an hour later, however, my companion complained of queer pains in his head and giddiness, which he attributed to the sun, and pulling up he dismounted. We were then in a lonely spot in a district utterly unknown to me. The general grew worse, being seized by strange cramping pains in the stomach and a curious twitching of the face. I gave him some water from a spring close by, and bathed his head, but he grew worse, and seemed to lapse into a state of coma. Suddenly he opened his eyes, and motioning to me that he wished to speak, he gasped faintly, 'Tell them I did it because those Jews were pressing me—I regret it—regret—but it is useless!' Then after a pause he managed to articulate, 'My wife!—my dear wife—my love to her, M'sieur Macbean—my love to her—I—I'—Then his jaw dropped, and I found him dead upon my arm! This fatal seizure appalled me. I shouted, but no one heard. I was miles and miles from civilisation in the centre of the wildest district of the Alps, therefore I covered the dead man's face with his handkerchief, tethered his horse, and rode back ten miles or so to a little village we had passed. The general was brought back to Mentone that night, and at the Villa Puget the scene was a sad and tragic one. I gave poor madame her husband's dying message, but his words about the Jews puzzled her. She could not understand them in the least. It was a mystery."

"They were words invented by you," declared Dubard in a hard tone. "Tell these gentlemen the truth! It was you who gave the poor fellow the cognac—you who poisoned him!"

"I gave him the brandy, I admit," exclaimed Macbean quickly, "but I swear I was unaware that it was poisoned!"

"You filled it from the bottle in your room. Now you have gone so far, tell the whole truth."

"I am not afraid," Macbean went on boldly. "On the night when the body of the general was brought home you came with Solaro to my room, locked the door, and charged me with administering poison—although three doctors had seen him, and as they had all previously treated him for a malady which they knew might terminate fatally on too violent exercise, they had decided that no post-mortem examination was necessary. Your allegation astounded me, but you asked for the key of the cupboard wherein I kept the bottle of brandy. There was some remaining, as well as the remains of that mixed with water in the flask. As I denied that I had poisoned him you both urged that, in satisfaction, I should seal both bottle and flask and submit them to some analyst in Paris. This I willingly did, entirely unsuspecting any plot. I packed them in a box, and myself saw them despatched."

"And the analyst's report is here!" exclaimed Dubard, waving the paper triumphantly before the speaker's eyes. "It proves that you deliberately poisoned General Sazarac, while Solaro, if he were here, could prove further that he found in your writing-case the draft which you stole from the dead man's pocket?"

"I know only too well the circumstantial evidence that was against me," said Macbean, addressing Morini. "I had been the victim of a clever and ingenious plot in which the unfortunate officer had lost his life. But why? There seemed no motive whatever. I returned to England a suspected man, and from that day I did not come face to face with Dubard until I recognised him last year driving on the Rugby road, and heard to my amazement that he was engaged to your daughter Mary. Ever since then I have desired to re-encounter this man, and to clear myself of the terrible charge he brings against me."

"And how do you propose to do that?" inquired His Excellency, astonished at the entirely new complexion placed upon that tragic affair which had caused him so much mental anxiety and so many sleepless nights.

"I can only declare my complete innocence. I was, no doubt, the agent who administered the fatal cognac, but I certainly was ignorant of it, and would never have poisoned the man who had showed me so many kindnesses."

"Then I think it is only in the interests of justice if this report of the analyst is given into the hands of the Paris police," remarked the Sicilian, who had remained silent, but whose active mind nevertheless had been at work to discern some means of effectually closing Macbean's mouth.

The young Englishman started. He had not expected such a suggestion. He foresaw the difficulty of proving his innocence when such witnesses as Solaro and Dubard were against him.

"For the present, we will leave that aside," said the Minister, in as quiet a voice as he could. "My first duty, as father of my child, is to investigate this allegation of Macbean's," and he touched the bell. To the man who answered his summons he said in English in a determined tone—

"Ask Miss Mary to kindly step down here for one moment. I desire to see her without a minute's delay. Say that I have some urgent news for her."

"Very good, your Excellency." And the door was closed again.

Dubard and Borselli exchanged uneasy glances; but a dead silence had fallen between the four men—a silence that was broken by the sound of wheels out on the gravelled drive. There were lots of coming and going in that bustling day, wedding guests arriving, and the bride's luggage being despatched, so as to meet her in London before they left for Paris on the following morning.

The pause was painful. Macbean looked at the pair who had for so long been united hand and glove against the Minister, and recognised the spirit of murder in their glance. They would have killed him had they dared, for they knew too well

ticed him to Rome hoping to ensure his secrecy over the Sazarac affair, had placed his own head in the lion's mouth by so doing. It was seldom he made an error in his clever schemes, but he knew that he had done so on this occasion, and that it would require all his ingenuity and cunning to escape from such a compromising situation.

The minutes passed, but neither spoke a word. Each man feared to utter a sentence lest it should be seized upon and misconstrued, while the Minister himself, silent and distinguished-looking, glanced from one to the other, and waited for his beloved daughter to enter and to speak.

CHAPTER FORTY.

THE STORY OF CAPTAIN SOLARO.

At last there was a light footstep out in the hall. The door opened, and she entered, radiant in her wonderful bridal gown and orange-blossoms, her long sweeping train behind, but without her veil, of course, her beautiful face revealed in all its haggard pallor.

Dubard sprang forward to welcome her; but ere he could take her hand he fell back in utter dismay, for behind her, silhouetted in the doorway, stood the figure of a man in a grey felt hat and a light overcoat.

"Great heavens!" gasped Macbean, who at the same moment recognised the new-comer. "Solaro! Felice Solaro!"

"Yes," replied the other, in a quiet, distinct voice, as he came into the room behind the Minister's daughter in her rustling silks. "I am fortunately here, not by His Excellency's decree, but by the generous clemency of the king himself, who, on the occasion of his birthday, three days ago, and in consequence of a petition of my family, gave me my liberty with others. I heard what was in progress, and so I have travelled here to ascertain the truth, and to clear myself of the base and scandalous charges those men who stand there have brought against me," and he raised his finger and pointed to the Sicilian and the Frenchman, both of whose faces had, on the instant of recognising him, become entirely changed.

"It seems, signorina," he said in Italian, turning his pale, emaciated face to Mary, who stood in the centre of the room utterly dumbfounded at the dramatic scene, "it seems that by good fortune I am here in order to save you, your father, and the Signor Macbean from these two men who have so very cleverly plotted your father's ruin, your own marriage, the disgrace of the Signor Englishman, and my own imprisonment."

"Do you allege that they conspired to obtain the conviction against you?" cried the Minister, amazed.

"Listen, and I will tell you everything. Then you yourself shall take what steps against them that you desire."

"I shall not remain to hear that traitor's insults!" cried the Sicilian, moving quickly towards the door; but Solaro, noticing his action, stepped back, locked the door behind him, and placed the key in his pocket, saying, "You will remain, general. You have to answer to me." Then, after a brief pause, he commenced—

"It may be news to you all, except the Under-secretary, that Jules Dubard is not a member of the French nobility at all, but a person who, while posing as a count, is one of the secret agents of the French Minister of War. It was for this rea- [illegible] been shown upon his papers."

"A spy!" gasped the bride, standing open-mouthed on the eve of her deliverance.

"That is the vulgar term for such persons," Solaro said. "It happened about four years ago that Borselli and he met, and the former, finding him a shrewd and clever adventurer, resolved to make use of him to gain a triumph over the Minister Morini. Borselli had also met General Sazarac at the Jockey Club in Paris, and had won from him several large sums at cards, accepting from him a number of promissory notes. Having done this, he discovered, to his delight, that Sazarac was actually in command of the Alpine frontier of France, therefore he proceeded with slow deliberation to win over Dubard from the French service, by promises of position when the Minister Morini was overthrown, and to unfold a plot which is a good specimen of his amazing ingenuity. Briefly, it was to place the promissory notes in the hands of some unscrupulous Jews in Antwerp, in order that they should press for payment, and when they did so, Dubard, who was attached to Sazarac's division of the French army, should suggest a course out of the difficulty—namely, to sell to the Italian Ministry of War certain plans of the frontier defences which we were very anxious to obtain. This was done. Sazarac, in desperate straits for money, listened to his friend Dubard's evil counsel, and agreed to allow the plans of the whole of the defences from Mount Pelvoux to the sea to be copied for a sum of two hundred thousand francs. These were the secrets which we had desired for many years to know, and the first I knew of the matter was a summons to the Ministry in Rome, where I saw Borselli, who introduced me to Dubard, and instructed me, because I spoke French perfectly and was a good draughtsman, to go to Mentone, take quarters at the Hôtel National, and make copies in secret of certain documents which Dubard would hand me from time to time."

"You were in our service!" declared the Sicilian.

"Certainly," he answered; and then proceeding he said, "I went to Mentone, and commenced the work of copying those plans which the general allowed Dubard to abstract from the safe at headquarters and bring to me in secret. While there we both became on friendly terms with the Englishman Macbean, who was secretary to the French general's brother-in-law, and who was of course in entire ignorance of what was in progress. After about two months, during which Dubard and I led the life of wealthy idlers on the Riviera, the copying was complete, I had sent the last batch of tracings to Rome by the official of the Ministry who came specially to convey them, and was awaiting further instructions, when one evening, after we had seen Macbean and the general going out for a ride together, Dubard entered the hotel and said he had heard in a café the startling report of the general's sudden death. We at once went round to the Villa Puget, and there sure enough he was lying dead, with madame inconsolable with grief. The doctors had declared death due to natural causes, as he had long been an invalid, and had been warned against riding too far. But Dubard took me aside in the garden and told me that he held a distinct suspicion that the general had been poisoned. The sum agreed to be paid for the plans had, he said, been paid on the previous day, and probably he had some of it upon him, which might serve as a motive for the crime. He suggested poison, and declared that he had suspicion of Macbean. At first I refused to entertain such a theory, but he persisted in it, and at his suggestion I accompanied him when he openly charged the Englishman with the crime. Macbean at once offered us every facility for the analysing of the cognac and the contents of his flask, sealed them up with his own seal, and packed them before our eyes, addressing them to a well-known chemist in the Rue Rivoli in Paris, and I despatched them. The report came back that there was an arsenical poison in both the bottle and the flask. It seemed that Macbean had tried to bluff us to the very last, but the most damning fact was that on searching his effects I discovered a draft on the Credit Lyonnais for fifty thousand francs from a firm in Genoa, but really emanating from our Ministry of War, and part of the agreed payment for the plans. This was concealed in the flap of his writing-case."

"So the natural conclusion was that Mr Macbean was a poisoner!" remarked Mary, standing dumbfounded.

"Of course," he said. "I certainly believed that he was, and that he was only allowed his liberty through Dubard's clemency, until about three months after the affair, when Dubard and I being together at the Grand Hotel in Venice, my curiosity was one day aroused, and I pried into his despatch-box during his absence. Among other papers I found this letter," he said, producing one from his pocket. "It is undated and unsigned, but it suggests that if some secret means were employed to induce S's (meaning Sazarac, of course) fatal illness, two ends would be achieved. France would never suspect that he had sold the plans, and the payment of two hundred thousand francs need not be made."

"Fifty thousand francs of that money Borselli handed back to me," the Minister admitted.

"And he kept the remainder himself," declared Solaro. "This letter is in his handwriting—and is in itself evidence that he instigated the general's death, and that this man, who is his accomplice, carried it out so cleverly that the whole of the evidence pointed to Macbean. Indeed, this is proved by recent events, and by the manner in which the pair have sought to close my mouth regarding the ugly affair. Last summer I was suddenly arrested, and was amazed to discover how very neatly the man Dubard, whom I thought my friend, had had me watched in Paris and in Bologna, had bogus plans of the Tresenta prepared and sent to Filoména Nodari, and how these and other documents—one purporting to be the mobilisation scheme itself—passed through that woman's hands into those of a French agent. Evidence—foul lies, all of it—was given against me; I was condemned as a traitor—I, the man who had copied all the plans of France in the interests of my own country—and then I realised how cleverly Borselli and Dubard, the ex-agent of France, were acting in conjunction, and that whoever was guilty of poor Sazarac's assassination it certainly was not the Englishman. I had, before my arrest, mentioned the death of Sazarac casually to Dubard, and inquired of the whereabouts of Macbean. It was this remark of mine which apparently aroused his suspicions, and which caused both he and Borselli to secure my imprisonment for a twofold reason: first, to ensure my silence; and secondly, so as to give the Socialists ing a traitor. This was the only way in which your Excellency's popularity and power could be undermined; but so craftily did they go to work, and so cleverly was every detail of the conspiracy thought out, even to the opening of your safe at San Donato with a key made from the impression of the original key taken by Borselli two years before. You made away with the key, hoping to conceal the evidences of your peculations; but their ingenuity was simply marvellous, for they were playing with the safety and prosperity of a kingdom."

"But General Borselli asked me recently to induce my father to release you," said Mary.

"In order to still further incite the popular feeling against His Excellency. He probably believed that I dared not denounce him as the instigator of the assassination of Sazarac, and that with my release his *coup* could be effected against your father after your marriage with his accomplice. It is, indeed, intended to strike the blow at the first sitting of the Chamber next month."

"Then I think we are now fully prepared to combat it," remarked the tall, grey-haired Minister in a cool tone, as he glanced at the Sicilian. "When I received the fifty thousand francs of the sum which was to have been paid from the secret service fund to General Sazarac, I was led to believe that, owing to a certain plan not being forthcoming, only half the sum had been paid to him. I had no knowledge of a tragedy until long afterwards, when, to my horror, I discovered for myself that there had been some foul play, and that I was morally responsible as an accessory."

"I am not to blame altogether," declared the Frenchman desperately. "Borselli sent me the cognac from Rome already prepared, and according to his directions I substituted the bottle in the Englishman's room and at the same time abstracted the general's flask from his holster. I also concealed, at Angelo's suggestion, the banker's draft in Macbean's writing-case."

"You scoundrel!" cried George, turning upon the white-faced criminal whom his well-beloved had so narrowly escaped. "And you, Borselli, have sent your spy, that woman Nodari, to investigate Mr Morgan-Mason's papers because you fear he holds something that incriminates you?"

"Silence!" cried the Minister, holding up his hand. "There must be no recriminations here in my house. I have been misled by Borselli as to this man's position and antecedents. The wedding will not take place, after these scandalous revelations, but there is still one duty before me, as Minister of War," and turning to his writing-table he took two sheets of paper, and upon each he scribbled some hurried words. One he handed to Borselli, who glanced at it and threw it from him with an imprecation.

It was his dismissal from the office of Under-Secretary of War.

The other, which he handed to Solaro, caused him to cry aloud with joy, for it was his reinstatement in the army and a declaration of his innocence of the crime of which he had been charged.

Then Solaro unlocked the door, and turning to the Sicilian and Dubard, who were standing together pale, crestfallen, and ashamed, he said—

"Go, you pair of assassins. Don't either of you put foot in Italy again, or I'll take it upon myself to prosecute you for your vile plot and my own false imprisonment. Then, at your trial, the whole affair will come out. You hear?"

"Yes!" muttered Dubard, with flashing eyes. "We hear your threats."

And in silence both the elegant bridegroom and his dark-faced friend passed from the study and out of the house, never to re-enter it.

Then, when they had gone, Mary, a pale, tragic figure in her bridal dress, flung herself into George's ready arms, crying—

"You have saved me—saved me!" and she burst into tears of joy, the outpourings of an overburdened heart.

For the first time Camillo Morini guessed the truth, yet then and there, before Felice Solaro, whose statement had liberated both of them, George Macbean openly confessed his great passion for her, a declaration of purest and strongest affection, of which she, by her own action, had already acknowledged reciprocation.

And so the Minister, on recovering from his surprise, gladly gave the hand of his daughter to the gallant, upright man who had placed himself in such jeopardy in order to save her and to unmask the conspirators, while Felice Solaro was the first to offer the pair his hearty congratulations. Hand in hand they stood, content in each other's love.

In order to preserve appearances, it was arranged that Mary should feign a sudden illness to necessitate the postponement of the wedding, and while there was great disappointment among the guests and the curious crowds of villagers, there was, in secret, a great rejoicing in Madame Morini's little boudoir when the glad news was revealed to her.

The pealing bells were stopped. Mary had thrown off her wedding-gown merrily, and when she tossed her orange-blossoms into the grate of the boudoir, she said to George laughingly—

"When we marry privately in London next month, I shall require no white satin—a travelling gown will be sufficient, will it not?"

"Yes, dearest," he said, kissing her fondly upon the lips, now that she was really his very own. "The dress does not matter when the union of our hearts is so firm and true. You know how fondly and passionately I love you, and how I have suffered in silence at the thought of your terrible sacrifice."

"I know," she answered softly, looking up into his eyes trustingly. "I know, George—only too well! Ah! you cannot think how happy I am, now that it is all past—and you are mine?" And then she raised her sweet face and kissed him of her own accord upon the cheek.

CHAPTER FORTY ONE.
A WOMAN'S FREEDOM.

Within a month of the abandoned wedding at Orton, Mary Morini and George Macbean were married quietly at St. James's Church, in Piccadilly, the Rev. Basil Sinclair assisting, and Billy Grenfell, as full of his bluff humour as ever, acting as best man, while among the various handsome presents the happy pair received was an acceptable cheque from Mr Morgan-Mason for ten thousand pounds—the sum he had offered to George for information as to the actual means by which his brother-in-law met with his death.

The millionaire was determined to place the assassins on their trial, and notwithstanding Morini's efforts to preserve secrecy regarding the affair, he actually gave information to the Chief of Police in Mentone. By some secret means, Angelo Borselli obtained knowledge of this fact, and on the very morning of George's wedding day he was found in a room in an obscure hotel in Brussels, quite dead, having committed suicide by swallowing some arsenical poison, probably the same as that used in the cognac which caused the unfortunate general's tragic end.

Felice Solaro was soon gazetted major, and is now transferred to the gaiety of Naples. As for Dubard, he did not long enjoy his freedom, for he was arrested as a traitor by the French police while passing through Bordeaux, and is now spending the remainder of his days on the penal island of New Caledonia.

George Macbean and his charming wife still live in Rome, and all in the Eternal City know them well by sight. The Cavaliere Macbean has been promoted to a very high and responsible position in the Ministry of War, but last year Camillo Morini, owing to failing health, resigned office, greatly to the regret of his new sovereign, King Victor Emmanuel, and of the gallant Italian people at large.

But before resigning he endeavoured by every means in his power to atone for the peculations of his earlier career, and by selling his palace and other properties, he paid back the whole of the money he had appropriated.

San Donato, the old-world estate above Florence, is, however, still his, and there, enjoying the greatest fame perhaps of any living Italian, he is spending with his wife the evening of his days.

Orton Court is still rented by him, and each summer they go there with Mary and her husband. But the village is still mystified why Miss Mary did not marry the Frenchman, and whether, after all, there was not a scene on that memorable day when the wedding was so abruptly postponed.

But in her fine dark eyes they now see the light of perfect love and sweet contentment, and they know too well the sterling worth and kindly heart of the man who is her husband.

In Orton village in summer, however, perhaps the most popular and important personage of any is the little round-faced, chubby boy, who so often sits between the happy pair when on bright afternoons they drive out in the smart victoria.

Much as she prefers England, Madame Macbean is compelled, on account of her husband's official position, to still move in Roman society, where, for her great personal beauty and the sweetness of her character, she is the most admired of women in the Quirinale set, that bright and brilliant circle of Italy's bluest blood—"The World behind the Throne."

Lector House believes that a society develops through a two-fold approach of continuous learning and adaptation, which is derived from the study of classic literary works spread across the historic timeline of literature records. Therefore, we aim at reviving, repairing and redeveloping all those inaccessible or damaged but historically as well as culturally important literature across subjects so that the future generations may have an opportunity to study and learn from past works to embark upon a journey of creating a better future.

This book is a result of an effort made by Lector House towards making a contribution to the preservation and repair of original ancient works which might hold historical significance to the approach of continuous learning across subjects.

HAPPY READING & LEARNING!

LECTOR HOUSE LLP
E-MAIL: lectorpublishing@gmail.com

Lightning Source UK Ltd.
Milton Keynes UK
UKHW010646090820
367908UK00002B/440